DAMEON GIBBS

Son of the Wilderness

GIBBS PUBLISHING CONGLOMERATE

First published by Gibbs Publishing Conglomerate 2025

Copyright © 2025 by Dameon Gibbs

All rights reserved. No part of this publication may be reproduced, stored or transmitted in any form or by any means, electronic, mechanical, photocopying, recording, scanning, or otherwise without written permission from the publisher. It is illegal to copy this book, post it to a website, or distribute it by any other means without permission.

This novel is entirely a work of fiction. The names, characters and incidents portrayed in it are the work of the author's imagination. Any resemblance to actual persons, living or dead, events or localities is entirely coincidental.

First edition

ISBN: 978-1-966856-28-3

This book was professionally typeset on Reedsy.
Find out more at reedsy.com

Train up a child in the way he should
go: and when he is old, he will not
depart from it.

Proverbs 22:6

Foreword

This novel is a work of fiction. While it draws inspiration from people, places, and events found in the pages of Scripture, its purpose is imaginative storytelling—not historical reconstruction. Within these chapters, biblical settings are expanded, untold moments are explored, and the life of Gershom—the firstborn son of Moses—is re-envisioned in ways that blend creativity with reverence for the sacred text.

Gershom is, indeed, a real figure mentioned in the Bible. However, the details of his life are brief, and Scripture offers only a few glimpses into his existence. Because of this, the character you will encounter in this story is shaped through artistic interpretation, narrative speculation, and thoughtful invention. This retelling should not be taken as evidence of actual events, nor should it be viewed as an authoritative account of Gershom's life or the historical realities of the Israelite in the wilderness.

Readers who desire to learn more about the real Gershom and his place in the biblical record are encouraged to turn directly to Scripture. His name appears in **Exodus 2:22**, **Exodus 18:3**, and **1 Chronicles 23:15**. These passages provide the foundation from which this fictional portrayal begins. Events mentioned in this novel can be found in their true form in the books of Exodus, Deuteronomy, and Joshua.

This novel aims not to rewrite Scripture but to explore the

spaces between its lines. May it inspire curiosity, reflection, and a deeper appreciation for the timeless stories preserved in the Bible.

Acknowledgments

Writing a novel is never a solitary journey, and this book is no exception. I owe an immeasurable debt of gratitude to the family and friends who have walked beside me with unwavering encouragement. Your belief in my ability to bring this story to life carried me through long nights, early mornings, and every moment of doubt in between. Thank you for listening as I talked through plot twists, for offering honest feedback when I needed clarity, and for reminding me, gently and persistently, why I began writing in the first place. Your love and support formed the quiet strength behind every page.

To my friends, thank you for the laughter, the conversations, and the space you gave me to create. Your patience through my missed outings, late replies, and "I'm writing right now" messages helped make room for this novel to grow. I am deeply grateful for each of you who read early drafts, asked how the book was coming along, or simply cheered me on when the finish line felt far away.

To my family, your encouragement has been a foundation throughout this journey. Thank you for your prayers, your advice, and the constant reassurance that you were rooting for me. Your faith in my calling and your willingness to celebrate each milestone, no matter how small, has meant more than words can express.

And finally, to you, the reader. Thank you for choosing to

spend a part of your life within these pages. In a world filled with responsibilities, distractions, and endless demands on your time, the fact that you paused long enough to explore this story is a gift I do not take lightly. Whether you are reading this book in quiet moments or between the rhythms of a busy day, I am honored that you allowed these characters and their journey to become a part of your own.

Your support makes stories like this possible. From my heart to yours, thank you.

Introduction

The story of Israel's long journey through the wilderness is one of the most enduring narratives in human history. It is a story of longing and loss, of divine provision and human frailty, of a people shaped not in palaces or fortified cities, but in barren places where every day demanded trust. For forty years the Israelites wandered through a landscape that tested them, refined them, and ultimately prepared them for something greater than they could see at the time. Their footsteps traced more than a route through desolate terrain; they marked a transformation of identity, faith, and purpose.

Beyond the trials and triumphs, the wilderness served as a crucible. It was where a nation learned to listen, to obey, to rise after failure, and to believe that the promises spoken to their ancestors would one day become real soil beneath their feet. When the people finally stood at the banks of the Jordan, the crossing into the Promised Land was far more than a geographic shift. It was the culmination of generations of struggle and anticipation, the moment when promise became possession, and when faith stepped into fulfillment.

This novel unfolds against that sweeping backdrop of movement, growth, and divine orchestration. While the events of the Exodus, the years of wandering, and the conquest under Joshua provide the historical and spiritual foundation, this story turns its gaze toward one man whose life rests quietly in the margins of Scripture: Gershom, the firstborn son of Moses.

Little is said about him in the biblical record. His name, his parentage, and a handful of references are all that remain. Yet the silence surrounding Gershom invites imagination. What was it like to be born into the household of a man who spoke face-to-face with God? To grow up in the shadow of a leader carrying the burden of an entire nation? To walk through the wilderness not as a figure of legend but as a son, a brother, a man searching for his own identity in a story larger than himself?

This novel explores those questions, weaving a fictional account into the historical journey of Israel. It seeks not to rewrite Scripture but to enter its atmosphere—to imagine the emotions, challenges, and inner conflicts of a man standing on the edges of greatness, caught between legacy and calling. Through Gershom's eyes, we revisit the wilderness, the Jordan, and the early days in the Promised Land, witnessing familiar events through an unfamiliar perspective.

May this story deepen the richness of the biblical backdrop, invite reflection, and stir the imagination as we journey with a man who, though scarcely mentioned, walked beside one of the greatest figures of faith and into the landscape shaped by promise.

Burden of a Name

"Take Joshua son of Nun, who has the Spirit in him, and lay your hand on him." Gershom repeated his father's words in his mind as he looked out over the host of Israel.

It was the air, as much as anything, that held the encampment together: a ceaseless, fretful force that tugged at the pegs and canvas, that whistled between the stakes, and in the absence of all order or certainty stitched the community with a restless, communal shudder. From the northernmost hill, where the ground tumbled in loose gravels before flattening into the great basin of Moab. The tents gleamed white as fish-bellies, ranged by the ten-thousand in tight lanes and ragged crescents, moored in the dusty heart of wilderness as if by sheer stubbornness of will. Above them, a haze of banners and woven signals shivered in the updrafts, their shapes rendering the names of tribes, lost forefathers, the incommunicable language of migration.

He had come here, perched at the hem of the encampment, arms folded and hands tucked in the blue sash of his outer garment, ostensibly to join the morning's lament, but the truth was not noble. He had not slept, had not wept, had not joined the men who paced the perimeter, raking the dirt with their sandaled feet in prescribed circles of grief. From his still vantage above the plain's nadir, the people streamed inward, settling to their knees in widening rings around the makeshift dais, the air tightening with a low, rising hum.

Already, before the second horn blast, the women had gathered, barefoot, veils abandoned, dark hair unraveling down their backs. They swayed together, hands laid flat on their bellies, the keening from their throats a minor third above the drone of men. The children, stilled by the gravity of the day, huddled behind mothers' knees or squatted in the lee of empty cooking pots, their fingers smeared with the remnants of morning's pulse cakes.

He would not join them. It was not a conscious rebellion; the capacity simply failed him, like the use of a limb lost in accident. He supposed this was what distinguished grief from mourning: grief had its own secret architecture, a system of rooms and closed doors, and his was hermetically sealed. He questioned whether anyone else suspected the magnitude of the vacuum where his own father's voice had been.

At the base of a wooden dais, men with oil-slicked beards bowed their heads to the dirt. He recognized the posture of penitence, the way the foreheads were ground into the soil until brows were left caked, the fine silt bright in the creases of their eyes. There was something performative, almost compulsory, in this display: as if the whole people must compact their sadness into a visible artifact, that the Lord above and the spies of Moab alike should see it and be satisfied.

He was not the only observer standing apart. Further down the slope, a knot of boys clustered near the refuse pit, muttering in the dialect of the second generation. To his left, an old man with a blackening birthmark on his neck braced himself on his staff. His stare raked across the gathering, sharp and unforgiving as the sun overhead.

It was the time of horns. The first note cut through the weeping like the blade of a scythe. It was not music or call but a brute signal, a reminder of order. The assembly shuddered, then focused; the second blast, lower and sustained, drew all eyes to the dais.

Joshua, the son of Nun, emerged, his cloak bunched at the top, his hands folded so tight the knuckles blanched to the color of sheep bone. His brow was unadorned, the simple band of goat-leather all that marked him now. As he mounted the steps, a woman at the rear of the company loosed a sob, then choked it down, shame rising to flush her cheeks.

There was a finality in the way Joshua walked. Not with the steady gravity of Moses, who carried his years like proof of command, but with unease, as if Joshua never trusted the ground to stay firm. Even from this distance, Gershom could see the flicker in his gait, the brief moment of hesitation before he reached the end.

On either side of the dais, the elders rose, their robes swept back, a dozen pairs of eyes flickering between Joshua and the vacated seat, shrouded in a linen wrap, the arms of the chair polished smooth by years of occupancy. The seat gaped like an open wound.

Gershom gripped the nearest guy-line. His thumb dug into the coarse hemp, working the strand until it bit his skin. He had rehearsed, in private, the words he might say if called: something to honor the legacy, to carry the Law from blood to blood. But no summons came. He was not needed, not even as an artifact. His name had not been read in the day's appointments. The future would be managed without the sons of Moses.

Darkness stretched across the dais as the sun neared its zenith, the tall forms of the elders projecting downward like the spokes of a wheel. Joshua's voice carried, flat and even, over the assembled host. He recited the names of the tribes, the cities yet unclaimed, the judgments and precepts to be sealed in the hearts of the people. His words held no poetry; they were the language of ordinance, of chain-of-command. Yet the people drank it in, heads bobbing in syncopation, as if the sheer inertia of their years in the wilderness demanded a figure to guide them.

It occurred to Gershom, not for the first time, that this was all the legacy amounted to: a relay race where the baton mattered more than the runners, the burden handed along until no one remembered who bore it first.

He watched as the elders closed in, one after the other, to lay hands on Joshua. Each bore down with an intensity that bordered on violence, as if to fuse the calling by physical force. Gershom noticed the line in some of their jaws, the strain in the knuckles as the force was applied. He registered Joshua's eyes flinch at the contact, a flash that slipped past his understanding.

The wind shifted, bringing with it the smell of scorched fat from a distant altar, the iron tang of blood, and somewhere behind it all, the faintest echo of incense, the scent his mother used to weave through her hair, years ago in Midian, before any of this began. He found himself suddenly, inexplicably, longing for that simpler aroma, the way it could mask the odors of pilgrimage and fear.

At the climax of the ritual, a second seat was dragged forward—the seat of the new judge, the placeholder for all time. Joshua bowed and sat, his frame swallowed by the expanse of wood and linen, a child playing king. The people stood as one, a field of bodies unfurling into verticality, and for a moment the entire encampment seemed to inhale, to swell with collective anticipation.

And then, in the hush that came after, Gershom's attention snapped back to the central void: the unoccupied seat, shrouded and prominent, its absence sharper than any presence. He stared, refusing to turn away, as if persistence alone could summon his father to fill it, to break this farce of succession.

His own heart was pounding, the rhythm loud in his ears. He questioned whether, in another world, his father would have left him words of instruction: how to grieve, how to yield, how to belong to a nation that had always belonged more to the Law than to its own children. But there had been no last testament, no final benediction. Only the recollection of a man who climbed a mountain and did not return.

Below, the congregation dispersed, the laments trailing off into small, shuddering breaths. Women gathered their hair, men wiped their skin and called for water, children scattered to the tents, the choreography of mourning already dissolving into the next necessity.

Gershom stood on his ridge, fist still closed around the hempen line. He released it only when the light shifted, and the outline of the empty seat lengthened, consuming the dais and the ground at its base.

It was a warning, or a benediction, or perhaps nothing at all. But it was his, and it was enough, for now.

The tent had never been large, but it felt diminished in his father's absence. Gershom ducked through the entrance, pausing for the second it took his eyes to adjust from the glare of midday to the interior's oily half-light. He breathed in the familiar scent: smoke from the altar mingled with the animal musk of rawhide and the sharper tang of anointing resin crusted on the tent poles. At the heart of it lingered the trace of his mother's hands, once busy with soaps and herbs but long stilled.

He had come here to disappear, to fold himself into whatever crevice remained unclaimed by the day's orchestrated sorrow. He found Eliezer: younger by five years but already grown into the slab-shouldered frame of a man who expected to command respect by mass alone. His brother sat at a wooden chest that served as both table and altar, arms braced on the lid, his face hidden in the dim of the tent's sloping wall.

There was no greeting. Gershom moved past, careful not to brush his brother's leg, and began the ritual of arranging the day's artifacts: the stylus abandoned at sunrise, a length of leather cording coiled with obsessive precision, the half-gnawed biscuit his father had left uneaten two mornings before the end. He set them side by side, aligning their sides, buying time.

"You missed the ceremony," Eliezer said, voice pitched barely above the hum of the wind in the guy-ropes. His foot tapped a muted cadence against the trampled earth.

"I was there," said Gershom, and kept his eyes on the biscuit.

"Not among the men. Not with the elders."

Gershom said nothing. He was busy locating a fold in the blanket that could be smoothed, a crease in the leather that begged for correction. He had become, in recent months, a man of small repairs.

"Did you even see him?" Eliezer asked, each word spat as if

it would rot the tongue if held a moment longer. "At the end? Or did you—"

"I saw him," Gershom interrupted. He would not describe the climb up Nebo, the tangle of roots and the dizziness, the moment he crested the last rise to find the prophet already face-down, lips dusted with grit. The way the light struck the tears caked on the old man's beard, as if even the land mourned him. "I was there," he repeated.

"That's not what I heard." Eliezer's fingers drummed the wood, a steady, punitive beat. "You could have spoken for us. You could have demanded—"

"There was nothing to demand." The words emerged thin, barely more than vapor. He risked a glance at his brother, who met it full-force, eyes bright as wet stones. "Joshua was charge with speaking to the congregation."

"Joshua is not our blood," Eliezer hissed in a harsh whisper.

Gershom allowed the stillness to spread, filling the tent like smoke. He moved to the back wall, where his father's traveling staff rested in its customary place, scarred by years, the top still greasy from daily use. He ran his palm over its length, feeling the indentations, the story told in nicks and darkened grooves.

"Our father said he would see the land," Eliezer pressed on, shifting to follow Gershom's movements. "He said he would bring us across, not send us like orphans. Why—"

"He did bring us." Gershom's voice cracked, the strain sudden and unbidden. "Just not the way you wanted."

Eliezer's mouth twisted. "You sound like one of them. The ones who forget."

"Maybe I envy them," said Gershom, surprised by the truth of it.

For a long moment, both were silent. Gershom scanned the tent, taking stock: two cots, a folding stool, a battered vessel of water and its chipped cup. On the far side, leaning against a trunk, the rolled sheaf of parchment that had accompanied them through every stage of wandering. He thought of the thousands of words inscribed there, the ink dark and indelible, a history that did not belong to him.

Eliezer broke first. "You could have asked for the blessing. It should have passed to you. Everyone knows it."

Gershom flinched. "Did you want it?"

His brother glared, fists clenching. "Don't put that on me. You are firstborn, and you know this."

"Firstborn of a man who never taught me to lead. Only how to survive. There's a difference."

"You're weak," Eliezer said, voice trembling. "He saw it. That's why he gave it away."

Gershom felt the words slip through him, seeking a nerve left untended. He reached for the parchment, unrolling it a few inches to see the familiar script. His father's hand, deliberate and even, each letter shaped as if chiseled from bone. He traced a line with his finger but did not read it.

"He didn't give it away," Gershom said, so soft it was almost a prayer. "He kept it until the end. Then it died with him."

Eliezer stood, pushing the stool aside so it rocked on two legs before settling. "You should leave," he said. "Go to Joshua. Bow and scrape. Maybe then the people will forget you ever bore the name of our father. Maybe the greatness of our family's name ends with us?"

"Maybe that was Father's intention all along, to leave behind two useless sons who never gave themselves fully to the law," Gershom said, his eyes fixed on their father's writings.

"How dare you," Eliezer growled through clenched teeth. He balled his fist and stepped toward Gershom, but Gershom turned his head slightly, cold and unflinching.

Eliezer froze mid-stride, fury tightening every line of his face. He drew in an even breath, forcing his hand to relax.

"Just like Father showed us... you're not worth it," Eliezer said at last, then turned and walked away.

Gershom let the man slip out; the tent flap snapped shut, a blade of sunlight cutting in as a distant goat shrieked. He lowered himself onto the folded blanket, the ache in his thighs reminding him of every mile he'd traveled in this wilderness.

He studied the artifacts laid before him: staff, stylus, cording, biscuit, and felt only fatigue. The legacy was crumbs and splinters. Still, he lifted the staff, cradling it in the crook of his arm. Its heft was unfamiliar, awkward, yet he held it close, as if it might anchor the world.

For a while, he let himself believe that it would.

The land cooled quickly, heat draining from the ground as the shadows began to elongate, tent lines melting into a dappled tapestry of ochre and indigo. Night on the plains of Moab arrived not as a shroud but as a gradual revelation, the darkness allowing new shapes to surface, new sounds to emerge. Where the air had howled in the day, it now lapped gently against canvas, shifting the seams of the encampment into a kind of breathing organism. Even the stars, first glinting in the east and then blooming across the black like the pollen of some otherworldly tree, lay closer than the world Gershom had known in daylight.

He slipped out of the tent as if escaping a mausoleum, careful to avoid the squeak of leather hinges and the collapse of his own resolve. The camp was transformed: the streets between the tents, which by day were choked with barterers, livestock, errant children, now ran open and silent, every so often punctuated by a knot of men or women clustered around an oil lamp. Here and there, the fire illuminated their faces, turning them into shifting masks, their mouths moving between chant and stillness. Grief, freed from its earlier choreography, became a series of private rituals. A mother traced words onto her child's back with a damp finger, a group of old men quietly recited the Law in a tongue only half-remembered from Egypt, and a girl sat alone atop an overturned basket, singing into her own lap.

Gershom wandered through them, feet dragging enough to stir a faint haze with each movement. He kept his eyes down, avoiding those who might recognize him. He did not want their pity or their speculation. He was not a prophet, not penitent, not inheritor, not mourner. He was, simply, untethered.

He moved past a circle of elders, seated cross-legged around a ring of stones. In their midst sat a boy, barely twelve by the look of him, staring into the fire with the intensity of someone bracing for an ordeal.

The oldest man in the circle spoke, his voice thin as a reed yet unwavering. "He parted the waters with nothing but a staff," said the elder, hands miming the miracle in miniature. "The sea rose up on either side, as if held back by the hands of angels. And when the last of our people crossed, the waters fell again, drowning every chariot, every horse, every man of Egypt who followed."

The boy's eyes were enormous. "And you saw it?"

The elder shook his head. "My father did. And he told me."

The others nodded, the story left unchallenged and unadorned. It was enough that the telling survived.

Gershom kept to the murk beyond the circle, the dimness holding him while the others went about their business. He wondered if there would ever be a story about him worth telling. He doubted it.

He continued on, drawn by the faint hum of music somewhere ahead. Beneath a line of pavilions, he found a group of women swaying together, their song braiding through the air in a minor, wordless lament. In the circle, a girl, older than the rest, her face half-veiled by the curtain of her hair, knelt quietly, hands folded in her lap. Something about her struck Gershom: the way her posture rejected both pride and despair, the way her lips moved in a whisper only she could hear. The torchlight wavered; he stopped breathing as the girl looked up, her eyes locking onto his through the smoke-blurred glow. For a moment she did not look away. There was no rebuke, no invitation; only a calm, appraising regard, as if she looked straight through his skin and into the circuitry of his failure.

Then she smiled, small, wry, almost apologetic, and bowed her head again, rejoining the muttered prayer. Gershom turned away, cheeks burning, though no one else registered his presence at all.

He wandered for a long time, not so much walking as drifting, until the ordered lanes of tents thinned and the camp finally fell away around him. Here, the density thinned, and the evening revealed its true breadth: a current, invisible in the dark, could be heard only as a deeper murmur; the slope of Mount Nebo stood silhouetted in the north, the moon cresting over its barren ridge. Far below, scattered fires marked the boundary where the sentries kept vigil against the unknown.

Gershom stopped at the base of a small escarpment, its rocky slope forming a natural overlook. He climbed, hands bracing on dry root and shale, until he could look back over the encampment. From this height, the people of Israel read more as a single organism than a nation, glowing at their core, darkening at the edges, restless in every limb. The columns of smoke, the grid of torches, the distant shapes moving like cells in a body: all of it, together, dwarfed by the impassive geometry of wilderness.

He did not know how long he stood there. The cold seeped into his feet, but he barely felt it. He cataloged the camps, the stories coiled inside them, the generations yet unborn. He thought about his father, not the prophet, not the miracle-worker, but the man who once bore him piggyback across a flooded wadi, laughing when the mud sucked at their sandals. He remembered the sound of his father's breath at night, calm and deep, the way his hand would settle on him, solid and reassuring, a promise that meant, "I will return, always."

He wondered if he would ever believe that promise again.

Movement drew his eye: down among the tribal banners, the largest tent, now the seat of government, was alive with activity. Figures entered and exited in quick succession, bearing tablets, scrolls, armfuls of new laws to be memorized by dawn. At the entrance, Joshua stood, flanked by his advisors, listening as a messenger reported in frantic gestures. Gershom held back in the half-shadow while Joshua leaned in, the messenger's words pulling his full attention. Joshua's fingers tightened briefly on the man's arm, a single nod answering whatever had been said. There was no performance, no thunder. Only the silent, patient absorption of yet another task.

Gershom felt a pang: not envy, but a kind of longing, the wish to be necessary in the same way, to be the vessel through which destiny might flow. But destiny had chosen otherwise. He was a witness, not participant. He was what remained when the fire passed over and left only a pillar of ash.

The air gusted, sharper now, and with it came a sound, a song, thin but rising from somewhere behind him. He turned. Below, at the margin of the camp, the girl from before (the one with the praying hands and the sharp, luminous eyes) was standing apart from her circle, gazing up at the stars. She sang without pretense, her voice not strong and not trained, but shaped by the plain need to be heard by someone, anyone, above the earth.

He wondered what she prayed for. Not for a miracle, surely. Not for the past to be undone. Perhaps only for the strength to endure the next migration, the next trial that would pass over their generation. Or maybe she prayed for someone like him, a stranger at the boundary, too proud to enter, too ashamed to leave.

He stayed where he was as the song thinned to silence and she slipped into the line of tents. The camp resumed its activity, each light flickering like a heartbeat in the night.

He turned back to the view, the dark land rolling away on every side, the old mountain rising up to the north, the waters out of sight but audible as a rumor. The stars above, indifferent and constant, claimed the night as their own. Gershom felt, for the first time in days, the trembling deep within, the knowledge that he was utterly solitary, yet still alive and still in motion.

He did not pray. But he did breathe, measured and controlled, until the chill forced him to shiver, and then he descended toward the camp, carrying nothing but the echo of her song and the burden of his unclaimed legacy.

Empty Tent

Three days after the passing, the tent held its breath, the canvas saturated with the echo of Moses' absence. Sunlight spilled through the east seam, bright and slicing, transforming each loose fiber and speck of grit into motes that revolved in the shafts, a silent blizzard orbiting nothingness. Every object inside was stamped with the finality of abandonment. Even the ceremonial bowl, upended in the far corner and still streaked with last week's ashes, suggested the careless precision of a man who always assumed a tomorrow.

Gershom sat in the lee of his father's cot, knees drawn tight, eyes weary from long nights. Around him, the fragments of legacy: the woven pouch, mouth cinched tight with a knot of lamb's gut; a phalanx of styluses, ink-dulled at their tips; a folded garment whose blue fringe was blackened at the hem from a fire no one spoke of. He moved as little as possible, as if to animate the contents of the tent would disturb its precarious peace.

On the lid of a lacquered chest lay the scroll. It was not the grand codex the High Priest brought out on feast days, nor the battered teaching scroll from Moses' circuit of the outer tents, but a personal version: a length of worn calfskin, the Law inscribed in tight, precise lines. The wood spindles bore the etchings of his mother's hand, her single indulgence in a world governed by cubit and rod.

He reached for it, and even that act felt treasonous, as if his father's authority might radiate through the parchment and scald him. He let his hand hover above it, tracing the grain of the skin, the spots where sweat had yellowed the corner or a careless ink-drop left an uncorrected blot. His fingers trembled, not with reverence, but with the familiar, recalcitrant fear that had followed him since boyhood. It was the same fear that had kept him silent during the first recitations, the same that caused him to stumble over the simple genealogies while his father thundered through the generations without pause or stutter.

The scroll, when lifted, was heavier than expected. He cradled it in the crook of his arm and ran a thumb along the seam where two sheets met, the join so skillfully executed it was almost imperceptible. He rolled it open, slowly, savoring the sound of paper unrolling. The letters themselves were astonishingly vital, as if they refused to fade with the hand that wrote them. Gershom had always been struck by their clarity: the blackness of the ink, the way each character stood alone yet bled into its neighbors, forming words that pulsed with a kind of muscular certainty.

He brought the scroll closer until the words blurred, letting the past come alive: the dusty heat of Kadesh-barnea, the rabble packed shoulder to shoulder, his father's voice rising above them like a current at the margins of a storm. Gershom, small then, perched on the stone boundary that marked the elders' enclosure, legs dangling, hands clenched so tightly between his knees that the skin went white. He felt the vibration of Moses' voice in his body, the Law sounding not as instruction but as the unraveling of the world, each commandment a stone cast into the abyss of the future.

He remembered, too, the chill that settled on him when his father's eyes swept the gathered people and rested, for a heartbeat, on him. There had been expectation in that glance, but also a kind of resignation, as if Moses read in his son not the inheritor, but the last link in a diminishing chain.

Gershom's jaw flexed. He pulled his lips tight, the bone tensing along the angle of his face. The muscles in his neck corded as he forced himself to read, line by line, the text he had never managed to memorize in its fullness. It struck him that the words were both salve and wound, a comfort in their repetition, an accusation in their permanence. He moved a finger along the verse, tracing the shape of each letter as if by doing so he might reanimate the father who had written them.

He found the passage about inheritance, dealing with succession and the transfer of blessing. The black-on-white of the Law distilled to a single imperative: the blessing did not pass by blood alone. He stayed there, the realization, familiar yet still piercing, unchanged by time. The scroll had always been a codex of exclusion as much as inclusion. What mattered was not descent, but selection.

He let the parchment rest in his lap, feeling the shape of the spindle dig into his thigh. His frame curved inward, folding as if to protect the hollow inside him. The morning outside had grown louder: a child's cry from the cook-tent, the braying of a tethered goat, the haphazard percussion of tent pegs being reset in the gusts, but within the canvas walls the only sound was his own breathing, ragged and uneven.

He read again, "Take Joshua son of Nun," letting the words blur, sharpen, blur again. He wanted to hate the object, to cast it aside and shatter the continuity it demanded. He rolled it closed, palms flat against the skin, and bowed his forehead to the wood as if in benediction. He did not cry. The well was long dry.

He heard the approach before it came into view: a cadence more purposeful than a servant's, softer than a sentry's. The rhythm faltered at the entrance, then resumed, as if the bearer hesitated before breaching a boundary best left untrampled. Gershom did not move. He kept his eyes on the coil of cord in his lap, as if by attending to its infinitesimal loops he could render himself invisible.

A figure darkened the entry slit.

"May I?" The voice was familiar, rounded in the vowels, impossible to mistake.

Gershom did not answer, but Joshua stepped through anyway, ducking to clear the frame. He filled the space in the manner of all natural leaders: never too quick to claim it, never so tentative as to betray uncertainty. The new judge's tunic was clean, the hem still crisp from its first wear; he had, perhaps, slept last night. The only outward concession to grief was the smear upon his brow and the cords of his girdle, looser than regulation permitted.

For a moment, Joshua regarded the inside of the tent with an expression that hovered between apology and duty. His eyes moved over the belongings with a care that bespoke both reverence and a desire not to trespass.

"Your brother said you would be here," Joshua continued.

"He is often right," said Gershom, keeping his tone flat. He did not look up.

Joshua's eyes narrowed, not with irritation but the studied neutrality of a man who had already weighed the day's necessary sorrows and would not add to them. "I have come," he said, "to see to your father's affairs. If you would help me, it will go the faster."

Gershom shrugged. "It is all here. Nothing's been touched." He rose, letting the coil slide to the floor, and gestured vaguely at the tent's accumulation of history. The movement exposed his own lack: the garment he wore was threadbare, one sleeve patched and darkened by the sweat of nervous hands.

Joshua knelt beside the lacquered chest and opened it. Inside, the scrolls were arranged in strict order, each bound with a different color of leather. Joshua removed them one by one, setting them on the blanket with a ritual slowness.

"He kept them well," Joshua observed, as if speaking of a body and not a set of texts. "They say no man could recite the Law as he did, not even among the Levites."

Gershom made a noise that could have been agreement. Joshua eased the scrolls open one by one, his broad grip exact, his nails pale and clean as polished shell. Gershom wondered if this was what respect looked like in the new regime: not the thunder of command, but the careful shepherding of relics.

The stillness threatened to swallow them. Joshua filled it, as was his way, with purpose. "He left instructions. I am to collect these"—he tapped the nearest scroll—"and the ceremonial rod. There is, also, the matter of the seal." He hesitated. "It will pass to Eleazar, of course. But the Law decrees you should witness."

Gershom nodded, still standing. He moved through the scene as a silent witness, the theater of his own dispossession playing out around him.

The rod, when produced, was a thing of beauty, almond wood burnished to a dark sheen, the tip worn smooth by years of invocation. Joshua examined it, turning it in his hands. "You know," he said, "he used to let me carry this when I was a child. I thought it gave me power over the wind." He smiled, the expression brief and contained.

Gershom said nothing.

Joshua laid the rod aside and rummaged through the pouch for the seal. He found it at the bottom, wrapped in a scrap of linen: a small, weighty cylinder incised with a symbol that only a handful of men could translate. Joshua offered it, palm up, to Gershom. "Would you do the honor?" His tone was gentle, but not patronizing.

Gershom took the seal. It was heavier than he expected, the cold stone against his skin a more honest memorial than any phrase or benediction. He wanted to say something, to invoke a thought or at least a fragment of his father's wit, but the tongue was a clumsy thing when grief was the only language left. He rolled the seal in his palm, feeling the engraved ridges bite against his callus.

Joshua regarded him, waiting. When it became clear Gershom would not speak, he rose. "Thank you," he said. "For keeping it safe."

Gershom's jaw worked, but still no sound came.

Joshua gathered the scrolls in the crook of his arm, tucking the rod tight against him, and moved to the exit. There, he turned. "If you should wish to join the council tonight, you would be welcome." The invitation was neither command nor request. "Or you may take your time. No one will judge you."

Gershom managed a nod.

Joshua left, his presence briefly reclaiming the space before slipping away. The tent rose enormous around him, all the more so for the items that were gone. Gershom studied the imprint in the blanket where the scrolls had lain, the faint indentation of the rod's tip on the battered mat. He opened his hand and gazed at the seal: the grooves cut deep, uncompromising, carrying a history both his and not.

He closed his fist around it, tight enough that its contours dug into the meat of his palm. Then he placed it, with as much ceremony as he could muster, on the chest. For a fleeting moment, the act restored the order he had always craved.

He stood in the tent, listening to the quiet around him. It was denser now, as if the removal of his father's legacy had also removed the only thing anchoring the air. He closed his eyes and tried to remember the last time the tent had felt like a home. Nothing came.

He stayed, breath shallow in the emptiness, until the sun shifted again and light poured back, stirring motes into their endless, pointless orbit.

He lasted as long as he could in the hollowed tent before the air thickened, pressing against his ribs, threatening to wring him out like a damp cloth. Gershom moved into the open, his frame bent forward as if bracing against an approaching squall. In truth, the day was so still that even the breeze held its breath. The world outside the canvas was bleached and brittle: a field of tents pitched in martial regularity, each tethered to its neighbor by shared history and mutual suspicion. The distant bray of livestock and the slap of a tent flap punctuated the calm, but otherwise, all was pause.

He pulled in a lungful of air; smoke and dung scraped his throat, stung his eyes, and left his chest tight.

It was not long before the voices found him. They traveled, as all things did in this dry basin, amplified by the acoustics of gossip and the inertia of a people trained to catalog every lapse in protocol. He recognized the cadence. Levites, the old guard, wrapped in their dusk-blue robes and clustered around a makeshift table in the sycamore's shade. Their dialect climbed to a tone reserved for sacred complaint, sibilants stretched thin and vowels worked like gristle.

"...saw him hand over the scrolls himself," said the first, his voice sandpapered by years. "Not even a word of protest. Just stood and watched them go, as if it were a loaf of bread to be divided."

A snort from another, sharper and more youthful. "He never wanted it, the burden. Everyone knows Joshua was the true heir in all but name."

A third, whose tone hovered on the brink of laughter: "The old man spent his life pouring the Law into vessels too cracked to hold it. Gershom, he flinches at the sound of his own lineage. I say, if it were up to the sons, we'd still be circling the Red Sea, arguing about the width of the tent cords."

The first speaker, more deliberate now: "Eliezer at least has a backbone. He would have kept the line, if not for..." A pause, as if to let the implication swell and settle. "Well. It is not our place to question what the Lord ordains. But the optics..."

Gershom's fingers curled, nails cutting into his palms. He kept his head down, feigning interest in the pattern of his footsteps, while each syllable drove inward toward his marrow.

"And yet," said the second, quieter, "I saw him at Moses' cot, the night before Nebo. He wept. Not like a man, but like a child afraid of the dark."

The others grunted, a sound equal parts sympathy and contempt.

A fourth voice, thin and almost avian: "The line is not broken, only changed. Some legacies are measured in strength;

others in silence."

There was a mutter of assent, then the conversation drifted to other matters: rations, the quality of the morning's water, the rumor of a new edict. He exhaled with the precision of someone holding back more than air. He clamped his hands to his sides, willing the tremor to subside.

He skirted the perimeter of their gathering, keeping to the line of shade where the dirt was still cool under his heel. Only when he was nearly past did one of them, an elder with a voice like honey and gravel, look up and meet his eyes. The old man's expression was neutral, but his eyes flickered, and for a second, with something like regret. Or perhaps it was only the sunlight, playing tricks.

Gershom inclined his head in respect. His pace held firm, betraying nothing of the tumult in his gut. His walk dragged with the gravity of a funeral march, each movement balancing pride against shame.

He made his way toward the periphery of the camp, where the river's murmur could sometimes rise above the din of daily commerce. He did not look back. Behind him, the elders' voices bore down, persistent and inescapable, the voice of the Law reminding him of his place, not at the center, but at the margin, always and forever watching.

Night descended with unusual deliberation, as if the day refused to be extinguished without ceremony. The camp at the heart of the basin became a theater: torches sprouted in ordered ranks, their fire magnifying the stature and significance of every assembled soul. The ground, tamped flat by generations of encampment, reflected the light in sullen streaks, and every face in the camp was half-illuminated, half-mask.

At the center, a platform high enough to impose hierarchy, had been hastily raised, the boards lashed together with rawhide and faith. Around it, the representatives of the twelve tribes clustered in concentric rings, colors and insignia woven into the sashes at their waists. The effect was geometric, a living emblem radiating outward from the core of authority.

Gershom found a vantage at the perimeter, wedged against the pelt-draped fence that marked the divide between sacred and profane. He had not intended to join, but the surge of bodies had borne him forward until resistance would have drawn more eyes than compliance. He kept to the margin, face turned from the torchlight, arms drawn tight, his frame a latticework of containment.

At first, the proceedings were rote: a succession of elders recited the day's mandates, their voices merging in the open air, each announcement a stone dropped into the collective will. The topics were practical: lists of inventory, the assignment of sentries, the rationing of oil and meal. But under the logistics pulsed a new anxiety: the knowledge that tomorrow would be different, that the Promised Land loomed as both prize and crucible.

It was in the interstice between two such announcements, a lull almost imperceptible, that Eliezer emerged from the knot of Levites and strode to the front, not waiting for permission. The assembly registered his intrusion with a rustle, the way dry grass reacts to the approach of fire.

He raised a hand and palm outward, and when he uttered the words, they cracked through the air with the precision of thrown flint.

"You all know me," he began, voice scaled to reach the back rows, "as the second son of Moses. You know my brother, too."

He did not signal toward Gershom, but the implication hung over the gathering like a snare.

"Young Eliezer, you speak out of turn," an elder interjected, his hair a mix of salt and pepper, framing a long beard that swayed slightly as he spoke.

"Let him speak," Joshua chimed in. "He has a right to," as he nods at Eliezer to continue.

"Tonight, you speak of order, of the tasks our fathers set in motion," Eliezer continued, words accelerating as if guided by a gust only he could feel. "But what of the root? What of the blood that carried the Law from Sinai to this very plain?"

A susurrus of assent, or perhaps discomfort, rippled through the front ranks.

Eliezer leaned forward, as if confiding a secret to the entire camp. "My father, your prophet, spent his last years transcribing the Law by torchlight, until his eyes blurred and his fingers bled." The image, vivid and unvarnished, settled over the people like a shroud. "And while he labored, where was his firstborn? Where, in the season of inheritance, was the one whose birthright was to carry the torch?"

He let the question fester, as only a brother could.

"Some say he is not fit. That he shrinks from the responsibility." Eliezer scanned the perimeter, his attention snagging at last on the patch of darkness where Gershom stood. "Others say he is more at home among the reeds of the river than among the scrolls of our father's house. But I say this: a man who will not honor the Law in his own blood has no place at the threshold of our people."

A ripple, then a tidal pull, as eyes turned to locate Gershom. The torchlight conspired, catching his features in half-relief: the hollow beneath his cheekbones, the line of his jaw locked against humiliation's force. Hundreds of eyes bore down, their verdict already delivered.

Eliezer spoke again, softer now but with a bite that could not be softened. "If a vessel leaks, you mend it, or you cast it aside. We are not so many, not so strong, that we can afford to be led by the lukewarm. Better an honest exile than a feigned heir."

The effect was immediate. The people drew back, not in deference, but in the involuntary recoil that precedes judgment. Gershom could hear the pulse in his ears, the faint sizzle of torches, the dry-click of a child's tongue somewhere nearby. He wanted to move, forward or back, it did not matter, but his feet had rooted, fusing with the ground.

Joshua stood at the dais, hands locked at the small of his back, face a study in restraint. Alongside him, the line of Levite elders held features schooled to neutrality, their eyes alive with calculation. Even the women and children, clustered at the edges, had turned toward him, some curious, some sorrowful, all complicit.

He could have spoken. There were a hundred refutations: pride, pain, the small stores of dignity he had hoarded his entire life. But every potential answer dissolved before it reached his lips. He kept his silence, and in that silence, every accusation was confirmed.

Those present held their breath, waiting for a sign. When none came, they began to dissolve, peeling away in ones and twos, each eager to be first to retell the evening's spectacle. Eliezer withdrew to his cohort, his stance rigid, already receiving the handshakes and half-embraces reserved for those who had spoken what others feared to voice.

Gershom remained where he was until the torches guttered and the voices thinned. Only then did he move, each step dragging with heaviness, toward the path that wound to the outskirts, where others kept away at such hours.

Wilderness Within

Gershom slipped through the ranks of sleeping tents, the canvas lanes pinched by the stillness of night, the embers at each threshold bright enough to sear the limits of sight. His footsteps found the hollows between scattered debris, each step rehearsed in the secret choreography of avoidance. He moved with the manner of one determined not to leave a wake behind him, the space he inhabited instantly collapsing in his passing. The chill of the hour bit through the weave of his tunic, and the thinnest ribbon of moonlight stitched a silver hem along the crest of his foot as he crossed the last cordon of Levite sentries.

The night beyond was an exhale, vast and vacant. The ground sloped away from the perimeter, then flattened into a series of blanched terraces where no tents rose to claim or partition. Gershom hesitated at the boundary, as if expecting resistance, then advanced, soles grinding through a crust of salt and powdered silt that drank the sound of his movement. In the space between the encampment and the first rise of hills, the air was thick with old smoke and something acrid, a tang of mineral decay that told of ancient riverbeds starved into stillness.

He did not look back. The firelight offered no comfort, and

the pulse of voices lingered behind him in a faint, continuous current. The only witness to his departure was a dog, feral and thin, slinking from behind a stack of broken amphorae, eyes glassy and intent. He bared his teeth in a silent snarl—whether at the dog or at Eliezer's words, he could not be sure—and the animal shrank away, melting into the brush with an ease he envied.

He angled toward the dark notch at the far side of the plateau, where the land fractured into gullies and stone. The moon was barely a crescent, a cuticle of cold light snagged in latticed clouds, yet it cast enough relief to map the way ahead: a field of stunted thistles, a dried wadi scored into the earth, the black-toothed silhouette of tamarisk trees clawing at the stars. The air here moved differently than on the plain, not steady but cunning, lying dormant between bursts, then striking without warning, grit stinging his calves.

The climb to the ridge was harder than he recalled, each step a negotiation with sliding gravel and the half-forgotten games of childhood once played in these outcrops. The soles of his sandals slipped on shale, fine scree rolling out from underfoot and hissing into the darkness below. By the second pitch, his thighs burned and sweat gathered in the hollow of his back despite the night's cold. He welcomed the sting, the animal ache in tendon and muscle.

At a ledge half-way up, he stopped to catch breath. The camp lay below him, an island of distant fires and swaddled bodies, the banners limp, the whole mass sleeping with the practiced insensibility of those who expect to rise and march at first light. He knelt, cupping hands over knees, and spat a clot of dust onto the ground. Above the line of tents, Mount Nebo loomed: not the thunderous Sinai of his father's tales, but a brute thumb of stone, bald and absolute against the horizon. The sight of it brought a taste of bile to his mouth. He remembered his father's voice describing the summit, how the land beyond would look in the moment of revelation.

He started up the final scramble. His knees barked against the rough, his hands raw from clutching at roots and loose stone. At the last shelf, he hoisted himself up and stood, unsteady, at the apex.

The world was infinite and uncaring. The ridge ran like a fossilized wave, curving east to west, and from its crest the land below fell away in a mosaic of barrenness: dun and ochre, pale blue shadows pooling in every depression, the vegetation sparse and twisted, as if scorched into stubbornness. In the west, the river Jordan was only a suggestion, a string of brightness lost between swells of terrain. Farther off, the faintest ghost of green, the Promised Land as his father had called it, looked to Gershom no more attainable than the stars reflected in the darkness above.

The air cut sharper here, slicing through the layers of his garment, prying at the sweat behind his ears and along his scalp. He drew the hood tighter, tucking chin to chest, and wrapped arms around himself. There was no warmth in the motion, only an attempt to keep his insides from spilling out.

He lowered himself to the ground, the stone leeching heat from his bones, and stretched his legs forward, heels digging shallow ruts. His eyes moved from horizon to horizon, refusing to linger on any one feature for long. If he looked at Nebo, he would see the hollowed face of his father, eyes fixed on a future he would never inhabit. If he looked at the Jordan, the unspoken disappointment pressed against him, thick between him and the men who now waited, below, for a new Moses to arise. If he looked up at the sky, so full of cold light, he would be reminded of his own smallness, his irrelevance mapped against the disinterested mathematics of stars.

He did not pray. He thought of the scroll, the passage on inheritance: selection, not descent. He let the words float up, inscribed in his father's hand, hovering out of reach, mocking him with their authority.

He recalled the last words his father gave him, or tried to; the past replayed them, but the tone always came through clouded, more syllables than meaning, as if the message were encoded for a different son altogether.

He let his head fall back, the chill of the night sky pressing against his throat. He exhaled, and the air left his body in a plume as pale as breath on a dying man.

He looked up, at the indifferent sky, and then down, at his own battered hands. The skin on his knuckles was abraded, the nails rimmed with black. He flexed them, then unclenched his jaw. The image of the council-fire rose again in sickening clarity: Eliezer's voice, the crowd's verdict, the mass of eyes refusing to blink or look away.

He tried to compose himself, but there was nothing left to marshal. The discipline that had held him rigid through mourning and humiliation had gone slack in the cold, and with it the last traces of composure. He remained hunched, fists planted in the scree, head bowed so deep that his breath steamed a small patch of earth.

At first the hush mocked him. Then, from some private hollow, the words began to rise, stripped of the cadence of his father's prayers, stripped of the stentorian rumble of a leader addressing the tribe, carried instead in a jagged, unfamiliar voice that shook with each syllable.

"Why?" His throat tightened, the word scraping raw. He tried again, louder: "Why him, and not me?" The sound fractured in the open air, returning as an echo from the far wall of the gorge.

He forced the rest through clenched teeth. "You made me firstborn, you made me son of the Lawgiver, and then you made me nothing. You left me nothing. What is a legacy if the blood is hollow?"

His face contorted, muscles tightening into a grimace that resembled a feral snarl. "Did you ever listen to my cries? Did you hear the heaviness of my heart when I begged for your guidance? Or was I merely a pawn in your grand design, a tool to spite my father?" The bitterness clawed at his throat, forcing a violent cough that doubled him over, and he spat another clot of phlegm onto the stone, the act mingling with his frustration. "What am I to you, O God? A shadow of greatness, an echo of a legacy that feels more like a curse? You chose him, the one who stands tall, while I linger in the dust. Do you even see me? Or am I destined to be forgotten, a whisper lost in the winds of history?"

The breeze shifted, a sudden downdraft rushing along the ridge, dragging loose grit and the bitter tang of distant ashes across his face. It howled in the cleft below, then faded into the hiss of sand on rock. He paused for a reply, an omen, a thunderclap, a shiver in the stars, but none came. There was only the regular pulse of his breath, the tremble in his hands, and the indifference of the earth.

Gershom leaned back, his knees falling apart as he bowed his head. Tears welled up, creeping down his cheeks in delicate rivulets, each drop leaving a trail of salt that chilled his skin. He made no move to brush them away.

He remained, thus, emptied, for a long interval. The first birds were hesitant in their song, the chirr of insects still muffled by the chill. Slowly, the east began to brighten: not with the pyrotechnics of a desert sunrise, but with a weak diffusion, a gradual lifting of black to gray to the barest yellow along the horizon.

He felt the change before he saw it. His body, wracked and spent, began to unclench. Shoulders sagged, fists uncurled. He drew in a breath, held it, and for a moment let the air swell his frame, the heart thudding constant under the breastbone. The pain in his muscles, the ache in his jaw, even the sting of dried tears, all of it lay upon him like proof, a reminder that he was still, after all, made of flesh and need.

He looked again at Nebo, its jagged profile softened, dusk spilling as the sun dragged across the world's last light. He looked, too, toward the west, where the thread of the river flashed in the new light, the promise of water drawing a line between now and what might someday be.

He closed his eyes and let the air have the last word. It did not comfort, nor accuse. It only existed, a presence as ancient and uninvested as the laws that had haunted his childhood.

When the sun finally breached the line of hills, it did so with a reluctance that suited him. He pushed himself upright, not with resolve but with the grim satisfaction of having outlasted the darkness. He brushed his knees, wiped the residue of salt from his face, and began an unhurried course down the ridge.

Each movement pulled him back toward the world of the living, tendons tugging, ligaments protesting, skin prickling as the newborn sun spread its warmth. The descent eased under his feet, the ground no longer jagged, as though the earth, in its own way, yielded to his surrender.

At the midpoint he stopped and looked back. The summit where he had knelt blurred in the brightness, his anguish already dissolving under the relentless advance of light. A final thought flickered, half question, half resignation, before he turned and continued down.

The sun had risen with no hesitation, burning off the paleness of dawn and imposing a new regime of light upon the plains. Gershom's eyes watered as he squinted against the glare, the world now harsh-edged, every outline shrunken and precise. The heat clung to him with the intimacy of accusation, sweat beading on the skin before evaporating in the same instant. By the time he reached the approach to the camp, his tongue felt thick, a dry animal caged behind his teeth.

He skirted a fallow swale, sandals sinking in the powder of ancient silt, and angled toward the nearest break in the cordon—an unguarded gap in the row of tethered beasts and empty wagons, always the least patrolled. He half-expected to walk in unmarked, but as he reached the second row of tents, a figure emerged from the shade of a lean-to, spear in hand, and called to him in the clipped dialect of the sentries.

"Halt."

He stopped, blinking to clear the sting from his eyes. The guard was younger than he, but wore the sash of a regular, a mark of those who had survived at least one campaign. He eyed him with a professional suspicion, not recognition; this was not a cousin or neighbor, but an extension of the Law.

"You were seen leaving last night," he said. "It's forbidden to wander after curfew. We are not yet in the Land."

He spread his hands, palms up, the gesture equal parts apology and defeat. "I could not sleep."

The guard frowned. "We have orders to report those who

break the perimeter."

Gershom shrugged, then forced a smile that didn't quite reach his eyes. "Nothing will happen to me unless it is divinely inspired."

The guard snorted and dipped the spear, signaling he'd heard worse before. "Next time, take a companion. There are leopards in the hills." His look shifted up and down, taking in the fatigue, the crusted blood at his knuckles, the haunted cast of his face. For a moment, he seemed to consider adding something, but he gave a nod and let him pass.

The walk to the heart of camp was a blur of familiar misery: the stink of livestock, the susurrus of gossip from women at the looms, the peal of children's laughter, always more biting in the morning, as if the new day cleansed away last night's grief. Gershom kept his eyes on the path, breathing through his mouth. He moved with the slowness of the sick, each motion controlled, each contact with the earth a reminder of the body's limits.

He moved past the Levite enclave, the men gathered around narrow tables, their words pitched to carry. His name came once, only once, sliced out of the air by a tongue that had already judged him. He kept going, rounding a corner into the sun-scorched open, where the communal well was located.

She was there, her back to him: the girl from the circle of mourners, the one whose song had found him on the margin of camp. Her sleeves were rolled to the elbow, forearms corded with effort as she worked the rope, hauling the water skin up from the depths. Her hair was tied in a loose knot, stray strands catching the light and making a nimbus around her profile. He recognized her not only by the bearing, but by the sense of purpose in each movement, each motion precise, untouched by the eyes around her.

She finished the pull, braced the jug on her hip, and turned. Her eyes met his, and she did not flinch or look away. She regarded him with a candor free of curiosity and untouched by pity, carrying only the awareness of another human being in need.

He stopped a few paces off, the distance at once respectful and unsure. For a moment, both remained silent..

"You look thirsty," she said, voice flat but not unkind.

He tried to muster a reply, but the words tangled on his tongue. He nodded, a single tilt of the chin.

She laid the jug on the well-stone and dipped a cup, hands firm despite the tremor in his own. She held it out, fingers wrapped around both the vessel and the space between, a motion as precise as an offering. Gershom reached for it, pausing before contact, half-expecting the vessel to be withdrawn, the offer rescinded by some hidden clause of social protocol. But her grip held, unchanging, until his hand took the cup and the coolness of it shocked him into the present.

"I'm Tima by the way," she introduced as he began to drank.

The water was a balm, slipping past lips and tongue and filling the hollow within him. Too refreshing to stop drink. He tipped the cup once, twice, the second swallow slower, as if the act of drinking had to be relearned.

When he finished, he handed the cup back, his eyes dropping to the stone between them. "Thank you," he said. It was the first time since his father's death that the words left his mouth without bitterness or armor.

"I'm Gershom," he finally responded, water dripping from his lips.

"Nice to meet you Gershom," he inclined her head, a motion

so slight it might have been sunlight, then bent to refill the skin.

He stood for a moment, uncertain if there should be more, but she was already occupied, tying off the jug, the line of her jaw firm in concentration. He waited for her to look up, to say something, anything, that might fill the void. But she did not, and in that restraint he sensed an unexpected mercy: the freedom to leave without further explanation, to remain a man who needed water and not the inheritor of a failed legacy.

He turned and walked away, feeling the coolness of her generosity linger inside him, radiating through the bruised machinery of his body. As he reentered the lanes of the camp, he glimpsed her one last time, standing by the well. A pull stirred in him, and he glanced back. Tima stood there still, her eyes fixed on him. Their eyes met again, hers unwavering and filled with strength, while his faltered under the pull of uncertainty. He swallowed hard, broke the connection, and continued toward the family tent. Behind him, the creak of the well-rope resumed, constant and unbroken.

Priestly Challenge

He sorted bronze clasps and socketed rods with reverence that edged toward fear, hands hovering as though the metal might flinch from careless touch. Gershom knelt at the open crate, knees pressed into the hardened earth, sleeves rolled to the elbow so the hair on his forearms glimmered in the morning's first band of light. Each joint of the Tabernacle's frame, each hinge and bracket, he inspected for residue: blood, old oil, the ghost of incense. Then he wiped each clean with a strip of lamb's wool before placing it in the shipping basket. The crate's interior was lined in felt, a small luxury wrested from the last campaign's plunder, and for a moment Gershom traced the lining with a knuckle, testing the softness of the padding.

A droplet of sweat skittered off his temple, darkening the wood in a shape reminiscent of script. His hand lifted to wipe it away, but the mark remained. He paused, fingers hovering as if to scrub it clean, then withdrew. The stain stayed, a quiet proof that even the holy demanded mortal upkeep.

The tent was already alive with the business of disassembly. In the near corner, two Levite cousins levered the top off a crate with the efficiency of men who'd spent a lifetime moving the furniture of God. Beyond them, silhouettes danced in the filtered light, hoisting skins of water, stacking ropes, barking instructions in terse, guttural phrases. The air held the faint sweetness of acacia wood, fresh-split lumber threading through the hum of sweat and ancient ash.

His task was simple, but he prolonged it. In the methodical sequence of removing, inspecting, and repacking each artifact, Gershom could simulate control, or at least competence. The items, bronze, gold, or simple wood, were stubborn in their simplicity; they did not expect interpretation, only faithful handling.

He reached for the last of the silver rings, a tremor flickering through his fingers, slight but undeniable. His thumb and forefinger clamped until the knuckles blanched, the effort visible in the strain of his hand. When he lifted the ring, it gave him nothing, no weight at all.

"Your father could pack a whole set of these without once looking at his hands," came a voice, sharp and close, slicing through the curtain of concentration.

Gershom turned, ring still pinched between finger and thumb. Phinehas stood at the threshold, backlit and immovable, his priestly garment flaring at the base as though the earth recoiled from him. The old man's staff was planted firm, but his grip was loose, almost contemptuous of the need for support. His beard was shot through with black, a detail Gershom found peculiarly reassuring, as if even the rigid old judge harbored an impurity.

"Phinehas," Gershom said, his voice neutral but edged with a hint of surprise.

"You missed the inventory yesterday," said Phinehas. "I wondered if perhaps you'd lost your interest in things that last longer than a day." He let the words hang, letting their ambiguity do most of the work.

Gershom returned the ring to the crate. "I thought the inventory was Eliezer's affair now."

"It is," Phinehas replied. "But the Ark remains family business. Until the crossing, at least."

He stepped into the tent, robes sweeping the ground as he moved, then squatted by the crate, knees creaking loud enough for Gershom to hear. Gershom turned the thumb-sized socket in his fingers, buffed it to a soft gleam, and eased it into its padded slot while Phinehas stood in the quiet beside him.

"They talk about you," Phinehas said, voice lowered now, a statement of both fact and warning.

"People always talk, and most of the time they are wrong," said Gershom, keeping his eyes on the inventory.

"They say you mourn your father more than you honor him. That your blood's grown cold for the Law." The old man's face creased at the word, the Law, as if he relished the taste of it even in accusation.

Gershom slid the lid closed on the crate. "Maybe they're right in some sort."

Phinehas reached for the rim of the crate, his fingers tapping with a steadiness sustained by control. "I'll not pretend you were your father's favorite. But you were never a fool." He raised his eyes, pinning Gershom in place. "Walk with me."

It was not a request.

They exited the tent into the glare, which struck like a thrown sheet. The sound of hammers and shouts drifted across the camp, while the ground lay beaten into a texture halfway between stone and flour. Gershom walked a half pace behind the priest, aware of every watchful eye in the camp. They threaded between rows of tents, canvas walls so near they breathed out the smells and voices of waking households: a baby's bleat, the scrape of metal on stone, the hiss of a kettle spitting steam into morning air.

At a crossroad, a knot of boys played with a sheep's skull, rolling it along the ground and arguing over the rules of their invented sport. As the two men moved by, the boys fell silent, their eyes fixed on them tracking until they turned the next corner.

Phinehas led them along a ditch to the periphery, where the tents gave way to open ground marked only by the scars of last night's fires, a place where Gershom found himself often after his father's departure. He stopped at a ring of stones, blackened and still warm, and gestured for Gershom to sit. He obeyed, perching on a slab, feeling the residual heat soak through the seat of his attire.

Phinehas remained standing, looming above like a pillar. "You know the story of your father's calling, yes?" he began, voice shifting into the cadence of teaching.

"How could I not? I lived with him," he thought before speaking.

Gershom nodded. "The bush. The voice. The staff, the snakes, the leprosy." He'd heard the stories since childhood, usually as object lesson or threat.

"Do you know the part that's rarely told?" Phinehas's eyes narrowed, as if peering through the years. "Your father ran. He fled Egypt. He was content to herd sheep for a Midianite priest, to marry and sire sons in obscurity. He even argued with God Himself at the mountain, claimed he was not fit to lead, that he could not speak."

Gershom met the old man's eyes. "But he did lead. He became the greatest of us."

"Because he returned," said Phinehas. "Because he submitted." The word fell like a stone.

Gershom looked away, down at his hands, still trembling in the residual adrenaline. "And if a man can't return? If the blood rebels or falters under its own weight?"

Phinehas's mouth compressed into a line so thin it seemed drawn on with ink. "Then he breaks the chain. And sometimes, that is the only honest thing a man can do." The old man bent, suddenly, and stabbed his staff into the ash. "But the Law will survive even your honesty, Gershom. And the people—" he gestured at the sprawling encampment, the frantic choreography of packing and movement, "—they will survive you, too."

The breeze kicked up a scatter of ash, spiraling it around their feet. Gershom took it in, wondering if even a passing breeze could be a whisper from the God on high. Yet, like so many others, he felt no real connection.

Gershom clenched his jaw. "So, what do you want from me?"

Phinehas straightened, the act costing him an effort he did not disguise. "I want you to remember your father's weakness as well as his strength. I want you to understand that inheritance is not a birthright, nor a burden. It is an invitation," he said with certainty as they lock eyes.

"To what?" The question was out before Gershom could temper it.

Phinehas turned to look out over the plain, squinting into the middle distance. "To serve something that outlives you. To lose yourself in the same way your father did, and, if you're fortunate, to find yourself remade by the attempt."

They stood without speaking, the only sound the hiss

through burnt grass and the faint, sustained cry of a bird somewhere above.

After a while, Phinehas turned back. "You'll assist with the Tabernacle's packing for the crossing," he said, but the sharpness was gone from his voice. "You'll see the holy things delivered as the Law prescribes. After that, you may do as your heart commands. To be one who leads or to be one that is lead."

He started to leave, but stopped after a few steps. Looking over his shoulders, "Gershom," he said, without turning. "Weakness runs in every line. But it is not what defines a man. Or a people."

He had only begun to sense a stillness when it fractured beneath something new. His brother's approach came without voice, without the shuffle of sandaled feet, announced by a shift in the air, an energy that sharpened the edges of all things.

"Eliezer," said Phinehas, stopping in his tracks. He sounded not surprised and not especially pleased as Eliezer came right to him.

Gershom felt, more than noticed, his brother's bulk occupy the void at his left, a presence looming over his shoulder. Eliezer's entry was a study in controlled dominance: he placed himself slightly off-axis from Phinehas, so that the older man was forced to pivot, and in doing so, set his own body between priest and sibling. The choreography unfolded before him, the familiar old pattern slipping back into place. If you cannot outshine, obscure.

"High Priest," Eliezer said, with the faintest bow of the head. "The incense measurements for tomorrow, have you reviewed them?" He produced a slip of parchment from the inner pocket of his robe, holding it aloft as if displaying a banner of alliance.

Phinehas's mouth twitched, a motion at once appreciative and weary. "I have," he said, voice gone administrative. "But we will need to reduce the galbanum. The aroma overtakes in this humidity."

Eliezer nodded, lips pursed in a show of thoughtfulness. "Should I instruct the assistants to adjust the recipe tonight?"

Phinehas accepted the parchment, running a finger over the notations. "Yes. And tell them to cut the stacte by a quarter measure as well. The wind will carry more than usual when we strike camp tomorrow."

All the while, Eliezer's back was an implicit wall. Gershom, seated behind and below, found himself staring at the fine salt crystals embedded in the fabric of his brother's sash. He shifted, intent on standing, but the act would only have driven him deeper into the scene, a bystander to the machinery of ritual. So he remained, hands resting together, his frame diminishing as the two men conversed over him.

The logistics of sacrifice and ceremony filled the air: which day's ashes to store, whether the firepans needed scouring, who should be assigned to the trumpets at dawn. Gershom understood every word, every nuance, but he might as well have been a foreigner in his own birthright. The conversation curled around him, never once seeking his input or glance.

At last, the matter was exhausted. Phinehas rolled the parchment and handed it back to Eliezer, who accepted it with a crisp, proprietary nod. It was only then, as the formalities concluded, that Eliezer deigned to look at his brother.

"You're still here," he said, tone even but heavy with private calculus.

Gershom held his look a moment longer than was safe. "For now."

Eliezer's eyes narrowed, a smile with no warmth in it. "You'll find your place, Gershom. The Ark needs carriers, too."

Gershom forced a small, brittle smile in return. "And the people need priests who can count beyond their own pride."

A flicker of color rose in Eliezer's cheek, but he did not take the bait. He turned to Phinehas, shoulders squared. "If you'll excuse me, there are preparations to oversee."

Phinehas nodded. "Go."

Eliezer retreated, his figure blocking the sun momentarily before it vanished behind the next row of tents.

Gershom felt the air refill the space his brother had left. He stood, brushed off his hands, and nodded to Phinehas, who met him with a look stripped of pity and free of condescension, carrying the weariness of understanding.

Gershom stood and turned from the ring of stones and started back toward the camp proper. He did not look back as Phinehas went his own way.

He moved through the arterial lanes of tents, each step a negotiation through the living body of the nation. Here, women pounded grain into meal, their pestles landing in rhythm that matched the deep drone of their singing. There, boys stripped branches from tamarisk for new tent poles, their laughter abrupt and bright as they snapped the green wood. Men knelt in rows, sharpening the edges of iron blades on whetstones, the hiss and grind underscoring the urgency of imminent departure.

The sun had climbed and with it, the temperature; the air rippled in sheets above the harder surfaces, making the tents shimmer at the horizon. Gershom moved with measured pace, eyes fixed on the path, careful to avoid the sprawl of sleeping animals or the cast-off refuse that marked the borders of each familial cluster.

No one called to him. No voice lifted to question his solitude. The encampment was a world in motion, every part engaged in its proper function, and Gershom alone drifted outside the choreography. He passed a mother scooping water for her child; the child stared at him, face sticky with date paste, until the mother pulled her close and whispered something that made the girl giggle and turn away. A pair of elders, hunched together over a clay tablet, looked up as he went by and resumed their discussion in undertones, heads bowed close as if sealing a secret.

He drifted, unmoored, until the noise and activity dwindled at the far limits of the camp. Here, the tents thinned out, and the ground sloped toward the river. Mount Nebo loomed, vast and unchanging, its presence a rebuke to all human striving. Gershom stopped at the margin, where the world stilled and the only sound was the muted murmur of water in the irrigation channel.

He sat, cross-legged, in the meager patch of shade from a thorn-bush. Around him the camp breathed on: labor humming, laughter lifting, meals made and unmade in their steady cycle, none of it touching where he stood. If he closed his eyes, he could almost convince himself he was already fading into the past.

His hands simply rested in his lap, empty and at peace with it.

The air shifted, carrying the scents of spice, and somewhere behind him, a song began again, rising faint and familiar above the din. He listened, not for comfort, but for proof that life continued, even at the margins.

He had chosen this place because it was overlooked by no

tent, concealed by nothing but geography and the world's inattention. Here, he could be alone with his thoughts, and with the trace of a man who, for all his myth, had not left a single word behind for his own sons.

Gershom hugged his knees to his chest, the shadows sliding over the far bank in slow, restless bands. He thought about what it might feel like on the day they finally crossed. Would the new land seem more inevitability than promise? Or would it, like every inheritance, taste of bitterness even as it sustained?

He did not register the approach until the footfalls were nearly beside him. He turned, expecting a child or a stray goat, but it was Joshua with a staff in one hand and the other resting on his hip. He wore nothing ceremonial, only the plain linen of the day's labor, his face marked by the trace of work. The creases at the corners of his mouth deepened as he smiled, equal parts apology and greeting.

"Is this seat taken?" Joshua asked, and before Gershom could answer, he lowered himself onto the ground, his legs dangling over the slope.

They sat side by side for a stretch, the quiet settling around them. Joshua seemed in no hurry to fill the air; he picked at a clod of earth, tossing pebbles down the incline, watching as they bounced to a stop.

"I've seen you here before," Joshua said at last, voice measured. "It's a good vantage. Makes the river look less of a boundary, more of a pathway."

Gershom considered the statement. "It's still a barrier. Water doesn't care what you want from the other side."

Joshua nodded. "No. But neither does land." He leaned back, propping himself on his hands. "We both know the terrain of in-between, don't we?"

A snort escaped Gershom's nose, involuntary but not un-kind. "You always talk like that? Or is it for the benefit of wanderers?"

Joshua chuckled. "Only for those who know how to listen." He let the smile fade. "May I ask something?"

Gershom shrugged.

"When you were a boy, what did you think would happen when we reached the Land?"

The question landed with unexpected force. Gershom sifted through the answers: obedience, glory, rest, but none sounded true to him now. "I thought my father would lead us in, and that I would help build the first house."

"Your father never told me that," Joshua said softly. "But I think he hoped the same."

Gershom kept his gaze on the horizon. "You're not here to tell me about hope."

Joshua shook his head. "No. I'm here because you have something I never did: a way to let go." He turned, met Gershom's eyes. "Your father saw in me what I didn't see in myself. But he never asked me to become him. Only to serve as I was made to serve."

Gershom pulled at a blade of dry grass, shredding it between thumb and forefinger. "You believe the Lord chooses as He will."

"I do," said Joshua. "And I believe the Lord's will can break a man, if the man won't let himself be changed by it."

They sat for another interval, the river's voice growing louder as dusk deepened.

"Does it bother you?" Gershom asked. "To be the one who follows? To know there will be songs, but not your own name in them?"

Joshua drew a slow breath. "It used to. Until I realized the only story worth being in is the one that matters to others. Not the one that matters to you alone."

He rose, dusting off the seat of his tunic. "We cross any day now. I hope you'll be with us, and I mean more than just in body."

Gershom looked up, searching the other man's face for irony, for the smallest betrayal of condescension. He found none. Only the calm of someone who had found, if not peace, at least a use for pain.

Joshua stopped at the top of the rise. "The mantle God gives is fitted to the shoulders that wear it. Not to the shoulders we wish we had." He inclined his head, and walked back toward the camp, melting into the blue haze of twilight.

Gershom sat until the last smudge of sun was gone from the water, until the only light was the thin glow from the distant tents and the cold, impartial light of the stars.

He tried, for a time, to remember what it had felt like to be a son. But the old ache was quieter now, replaced by something unfamiliar. He did not have a word for it.

When he stood, he felt taller. Not lighter, exactly, but no longer afraid of how his form might appear when cast across the river.

Mother's Wisdom

Gershom found himself a child once more, the tent looming above him like a fragile shell, its lambskin and woven reeds barely holding back the encroaching shadows. He sat cross-legged on the well-worn mat, its intricate patterns faded to whispers of their former vibrancy, and he focused intently on his mother's hands. They moved with a practiced grace, coaxing a tangled mass of wool into the nascent form of a cord. Each motion was deliberate, as if she were weaving not only fibers but lessons into the very fabric of his being. He could almost visualize the journey of each strand, the first twist melding seamlessly into the next, the gathering of individual threads creating a tapestry of strength that conveyed unity born from diversity.

Zipporah's face was illuminated only by firelight, but even in that shifting, orange glow her eyes were the same—reflective, knowing, ringed with the fine lines of a woman who had learned to smile in a world that seldom rewarded it. The features were not as the Israelite women wore theirs: the cheekbones cut high, the mouth broad and quick, the voice tinged always with the music of her home past the wilderness. She did not simply speak to him; she narrated, as though the very air required an explanation to allow her words passage.

"Do you know why we spin cord, Gershom?" she asked, her gaze not breaking from her work. Her accent softened the edges of the consonants, gave the sentence a gentle dip and rise that made it sound like something sung rather than spoken.

He shook his head, fingers knotted in the fringe of his own garment. The desire to please her warred with his fear of answering wrong. "To tie things?" he offered, voice thin and reed-like.

Her smile was audible before it appeared. "To bind, yes. To mend, to hold fast, to build a thing from what is scattered. But mostly to remember." She brought the nascent cord up to his nose. "Smell this, child. What do you find?"

He obeyed and leaned forward, inhaling the faint musk of lanolin, the sharper tang of ash from the hearth, and masked by it, the secret sweetness of the acacia box where she hid her best wool. "Smoke," he said. "And sheep. And something else."

She nodded, satisfied, and resumed her spinning. "Every knot holds a little memory, Gershom. When you are grown, you will see: the world is not kept together by strength alone. Sometimes, it is only the small acts, overlooked, quiet that hold the world in place." Her eyes flicked to the stew pot, where hunks of lamb shivered on the surface, the aroma thickening with each simmer. She leaned to stir it, the spoon swirling up a cloud of rosemary and bitter greens.

She moved, and he went motionless, her smallest gestures imprinting themselves on him, as though the answer he'd chased for years might flicker in the lift of her wrist or the turn of her shoulder.

"Mother," he began, the word strange in his mouth, for she

was always more than that, and never less. He stared at the fire briefly before returning his gaze back to her, "do you ever wish you had not come with him? With Father, I mean."

Her hands went still, the cord pinned between her thumbs. The question, he realized too late, bore more force than he had meant, yet she offered no rebuke Zipporah laid the wool aside and drew her hands across the hem of her garment, the motion deliberate, ceremonial.

She turned, resting elbows on knees so their faces drew close in the furnace-warm dark. "There are things you must understand, Gershom. We were not called as others were. Your father was not chosen for his birth, not for his strength, not for his cleverness. He was chosen because he ran from what he feared, and in running, he found the place he could be met. Even a shepherd can hear the Voice, if his ears are open. Even a foreigner can serve, if her heart is willing."

He absorbed the words, though some part of him understood they were meant as much for herself as for him.

She brushed a coil of hair from his brow, her fingers rough but gentle. "You are not like the other boys. You have their games, their hunger, but you see what they do not. You look for the story behind everything, even if you do not yet know it. This is a blessing, my son, and a trial. There will be days when it feels only the latter."

He looked down, ashamed by the confusion the compliment bred in him.

She tilted his chin up. "Listen. You will hear it said that the sons of the prophet are set apart, that they are heirs to a destiny. This is true, in a way. But what matters is not the mantle you inherit, but the hands you use to shape it. No one can wear a father's skin; even you must grow your own."

Gershom flinched at the imagery, but she only smiled, shaking her head. "I mean this: you do not need to become him, only to become yourself. That is all the Maker ever asks of any man."

A sudden draft, harsh and uninvited, threaded through the tent seams. The fire guttered, and for a moment the world danced reddish-orange, steeped in recollection. In the stillness, a woman called for her child, the name lost in the draft but the intent unmistakable.

Zipporah reached for the spoon again, tasting the stew, then wrinkled her nose. She gestured for him to join her closer to the hearth, and he did, settling beside her on the warm dirt. She placed the handle in his hand, guiding his motion as he stirred. "Careful," she murmured. "Too much and you cloud the broth. Too little, and it will burn at the bottom."

He tried to match her pace, but the motion was unfamiliar. His hand jerked, and a slop of stew leapt over the side, spattering his bare ankle with hot fat. He hissed, but she only laughed—a sound so unguarded it startled him.

"See?" she said. "This, too, is part of learning. Even a scar has its lesson."

He wanted to ask her about scars: how many she bore, how many his father had given, how many were still forming unseen. But the words knotted in his throat.

She reached for a clay bowl, ladling a portion for him, then another for herself. They ate without speaking, the only sound the soft slurp of broth and the crackle of embers.

After, when the pot was empty and the fire reduced to a seam of red in the ash, she gathered her wool again and beckoned him toward the tent flap.

"Come. It is cool now. Let us see what grows in the dark."

Curiosity drew him after her, and together they stepped out into the night. The air bore a keen clarity, the sky a bowl of ice and stars. She moved ahead, pulling him from the fire's comfort, past the loose perimeter of their tribe's tents, past the stacked amphorae and the sleeping beasts. The earth lay bare, marked only by faint, dragged patterns across the soil and the errant print of a stray animal.

"Look there," she said, pointing to a patch where the dirt crusted white over a shallow depression. "What do you see?"

He squinted. "Nothing."

"Look again. Use more than your eyes."

He knelt, feeling the surface with the tips of his fingers. The soil gave way, and in the tiny furrow he found a cluster of spiny shoots, no taller than his thumb.

"Desert cress," she said, kneeling beside him. "You would not think it worth the space, but come spring, it makes the best green for a hungry man."

He pinched off a leaf, pressed it to his tongue, and chewed in silence. It was sharp, almost sour, but not unpleasant. She smiled at his reaction.

"You see, Gershom? Even what grows unnoticed can save a life. It does not need the world's permission to exist. It only needs to root, and to wait."

He looked at her, understanding more than she said.

As they wandered and took a longer route back to the tent, she pointed out the other survivors: a twist of wild onion, the collapsed skeleton of last year's fennel, a stubborn clump of moss clinging to the side of a discarded stone. Each, she named and explained, her voice a catalog of what the world overlooked. By the time they returned, his hands were stained with sap and his mind crowded with unfamiliar names.

They ducked inside, warmth blooming over him as the fire's glow welcomed their return. She set the day's harvest on the mat, arranging it with care.

"Gershom," she said, "what you carry with you may not be what you hoped for. But it is enough, if you tend it well."

He nodded, not trusting himself to speak.

She drew him into an embrace, her arms strong, her voice low in his ear. "Never forget, my child: the world has need of things that do not announce themselves. Even the least seed can outlast the greatest fire."

He closed his eyes, the scent of her hair and the heat of her body sinking deep within. When he opened them again, the fire was cold, and the tent was gone, leaving only absence.

He woke with the sensation of falling, though his body lay flush against the hardened bedding, his blanket twisted about his legs. The dark within the tent was absolute, a velvet pressure, suffocating and close, as if the very air had thickened in conspiracy with his heart. He lay still, eyes open, seeking the crack of light that would orient him, but there was only the faintest ember on the dying hearth, a single red bead pulsing faintly with every draft.

His breathing came in short, sharp draws, the echo of the dream, no, the vision, still rippling through the latticework of his mind. He could see, behind his eyelids, the exact grain of his mother's face as she leaned in to teach him; hear the timbre of her voice, even as he strained to recall the precise words. The absence of her in this moment was as palpable as a wound. He drove the heel of his hand to his chest, as if to tamp down the ache before it consumed what little dignity remained to him.

Gershom turned on his side, the motion calculated to disturb nothing. His brother's cot, across the narrow divide, was empty—Eliezer already vanished to whatever duty or ambition roused him at this unholy hour. The knowledge left Gershom both relieved and diminished: relieved not to be witnessed in this raw, shuddering state, diminished by the realization that even now, Eliezer moved in lockstep with the expectations of a world that had never wanted for certainty.

The dream clung to his mouth: wool, ash, and the faint sweetness of long-ago comfort. He clung to the afterimage, unwilling to cede it to the rising tide of obligation that would, soon enough, pull him into the day's machinery. He considered, not for the first time, what counsel Zipporah might have offered if she were still alive. He imagined her voice, cool and even, cutting through the fog of self-pity: *"There is more mercy in the dawn than you can see from your blanket, Gershom. Rise and find it."*

He did not rise at once. He lay there, allowing his mind to wander the old corridors: his father's proclaimed death, the hollow it had opened in the narrative of their family, the unbridgeable gulf between expectation and capacity. Again the torches of the night assembly lit the shifting faces of the elders as they pronounced the verdict of succession, and the sky loomed over him with its blank, unswerving attention. He imagined the legacy of Moses, grand and unyielding, pressing down on the tent and shrinking the world inside to the size of a sarcophagus.

At last, with an inward curse, he forced himself up. The blanket snagged on his knees, and he had to peel it away finger by finger, each tug a small capitulation to the day. He sat for a moment, elbows propped on thighs, head in his hands, willing the tremor in his stomach to subside. The air was cold, or perhaps it was simply that his body refused to hold warmth; he reached for his outer tunic, drew it on with deliberate slowness, then cinched the sash tight enough to leave a shallow furrow in his midsection.

He stood, steadied himself, then gathered the tools for morning: the cup, the water skin, the length of cording his mother had once made and which now served to hang the little lamp from the tent frame. He moved about the space with the economy of one who has learned to leave no trace, each movement calculated to avoid noise, to leave the world undisturbed. Even the way he fastened his sandals, carefully, thumb following the seam of the leather before tightening the strap, was a study in containment.

The tent's flap was stiff with cold; he worked it open with both hands and ducked through, drawing it closed behind him as quickly as possible. The shock of air beyond the tent was a rebuke, piercing, hinting that the sun would soon climb and render the night's failures moot. The camp lay in quiet, the lanes between the tents dark but not empty: here and there, the glow of a charcoal brazier, the distant shuffle of feet on packed earth, the indistinct murmur of early risers preparing to meet the day on its own terms.

He fixed his course toward the water basin, where the first light would find him and where, if luck held, he might go unrecognized. The sky above was inked with a deep indigo, the stars still bright and untarnished, but along the eastern rim a line of pale gold announced the inevitable. He kept his eyes down, watching the silhouette of his own body stretch and fold with every stride. His gait wavered, the residue of a sleepless night manifest in a subtle limp.

The ground at his feet was uneven, the old river terrace

rutted with the scars of a thousand migrations. He stepped over loose stones, skirted the occasional pile of refuse, and avoided the makeshift oven where a girl huddled, tending her family's morning bake. The air was rich with the smell of yeast and charcoal, a combination so elemental it lodged in the core of his being. He felt, in that instant, both hunger and the echo of hunger, a duality which defined his condition with unsettling clarity.

As he reached the outer boundary of the camp proper, the world opened up: the basin spread out before him, a landscape of empty lanes and sleeping tents, bounded to the west by the first blue shadows of the hills. The mountains loomed in the middle distance, their edges blurred by the uncertain light, and for a moment Gershom imagined them as the shoulders of a giant on which his whole future was perched, teetering, waiting for the chance to fall.

He walked on, the path to the basin familiar but never entirely the same. The rocks shifted underfoot, the dry grass snagged at his hem, and the draft found every gap in his clothing with the skill of a practiced thief. He wrapped his arms around his body, bowing his head against the current, and forced himself onward until the sound of water, faint and rhythmic, began to register above the background murmur.

The world was still in that suspended moment before dawn, when nothing is required of a man except to endure, and Gershom, for all his doubts, found a perverse comfort in the emptiness. He stopped at the rim of the basin, lowered his cup, and stared into the black pool. His reflection was a ghost, rippled by the breeze, the features indistinct but the hollows unmistakable.

He dipped the cup, filled it, and drank slowly, savoring the sharp cold as it scoured the back of his throat and shocked his mind into alertness. The sensation was not pleasant, yet it was refreshing in an oddly unexpected way.

For a long while, he stood at the basin, cup in hand, watching as the sky lightened in imperceptible degrees. He let his mind wander the circumference of the basin, let it drift over the sleeping masses and the endless labor of the coming day. He considered what it might mean to live without expectation, to simply be another figure in the camp. The thought was at once terrifying and intoxicating.

He remained as the sun lifted above the ridge, its pale light stretching across the basin. From behind came the shuffle of feet, a cadence of familiarity rising and falling in the air. The women swept into the clearing, their movements quick and sure: water sloshed into jars, pestles ground against stone, roots and seeds broken down for the day's ration. Gossip threaded through instruction, laughter cutting through the cadence. They moved in practiced harmony, bodies weaving past one another with precision, each action bent toward guarding the water they bore.

He made sure to keep to the periphery, unwilling to disrupt the order, but as he filled his cup from the communal basin. That is when he heard the voice, steady and comforting to both his ear and his inner thoughts.

Glancing down the line of women, he spotted Tima, sleeves rolled to her elbows, muscles corded with effort as she cinched the top of a water skin. Her hair was braided close to the scalp, an uncommon practicality, and the sunlight glimmered along the arch of her cheek as she leaned in to tie off the knot.

There was a competence in her posture, shoulders squared and motions unhurried, that suggested both pride and the faintest trace of defiance.

Their eyes met, briefly, in the way of people who have already calculated the risk of contact. Gershom looked away, feigning interest in the ripples of the basin, but he felt the charge linger, as if the mere fact of recognition threatened to destabilize his carefully curated anonymity.

He made his cup full and turned to leave, but Tima intercepted him, water skin slung over her shoulder like a badge. She did not smile, and she withheld the rote pleasantries that often signaled the beginning of an encounter. She held out a second skin, its surface still damp with condensation, pausing until he took it.

He reached for the vessel, and their hands brushed, a brief electric contact that left a warm print on his palm. He tightened his grip around the neck of the skin, surprised by the strength in her fingers, by the way they seemed to communicate not invitation but expectation.

"Thank you," he managed, voice barely above a whisper.

Tima shrugged, eyes sliding past him to the line of tents in the distance. "It's heavy," she said, "and you looked like you could use it."

He wanted to bristle, to reject the implication that he needed anything, but the exhaustion in his bones and body conspired against him, compelling him to stay. He nodded, shifting the load across his chest. For a brief pause, both stayed still; the world contracted to the small triangle between them, filled with unsaid things.

Tima was the first to break the silence. "You don't usually come here this early."

He considered denying it, but the lie felt too brittle for the morning. "I couldn't sleep," he said, "and the tent... it's quieter when I'm not in it."

Her mouth quirked, almost a smile. "It's loud, isn't it? Even with no one speaking."

He glanced at her, glimpsed the flash of understanding in her eyes. "Yes," he said. "Sometimes it's worse when it's quiet."

She nodded, as if this were a truth she had borne for a long time. "I used to hide in the goat pens, when I was a girl. The smell kept the others away."

This drew a surprised laugh from him. The sound was small, unpracticed, and genuine. "I used to hide under my mother's loom," he admitted. "She would drop the thread ends on my head, and pretend not to see me."

Tima's face softened, the recollection casting a gentle veil over her features. "I remember your mother," she said, "though I was very young. She had a way of making everything seem important. Even the small things."

He looked at her, the image of his mother still vivid from the night's dream. "She believed the small things were what held the world together."

Tima let the thought settle, then said, "Maybe she was right."

They lapsed into a lull, the kind that felt more like a shared retreat than an absence. Around them, the other women continued their work, some glancing over with practiced indifference, others ignoring the presence of a man at the well entirely. It struck Gershom that he was invisible again, not because he had willed it, but because their attention was simply elsewhere.

He shifted the water skin, clearing his throat. "You're preparing for the crossing?"

She nodded. "I volunteered to help. It keeps my mind off... everything else."

He hesitated, then said, "It's strange to think it will happen without him."

Tima did not need to ask who "him" was. She replied, "It will be different. But I suppose that's how we know it's time."

He wanted to say more, to confess the knot of anger and envy and loss that had lodged in his gut, but the words would not come. He asked, "Do you ever think about leaving? Not just the camp, but... all of it?"

he did not answer immediately. She bent to rinse her hands in the basin, the water drawing rivulets down her forearms. "Sometimes," she said. "But there's nowhere else to go. We're all caught in the same net and in the same wilderness."

He considered this, then said, "My mother used to tell me that even a desert weed has a purpose, if you know how to use it."

Tima straightened, drying her hands on the hem of her skirt. "She was a wise woman."

He nodded, feeling the compliment as both balm and accusation.

She fixed him with a level stare. "I saw you at your father's memorial. You stood apart from the rest."

He felt the old defensiveness flare, but she held up a hand. "It's not a fault," she said. "Some people have to see the world from the edge, or they can't see it at all."

He blinked, surprised by the clarity of her perception. "That's how she was, too. My mother, I mean. Even when she stood next to him, she was always a little bit outside."

"Maybe that's what made her strong," said Tima. "Maybe that's what made her yours."

He did not know how to reply, so he let the pause settle between them, no longer awkward, but companionable. She fitted the final water skin among the others, each motion clean and certain, and he remained where he was, drawn into the quiet rhythm of her work.

A sudden shout from across the camp signaled the arrival of a new chore: a cluster of girls ran up, all talking at once, each demanding Tima's attention. She glanced back at Gershom, apologetic.

"I have to go," she said, adjusting the bundle on her shoulder. "But if you ever want to talk... I'm usually here."

He nodded, the words catching in his throat. "Thank you," he managed. "For the water."

She offered a half-smile, then turned and walked away, her braid swinging in time with her stride. Gershom's eyes settled on her, as she stepped into the brightening day, and the air she left behind carried a faint disturbance, like ripples settling after a passing body.

He remained by the well for a while, sipping from his cup, feeling the day's heat begin to gather in the stone. He tried to make sense of the conversation, of the ease with which Tima had drawn out memories he had long kept submerged. It left him unsettled, but also, inexplicably, lighter, as though for a few moments the burden had shifted from inevitability to choice.

He finished the water, slung the skin over his shoulder, and made his way back to the main body of the camp. The day had begun in earnest now, the lanes crowded with people and the air thick with purpose. But as he moved through the press of bodies, he found himself replaying the conversation in his mind, the words hanging together like beads on a string: small, perhaps, but stronger than they appeared.

He touched the spot on his hand where hers had rested. The warmth was gone, but the image of it, like the knots in his mother's cord, held fast.

He returned to the camp with the cup in hand, the skin still beaded with dew where the morning's chill had not yet surrendered to the sun. The main thoroughfares were no longer deserted; they vibrated with the purposeful traffic of a people bent on motion. Men hauled bundles of timber and tools, their faces hardened in the grim focus of those who knew there was more work than daylight; women exchanged handfuls of grain and soft commands, their voices rising and falling in a counterpoint to the clatter of pots and the periodic squall of an impatient child. Even the animals seemed animated by the coming departure, the goats bleating and surging against their tethers, the sheep staring with placid, implacable judgment.

Gershom moved through the lanes as though walking a path underwater, the ease of his conversation with Tima trailing him like a faint current but already thinning in the wake of returning expectation. He skirted around the Levite section, instinctively taking the narrower, more concealed paths between the rows of canvas. It was here, where the sacred implements were kept and the business of ritual converged with the politics of inheritance, that he felt the pressure of scrutiny most keenly. Every gesture in this sector, every greeting or omission, carried an unspoken calculus: who belonged, who merely endured, who drew eyes for any hint of failure or prodigy.

It was at one of these crossways, a junction marked by the fading print of his father's staff against the packed dirt, that Gershom spotted Eliezer. His brother was in full form, holding court at the center of a loose ring of tribal elders and priestly officials. He gestured with open palms, punctuating his statements with the half-remembered authority of their father, the sway of his body echoing the old man's cadence so precisely that for an instant Gershom recognized not Eliezer, but a ghost reanimated.

The elders held the space like men braced for an old blow, their eyes moved without their bodies, measuring every word, every pause, as though the past still breathed down their necks. Some nodded in approval; others exchanged brief, calculating glances, each measuring the younger son's performance against their own interests. One, a scarred old man with a voice like gravel, laughed at something Eliezer said, then clapped him on the back hard enough to stagger him forward a step.

Gershom stopped, half-concealed by the side of the tent, unwilling to intrude and yet unable to look away. In the ebb and flow of the conversation, Eliezer's posture rose and folded like a tide, deference slipping into quiet insistence before retreating again, never overstepping but always pushing the boundary. He caught the unconscious curl of Eliezer's left hand around the signet of their house, thumb grinding the engraved lines as if pulling power from the past. In that moment, Gershom felt the old ache flare, pride and envy tangled with the bitter certainty whatever story was being written here cast him as footnote or cautionary aside.

The water jar grew heavier in his grasp; he tightened his hold, the muscles in his forearm tensing until the skin shone taut and pale. He felt his shoulders hunch, the old instinct to shrink from attention asserting even in anonymity. It would be easy, he knew, to step forward, to announce himself and take a place at his brother's side, but the thought filled him with a dread so immediate it threatened to collapse his chest.

He turned away, taking the long route through the clutter of storage tents and half-packed bundles. Two boys paused in their banter, eyes sliding toward him before darting back again. A woman bent over her lentils kept her hands moving, never lifting her head. Even the dogs in the shade gave him only a twitch of their ears before sinking deeper into sleep.

By the time he reached his family's tent, the pulse in his wrist had settled into a dull, resentful throb. He ducked inside, setting the water skin down with more force than intended, the slap of clay on mat echoing in the close air. The tent was empty, as he knew it would be, but he hovered inside the entrance, unwilling to keep the tent open and allowing the light in, or do anything that would signal to the world that he was home.

He stood there, hands at his sides, and let the morning's events replay themselves in the dark: Tima's words, his own halting confessions, the image of Eliezer surrounded by elders, soaking up their deference as though born to it. He wondered, not for the first time, what genetic defect or twist of soul had rendered him so ill-suited to the script that had been written for his bloodline.

He thought of his mother, of the lessons she had tried to teach him—patience, humility, the discipline of tending to small things. He wondered if she had known, even then, that her son would grow up to haunt the margins of his own inheritance, unable to claim or renounce it. He wondered, too, if she would have approved of the conversation with Tima, or if she would have advised him to retreat further, to withdraw until the ache was manageable.

A gust of wind rattled the tent poles, and for an instant he imagined her voice in the sound, a memory so vivid it threatened to undo him. He clenched his fists, nails digging into the callus of his palms, and forced himself to breathe. Hoping it would be enough to get him through the day.

The Law and the Heart

The day had ripened past the second watch by the time Gershom found the courage, or perhaps the absence of it, to approach the assembly hall, a place for the leaders and priest could gather and deliberate. In the shadow of the great tent, the light was filtered, made thin and refracted by layers of woven goat hair and linen, each dyed band testifying to the Law's gradations. He had not been summoned, and no man had hinted at his obligation, yet the current of the camp had shifted unmistakably toward this locus, and so here he was, awkward, untidy, lingering at the threshold like a rumor.

Within, the space was already crowded. Elders from each tribe, their beards combed and faces freshly oiled, formed an uneven perimeter around the central aisle. They sat on mats in tight ranks, sandals aligned at the edge of each reed rug, hands folded, postures braced against the expectation of a reckoning. The effect was of an audience arranged to witness a trial or a coronation, though the precise charge had yet to be named. At the heart of the tent, atop a raised platform scavenged from the boards of broken wagons, stood Joshua son of Nun, monumental in the shadow and sun leaking through the vented ceiling.

The air was hot, held close by bodies and the canvas, and

thickened further by the vapor of crushed myrrh and sweat. Gershom stood a moment, surveying the interior, every nerve tuned to the possibility of rejection. But the congregation was preoccupied, attention drawn to the front, where a cluster of scribes fussed over a pair of scrolls as if their lives depended on the fidelity of the transcription.

He crept along the wall, avoiding eye contact, and sank into a strip of obscurity behind a stack of surplus amphorae. The spot was not dignified and not invisible, but it afforded him a view of the proceedings and a sliver of anonymity. From this vantage, the conclave revealed as a living diagram, each elder a node, each scribe a circuit, all humming with an energy at once sacred and transactional.

A stillness descended as Joshua raised his arm, a signal both imperious and matter-of-fact. Even the persistent drone of flies stilled for a moment, as if the insects recognized the gravity of the hour.

"We are called to remembrance," Joshua intoned, his voice neither as resonant nor as sinuous as Moses', but suffused with an authority born of survival. "Today we recount the Law, not as a monument to our fathers, but as a guide for those who will dwell beyond the river. The land will not forgive ignorance. Nor will the Lord forgive forgetfulness."

Gershom felt the words settle upon him, heavy and chill, like the cloak of a man not yet dead but already memorialized.

A scribe, hunched at the periphery of the dais, began to read—his voice nasal, the accent of the wilderness unsoftened by any courtly affectation. The Law unspooled in phrases at once familiar and alien: statutes on the inheritance of land, ordinances for purity and expiation, instructions for the division of spoils after conquest. The elders listened with a detachment that was almost brutal, their faces impassive, as if daring the text to contradict their lived experience.

Gershom tried to focus, but his mind wandered to other readings, other assemblies. He remembered the last time his father held such a council: the tent was smaller, the group thinner, but the stature of Moses had made the air electric. The old man read with a cadence that bent the words to his will, emphasizing mercy where others would have found only law, inserting pauses that forced the mind to reckon with the distance between command and consequence. Gershom, a boy then, sat at his father's feet and imagined himself invisible. Yet he knew, even then, that Moses read for him, as if each phrase was a stone laid on the path of his own uncertain future.

He was shaken from his reverie by a motion in the front row. Phinehas, the priest, leaned over to Joshua and whispered, his eyes flickering toward the back of the hall. Gershom instinctively ducked, but it was too late: the priest's eyes found him, held him, then dismissed him as one might assess a crack in the tent seam, annoying but not urgent.

Joshua continued, this time more softly. "It is not enough that we recite the Law. It must be internalized, made flesh and breath among us." He paused, scanning the crowd. "There are among us those whose fathers wrote these words with their own hands. The Law must live in them, or it will die in all."

For a heartbeat, Gershom believed Joshua called to him directly, but the moment passed as quickly as it arose.

The reading continued. On and on, the catalogue of ordinances, the genealogy of obligation. At intervals, elders rose to offer clarification, or to dispute the precise rendering of a phrase. Each intervention was greeted with a bow from Joshua, who then ruled with a clarity that brooked no debate.

Through it all, the tent grew hotter, the air more saturated with the aroma of men stewing in their own importance and uncertainty.

It was near the close of the second scroll that Phinehas again looked to the rear and, with a movement as subtle as a whipcrack, called out, "Gershom, come forth."

The effect was immediate: every pair of eyes in the hall swiveled to him, a hundred pupils dilating with a mix of curiosity, suspicion, and—he fancied—pity. He remained there motionless for several more seconds, thinking Phinehas would pause for a second thought and move on. He was wrong.

"Gershom, arise and come forth. Only men here, no need to hesitate," Phinehas called out once more.

He stood, knees uncooperative, and advanced down the aisle, every footfall loud against the trampled matting. The elders made no effort to disguise their scrutiny; a few drew back their robes as he passed, as if expecting contagion. He reached the platform, the world compressed to a circle of lamp smoke and the faces of men who had buried his father and were, in their own way, still digging.

"Perhaps," said Phinehas, he paused as if gathering his thoughts, "the son of Moses would honor us by reading the passage of inheritance."

Joshua nodded, eyes unreadable.

A scribe handed Gershom a scroll. The parchment was cool and slick with the oil of countless hands; the ink, though faded at the edges, retained the peculiar vitality of a text written in moments of crisis. His own hands trembled as he unrolled it. He knew the passage, of course. Everyone did. But to read it here, in this place, before these men, it was an exposure more intimate than any confession.

He cleared his throat, the sound small and insufficient.

"And the Lord said to Moses, 'The daughters of Zelophehad are right in what they say: you shall indeed let them possess an inheritance among their father's brothers and pass the inheritance of their father on to them. And you shall speak to the people of Israel, saying, If a man dies and has no son, then you shall transfer his inheritance to his daughter...'"

His voice faltered at first, but found a rhythm, less the practiced chant of a professional reader, more the cadence of a man rediscovering his own tongue. The words poured out, awkward at first but gathering a strange momentum, as if the language longed to be heard above the shuffle and snort of the camp.

He felt the shift in the room. Heads inclined, backs straightened. Somewhere amongst the group, a voice whispered, "He sounds like the prophet." Another, softer: "He has his father's voice."

Gershom read on, allowing the words fill the space, not as an act of performance but as an invocation. He came to the end of the passage, rolling the scroll shut with hands that no longer shook. He stood, uncertain what to do with himself, and looked up.

Joshua began first. "Well read. The Law is safe in your keeping, even if the mantle is not." He said it gently, but the phrase sliced through Gershom all the same.

A murmuration moved through the elders, approval perhaps, or the echo of an old grief. Phinehas leaned forward, his expression unreadable.

"You see, sons of Israel," he said, voice pitched to carry, "the Law is a river, and its source must be clear. Let no man question the blood that carries its current, nor the vessel that bears it onward." He nodded to Gershom, an act that was both dismissal and benediction.

Gershom backed away, face flushed, the scroll pressed close to him. He did not look at the elders as he returned to his place in the shadows, but he felt their eyes upon him, cataloging the shape of his defeat and the outline of his resemblance.

The reading concluded with a prayer, a formulaic utterance that left the air oddly empty. The men stood in twos and threes, collecting their belongings and their unresolved anxieties. Joshua and Phinehas spoke in sharp, urgent threads at the platform, the discussion clearly left open, while Gershom kept to his position.

He stayed until the tent had half-emptied before making his escape. As he crossed the threshold, he heard the faintest echo of a conversation between two elders:

"He reads well," said the first.

"Better than he listens," replied the other.

The tent flap closed behind him, and the heat of the day, so harsh before, now felt bracing, almost clean. The sun had dipped enough to cast elongated shadows across the camp's thoroughfares, each tent stake and rope-line inscribing lines of demarcation held as fixed as any statute.

The area outside the hall lay thick with human detritus: leftover bread crusts, bits of wax from discarded seals, the heel-drag of men too weary or too angry to lift their feet fully from the ground. He made it three paces before Eliezer materialized from the blind side of a stacked cart and gave him a soft shove, enough to throw Gershom off balance. Regaining his footing, he turned swiftly to see his brother's face, usually a study in controlled emotion, stretched tight this evening with something closer to pain than fury. Eliezer closed the distance in three long strides, planting himself squarely in Gershom's path.

"Suddenly interested in the Law, brother?" The words were not shouted, but they cut cleanly through the background hum of the camp.

Gershom tried to step past, but Eliezer anticipated and matched his movement, blocking him with the implacable certainty of someone used to being obeyed.

"Eliezer, I'm not up for this today," Gershom said, keeping his voice low.

Eliezer's lips twitched, not in amusement, but in the effort of containment. "That's not what I see. Especially with you parading yourself at the assembly."

Gershom shook his head. "I didn't parade anything. I was called on, same as anyone."

A derisive snort. "You could have declined. You always did before. But today? Suddenly you want to be seen on the eve of crossing over, to read what you never bothered to learn?"

The bite in Eliezer's voice drew attention. Two Levite assistants, arms loaded with bundles of rushes for the morning's torches, slowed as they passed, their eyes doing the quick math of risk and interest.

Gershom kept his focus on the ground. "It's not about being seen. You know that."

"I don't know anything about you anymore," said Eliezer. "Except that you show up when it suits you, then vanish beyond the camp when the hard work begins."

Gershom felt the old shame flush his neck, but he stood his ground. "You think you're the only one who worked? Who hurt? I buried him, too."

Eliezer's hand shot out, grabbing Gershom by the forearm.

The grip was not gentle; it compressed bone and tendon.

"Don't talk about hurt," Eliezer hissed. "You don't know what it is to serve. You don't know what it is to lead men who would rather die than follow a coward."

Gershom tried to pull free, but Eliezer's hand tightened. "Let go," he whispered, aware of the ring of attention now circling them.

"Make me," said Eliezer, face inches from Gershom's. "Say it. Say you want the Law. Say you want his place. Or leave and never come back."

Gershom glared at him, the words boiling up. "I never wanted his place. I only wanted—"

Eliezer's other hand jabbed, index finger pressed hard into Gershom's chest. "You wanted to run. Like him, before they made him turn back. Like her, before she died. You think the Law is a story, something to read when you feel like it. But it's a yoke, brother. A chain you wear until it grinds you down to powder. And you—" He shoved Gershom backward, causing him to stumble. "—you would rather break than wear it for a day."

Gershom steadied himself. The impact hurt, but not as much as the echo of "like her, before she died," the implication as sharp as the physical shove.

"You think you're better than me," Gershom spat. "But you're simply another one of their dogs. Hungry for scraps, ready to bark when the master whistles."

Eliezer's eyes went wide, then narrowed to slits. "I'd rather be a dog than a ghost. At least a dog is loyal."

The tension in the courtyard now verged on spectacle. Several men from the tribal council lingered at the margins, their faces stony, waiting to see who would flinch.

The tent's side-flap stirred, and Joshua stepped through, his cloak hanging open and dust clinging to his knees. Without a word, he moved between the brothers. One hand settled on Gershom's shoulder, the other on Eliezer's, his grip relentless enough to bend their stances toward stillness, the kind of pressure that needed no explanation.

"Enough," he said. It was not loud, but the force of it silenced even the distant argument of crows by the refuse pit.

For a moment, the brothers did not move. Then Eliezer shrugged off Joshua's hand, his breath rising and falling, his knuckles gone white from the residual tension.

"You will never be our father," he said to Gershom, voice thick, then turned away, nor did he acknowledge the ring of onlookers who immediately busied themselves with invented tasks. Eliezer's back receded up the path, the faint hitch in his stride breaking through the mask he tried to keep, and nothing in Gershom stirred in response.

Joshua kept still until the group had dispersed before speaking again. "You read well today," he said, not as a compliment, but as a statement of fact.

Gershom nodded, not trusting himself to answer.

"I didn't do it for him," he managed finally, "or for them. I wanted—"

Joshua stayed, patience infinite.

"—to remember what it was like to hear the words before they became a weapon."

Joshua considered this. "Words are only weapons when a man gives them sharpness," he said, then smiled—a weary, crooked thing that nonetheless softened the lines of his face. "Your father would be pleased you came today."

Gershom looked at him, not as the leader but as the friend

who once helped him gather wild figs at the riverbank, who once splinted his finger after a foolish dare. He felt the edges of anger dull, replaced by a confusion that was almost more painful.

"Thank you," he said, then immediately hated himself for the inadequacy of it.

Joshua patted his shoulder once more, this time with something like affection. "Give your brother time, he will come around," he ended and headed back toward the tent.

Gershom stood alone in the now-emptied courtyard, the sky above paling into the indifferent blue of coming night. The evening bell rang, a flat clang that signaled the beginning of the last meal before the night watch. All around him, the camp stirred back into motion, every lane alive with the shuffle of feet and the faint murmur of exhausted voices. Gershom lingered in the open, unwilling to join the flow, the afterimage of his brother's anger lingering in his vision long after the man himself had disappeared.

He thought of what Joshua had said, about weapons and words, and wondered if he would ever learn to blunt one without destroying the other.

It was not long before Gershom found himself climbing the same outcropping, he has been climbing upon since camp had settled on the basin of Moab. The same place where he could see the whole camp arranged in its careful, concentric rings, each tribe a wedge of color, each light a heartbeat. From this vantage, the world held itself both intimate and impossibly remote. He sat cross-legged on the cool slab, the seam of the rock pressing up through the thin fabric of his garment and let the silence wash over him.

He closed his eyes and reached for the prayers his father had taught him.

"The Shema," he whispered to himself, steadying his breath the way Moses once showed him. Inhale. Exhale. Let the words carry you upward.

"Hear, O Israel..." The familiar line slipped from his tongue, but it landed flat, a shape without substance. He stopped, tried again, the next syllables forming slowly, as if meaning might return if he uttered them gently enough. Nothing stirred inside him.

He switched to the evening invocation, the blessing for the body, the song meant to gather the fading light into something sacred.

"Blessed are You..." he murmured.

The phrases came out smooth, practiced, but they echoed around him like sound inside an empty vessel, loud enough yet hollow, lacking the pulse they once possessed.

He opened his eyes. The dusk had thickened to blue–black, the moon not yet risen. Somewhere in the near distance, a jackal barked, the call returned by another, then another, until the whole escarpment pulsed with the music of creatures more at home in the dark than any man could ever be.

Gershom tried once more, with the opening lines of the mourner's prayer, or kaddish, as it slipped out, the words fitting against his tongue like the bones in his wrist.

"Yitgadal v'yitkadash sh'mei raba..."

The cadence settled into rhythm, guided by the echo of a voice he had once pursued as faithfully as others trace a path in the sand. By the third phrase, his throat cinched without warning, the next word snagging in his voice and dissolving before it could form. He drew a breath, shallow and uneven, the prayer dissolving in his mouth.

He sat quietly, feeling the ache in his hands, the thrum of blood behind his eyes. It occurred to him that he did not know how to pray, not really. He knew only how to copy, how to repeat. Everything he had ever said to God was a translation, a ritualized echo of a conversation that had never included him.

He thought of the day's reading, the way the words had felt alive and dead at the same time. He remembered the heft of the scroll, the hot glare of the elders, the searing contempt in Eliezer's voice. He thought of his mother, the way she made her own rules for prayer, the way she taught him to look for the face of God in the pattern of wind on water, or in the persistence of weeds along the banks of a dried-up wadi.

He tried to imagine what she would say now. Probably nothing; she would let the stillness do its work.

He cleared his throat. "I don't know how to do this," he said, the words unsteady as they left him. "I was never taught the way you wanted. Father always knew the right words, but I—"

The rest snagged in his throat. "I don't."

Heat climbed up his neck, tightening behind his eyes. Frustration roiled beneath his ribs, tangled with something sharper, something he didn't want to name. His breath hitched once before he forced it steady, holding back the tears that pressed hard against the limits of his composure.

He stood still, as if expecting a sign. The only answer was the wind, cooler now, brushing against his sleeve.

He tried again, the words tumbling out, unmeasured and unremarkable. "I came today because I missed him. Not because I wanted his place. Not because I think I'm worthy of anything. I just—" He faltered, then finished, "didn't want to be forgotten."

He looked up at the stars, burning in their uncaring arithmetic. He wondered if they remembered the man who once called them forth by name, or if every generation was required to start the naming all over again.

"I don't know what you want from me," he breathed out, the weight of his uncertainty hanging heavily in the air, directed toward the God of his fathers, yet perhaps also a plea to the very echoes of those fathers themselves. The night sky loomed above him, indifferent and vast, as if holding the answers beyond reach. "But I'm here. I am here," he continued, his voice trembling with a mixture of desperation and defiance, a quiet declaration against the heavy calm surrounding him.

He remained for the surge of shame, the automatic self-flagellation that usually followed any moment of vulnerability. But it did not come. Instead, he felt a spreading calm, as if the admission of not knowing held its own wisdom, releasing him from the old, inherited urge to posture or command the quiet around him.

He stayed there a long while, words coming in uneven bursts. Nothing ritualistic, nothing polished. Halting, plain speech from a man who had never learned how to lie to the open air.

"I don't know what to do with him," he muttered, rubbing the heel of his palm against his brow. "Eliezer... he looks at me like I'm already a failure he's just waiting to confirm."

The wind shifted, brushing his cheek, and the next confession slipped out before he could tame it.

"It's like something's eating at me. I wake up angry. I go to sleep angry." He swallowed, voice thinning. "And I don't even know who I'm angry at anymore."

Silence opened around him, wide and patient.

He let out a slow breath. "I keep seeing him," he whispered. "My father. The way he looked near the end. Always hoping

I'd catch on this time. Always waiting."

More words followed: quiet, scattered, half-formed truths he had never allowed another soul to hear. Thoughts he had refused to let himself think in the dark, now slipping free into the night air as if they had been waiting for this moment to surface.

He did not expect a reply, and so when the tears came, first slow, then sudden, he did not resist. He let them fall, each one a bead of salt that traced a new path down his cheek, pooling in the hollow above his collarbone. It was not relief, exactly, but it was not despair either. It was the feeling of something real, and that was enough.

The night deepened. In the camp below, the torches were gradually extinguished, the lanes emptying as the people withdrew into their shelters. Above, the stars pulsed brighter, mapping out patterns he had never bothered to learn.

He stayed on the rock, watching the slow arc of the heavens, until his legs numbed and his jaw stopped trembling. When he finally rose to leave, he felt lighter, if only by a fraction, the old heaviness spread into places he could manage.

Jordan's Edge

At dawn, Gershom's body registered the cold before it registered the summons, the ingrained reflex of a thousand mornings spent roused to duty in the service of a will not his own. The camp stood still, the calm enforced by the discipline of a people who had spent generations living by the drumbeat of other men's imperatives. Somewhere in the distance, a sheep coughed out the remainder of a bad dream; the noise threaded through the interval before the next breath, then was gone, leaving only the brittle, pre-light expectancy of a day about to demand its presence.

The runner appeared right when Gershom had finished cinching his outer wrap, a boy with arms too long for his frame and the voice of someone still uncomfortable with authority. "You are called," he said, neither deferential nor rude, merely a conduit for the instruction that awaited. "The tent of Joshua, at once." No elaboration. The message was sufficient; no one summoned at this hour needed explanation.

He followed the boy, keeping a respectful distance, his feet leaving twin furrows in the fine grit that overnight had blown in from the open lands east of the valley. The other tents were silent, their occupants cocooned in a final hour of borrowed comfort. The air stung with the possibility of frost; his breath smoked out ahead of him, dissipating quickly in the direction of the new sun.

At the perimeter of the command enclosure, two guards stood at the threshold, men of the old stock, faces carved with the lines of a life spent between hunger and discipline. They eyed him, registered his status, then stepped aside in perfect synchrony, the gesture as automatic as the blink of an eyelid.

Within, the tent's interior was already aglow with the warmth of a brazier. Joshua sat at a short table, hunched over a spread of parchment and twine. His face was half-illumined by the glow, the planes of his cheek thrown into stark relief; he looked older than yesterday, but his posture retained the same measured composure as ever. Beside him, two officers, Shammah and Elead, both veterans of the southern campaigns, hovered, their attention fixed on the materials before them rather than on the man about to enter their orbit.

Gershom hesitated at the entrance, waiting for acknowledgement. Joshua looked up, and for a moment the two men regarded each other through the haze of their shared, unspoken history. "Come," said Joshua, his voice roughened by sleep but clear enough to carry through the thickness of the air. "We are nearly ready."

Gershom stepped inside, his senses immediately assaulted by the tangle of sweat, old leather, and the resinous sap that fueled the brazier. He stopped shy of the table, folding his hands behind his back, the pose of someone long accustomed to being observed but seldom addressed directly.

"We leave at first light," Joshua began, not as a preamble, but as a pronouncement. "The scouts will go before the main body. We will assess the approaches to the river and report at dusk. Your task is to observe and record. Nothing more, unless I say otherwise." He did not glance at the officers for confirmation; his words settled on the men as if carved into the tent's supports.

Gershom nodded, but said nothing. His throat was still raw from the previous night, and he sensed any question would be unwelcome.

Joshua gestured to the table, where a crude map had been sketched in ink and scored with the point of a dagger. The river was marked as a fat, uneven line, the territory beyond a series of unlabeled notches and hollows. "You will travel with these men," Joshua continued. "Do not separate, unless there is a threat, in which case you will return here at once. Is this clear?"

Gershom nodded again. He studied the map, noting the subtle corrections that had been made: a crossing point erased and redrawn farther south, a path through the reeds abandoned in favor of a higher ridge. He wondered who had made these amendments, whether they had been born of revelation or of panic.

"Questions?" said Joshua, it was clear there was room for only one kind of question, the kind that revealed more about the asker than about the mission.

"Why me? There are so many others more fitting for this task," Gershom thought.

Gershom shook his head. The officers said nothing, their attention fixed now on their own preparations: one testing the edge of his short sword, the other tightening the cord of a waterskin. The message was obvious: everything that mattered had already been said, and anything left unsaid was either extraneous or dangerous.

Joshua leaned back, exhaling through his nose. "Good. You

are dismissed. Meet at the east gate in twenty minutes. Bring nothing you can't afford to lose."

Gershom backed out of the tent, his pulse quickening as the cold reasserted beyond the canvas. He walked the perimeter once, his steps striking with a force that drove out the residue of the meeting. The sky above had begun to pale, the first hint of gold brushing the undersides of the ragged clouds. He ducked into his tent, pulled out the battered pouch and the coil of cord his mother had spun, then strode back to the meeting ground.

The scouts had already gathered. Shammah and Elead, their gear cinched tight, conferred in the low, muttered code of men for whom every word was an increment of risk. The others, four in all, none of them Levites, stood in loose formation, eyeing one another with the practiced suspicion of comrades who might, at any moment, be ordered to leave the slowest behind.

Gershom found his place at the rear of the group, not welcomed yet not excluded. The signal to move came as a flick of Shammah's hand, and they departed at a pace that would have strained lesser men. He matched strides with the last two, both seasoned in the old wars, their names irrelevant but their bearing unmistakable.

Gershom found himself relieved that all those days spent walking the wilderness and climbing the nearby hills had not been in vain. *"Was this the reason Joshua chose me? He did say he saw me,"* He thought.

The camp fell away quickly behind them, replaced by the sprawl of the plain, a featureless expanse poised to sap the resolve of anyone who stared at it for too long. The ground was hard, cracked by weeks without rain, and the breeze carried whorls of fine powder that coated their sandals and crept into the seams of their clothing. Overhead, a single kite hawk circled, its cry so high-pitched it was nearly indistinguishable from the shriek of a flint blade against stone.

For the first hour, no one uttered a word. The labor of movement consumed all available breath, and each man conserved his voice as he would his water. Gershom found his mind wandering to the odd mechanics of the journey: the way the men kept their spacing, the unconscious choreography that prevented them from bunching up or straying too far. He counted their steps, then stopped, realizing that the act alone was a kind of prayer, a hedge against the anxiety that came with not knowing what lay ahead.

They crossed a gully where the remnants of a goat carcass steamed in the morning sun, the flesh picked clean, but the eyes left intact, staring up in accusation. Elead pointed at the bones with the tip of his staff, then made a sign against the evil eye. "We're not the first to try this route," he said, voice low enough that only the men closest could hear.

Shammah grunted. "The river is different every year. Last spring it ran high enough to drown a camel. Now they say you can wade it if you know where to walk." He did not slow as he spoke; the pace was relentless, designed to punish any doubt.

One of the other scouts, a man with the ragged beard and the bearing of a failed merchant, spat into the dirt. "Wading is fine for a handful of men. Try it with a whole camp behind you and see how far you get."

This prompted a round of sardonic laughter, quickly stifled. The air was too thin for frivolity.

Gershom listened, but did not contribute. He was aware of his own outsider status, the way the other men glanced at him only when they thought he was not looking. He felt his father's absence settle upon him, in his body and in the air around him. Where authority should have stood, there lingered only a vacuum, patched together by men joined more by need than by faith.

They walked through the changing terrain, the first four hours a study in incremental suffering: the dust grew thicker, then abated as the ground sloped into a shallow basin, where the earth was crusted over in white, brittle patches like the scab of an old wound. At intervals, the landscape offered a brief mercy: a windbreak of wild grass, a stand of stunted tamarisk. Mostly it was a relentless canvas of the same, the variations subtle and demoralizing.

By midday, the sun had risen to its punishing height. The group stopped below a scrap of overhanging rock, its shade barely enough for two, but they crowded in anyway, hands cupped over eyes as they assessed the path ahead.

"We're on time," said Shammah, scanning the horizon. "The river's less than an hour now, if we keep straight."

One of the others, a younger man with a jagged scar down the side of his face, uncorked his flask and took a sparing sip. "What's the plan when we get there?"

Shammah shrugged. "We observe, we make a record, we don't get killed. Same as always."

The nods ended the exchange. Gershom unwrapped a piece of dried fruit and chewed it with unhurried bites, the sun casting a bright, slender trail along the river's far-off bend. He tried to recall what his father would have said, had he been present, but the recollection was slippery, words displaced by the burden of the world that came after. He settled for the comfort of the routine: eat, drink, wait for the order to move.

When they set off again, the air had grown thick with the scent of water, a richness that clung to the skin and reminded even the most jaded scout of why men risked everything to cross from one world into another. The grass grew greener in patches, and here and there the ground softened, forcing them to adjust their footing lest they sink in the mud. The hawk had vanished, replaced by a cloud of insects that rose and fell in intricate, meaningless patterns.

As they neared the river, the landscape changed: the dust gave way to alluvial sand, the plants grew in denser, tangled clumps, and the ground trembled with the faint, continuous percussion of water moving at speed. They crested a low rise, and there, not more than a quarter mile ahead, the Jordan ran: a brown, muscled current, wider than Gershom had expected, its surface breaking in eddies and whorls that revealed nothing of the treachery below.

The scouts stopped in unison, as if arrested by an invisible hand. Even Shammah took a moment before speaking. "There it is," he said. "The last line."

No one responded. The river was not a metaphor to these men, but a reality, one that had claimed better men than themselves, and would again.

Gershom stood at the edge of the group, his gaze fixed on the far bank, where the land was rumored to be as fat and forgiving as any in the world. He felt the old, familiar sensation of standing outside himself, the observer rather than the actor, and for a moment he allowed the feeling to settle. It was easier this way, to see the task as a series of problems to be solved, rather than as a destiny to be either embraced or declined.

The men fanned out along the bank, each one assessing the current, the lay of the stones, the depth of the far channel.

Gershom trailed after them, careful to keep his distance but attentive to every word exchanged.

"It's high for this season," said the merchant-scout, squatting at the water's edge and letting his hand skim the surface. "If it doesn't drop before the crossing, we'll lose people."

Elead nodded, eyes narrowed. "You see the color? It's carrying silt. There's been a storm upstream."

Shammah walked a few yards upstream, scanning the terrain for a more forgiving approach. "We'll mark the shallowest point and double back for the main body. No reason to risk the crossing until we have a clear plan."

The others murmured assent, then dispersed to gather samples of the riverbank—handfuls of mud, sprigs of reed, a single, perfect stone plucked from the water as if it might contain the secret of what waited on the other side.

Gershom remained at a distance, the low hum of the group's voices merging with the drone of insects and the constant, tireless rush of the river. He was aware of his own posture, tense and tight-jawed, his hands twitching with the urge to write or maybe to pray, and he wondered if anyone else noticed. He doubted it; these men had survived by knowing exactly how much to ignore.

The Moabite

The river was not merely a line on the map, nor even a destination; it was a voice. A sibilant, ceaseless whisper, more present than the wind or even the insistent hum of insects, its message both invitation and rebuke. By the time Gershom reached the embankment, sweat ran down the small of his back, his sandals heavy with the silt of the alluvial approach. The sun hung directly overhead, its reflection off the water so blinding it forced light through his eyelids, burning away the last residue of sleep or self-pity.

He stopped at the margin, toes over the lip of the clay, and stared across at the far bank. The water was thick, brown, muscled with the promise of undertow, but beyond it the land lifted in terraces: a half-hidden geometry of new greens, pale and gold at the edges, the occasional shock of wildflower like an error in the logic of the wilderness. The transition was abrupt; here, the battered weeds and exposed roots clung to life, while there, a lushness began almost immediately, as if the very act of crossing conferred favor.

Gershom felt the familiar tightening in his throat. He tried to swallow it, but the taste was coppery, as if he had bitten his own tongue.

Along the riverbank, the voices of the scouts played a

syncopated counterpoint to the river's monotone.

"—measure at the break in the reeds, its narrowest there—"

"I've seen worse at harvest, but it's fast, maybe a cubit and a half per second—"

"—you can see the striations on the rock, it's undercut, probably collapses after the first flood—"

Shammah's voice was a dull grind, harsh and unrelenting: "If we have to ford here, we'll need to build a causeway or risk losing a third of the baggage. There's no margin for error."

The men spread out, one doubling back to flag the best approach, another using a staff to probe the depth at the point where the current, at a glance, offered its most forgiving face. They were thorough, precise, skeptical of the river's calm; the tension in their murmurs made it clear they did not trust this passage, or perhaps they did not trust the fate that had led them here.

Gershom let their words drift past, a haze of professional paranoia that failed to touch him. He stepped away from the main group, his feet finding the uneven, stone-studded margin where the water nibbled at the earth in small, incremental bites. The stones were slick with algae, their surfaces rounded by years of patient abrasion. He bent to pick up a black river stone, flat and ovoid, heavy enough to press certainty into his palm. He ran his thumb over its surface, noting the tiny scars and pocks, the evidence of a thousand collisions.

He squatted near the water, balancing the stone in one hand while the other hand traced lazy patterns in the silt. The water was colder than expected, even in the heat of the day; it numbed his fingers almost instantly, the nerves firing quick, panicked signals up the length of his arm. The little snail crawled the length of his hand, each movement a damp tick of time, before dropping into the current and disappearing like a thought wiped clean.

He looked up, eyes stinging from the glare, and for the first time let himself imagine the multitude: the mothers and children, the animals, the sick and the hungry, queued here. Their lives were balanced on the whim of a river that owed them nothing. He tried to conjure the sound of that future moment, the shouts, the prayers, the chaos, but all he heard was the river, uncaring and monotonous.

He glanced back at the men. The scouts were now clustered around a makeshift staff, marking out spans with the twine they bore for such a purpose. Elead had rolled up his trousers and waded knee-deep into the channel, his calf muscles straining against the pull. He shouted back some measurement, but Gershom did not register the number. He stood, drying his wet hands against the coarse linen at his legs, then drifted farther downstream, away from the others yet still within their line of sight.

Here the bank was overgrown, the branches of an old acacia dipping close enough to nearly brush the surface. The air was denser, thick with the green, living smell of riverweed and wet bark. He reached for a branch, his hand closing around the roughness of the trunk. The sensation was grounding, a reality check against the unreality of the moment.

For a long interval he stood like that, fingers hooked into the ridges of the tree, toes curling into the cold mud, body oriented toward the impossible distance. He thought of the stories, the ones his father used to tell at the end of a long march or in the comfortless dark: the splitting of the sea, the plagues, the bread from heaven. They were stories of rupture, of world turned upside down, of nature bending to the will of a God who sometimes gave voice and sometimes remained silent. It struck Gershom, with a clarity he had never before allowed, that he did not believe the river would part for them, not unless someone was willing to walk in first and let the current take them under.

He stood at the riverbank, the current glinting like hammered bronze beneath the sun. A cool shiver ran up his spine as the water whispered around his ankles. Then the world tilted, light bending and sound thinning, and the river rose to take him inward, its touch both weightless and overwhelming. In the next heartbeat, he felt like he was no longer standing but falling gently, he blinked rapidly to keep the world from swallowing him whole.

"You are from the camp," a voice said from behind him, the words shaved down to their simplest form, no effort wasted on embellishment.

Gershom shook off the weird feeling and spun to face the voice, his posture that of defense, only to find a Moabite leaning against the old acacia. He was certain that the figure was not there before or maybe he was too focused on the river to notice him. He took in the man, the cut of his tunic and the patched trading cart at his side. Age had carved his face into a topography of creases and burnt umber, his hands resting palm-up on his knees as if he had finished a long calculation and found the answer unsatisfactory.

"Don't worry young man, I've traveled too far and wide to be one of danger," the old man said.

"One, can't be too careful," Gershom said, relaxing his posture. "I did not see you there."

"You're fine. No crimes committed, the heat can do weird things to the mind," the old man smiled. "You from the camp of Israel," he repeated.

"We're marking the river. It's high this year." Gershom answered keeping his tone level, conscious of the fragile detente that governed such meetings in the borderlands.

The Moabite gestured at the river with a tired sweep of the hand. "It's always high, until someone proves it's not." There was a wryness to his voice, not quite mocking but edged with the survival instinct of a man who had witnessed many cycles.

Gershom stepped closer, taking care to keep his hands visible. "Are you alone?" he asked, though the question was less about numbers than about intent.

The Moabite nodded. "I wait here for whomever comes pass. And today, that appears to be you." He shifted his weight on the root that served as a bench, then, after a moment's deliberation, gestured for Gershom to join him.

Gershom lowered himself to the ground a meter away, his back against the cool, rough bark of the acacia. The two men sat, side by side but not together, each angled slightly apart, the air between them holding a quiet tension which kept pressed for distance.

From this vantage, the river lay before them not as a raging torrent but as a long, unbroken cord, its surface glinting as though it stitched the familiar shore to the mysteries beyond. The Moabite produced a strip of leather and began to work it between his fingers, hands moving with the idle, unconscious precision of someone trained since childhood to never let the body go slack.

"I have heard about your people," he said, voice low, pitched above the river's murmur. "They say you have a God who does not forget."

Gershom weighed the phrase before answering. "Sometimes

He remembers more than we'd like."

The Moabite nodded, lips curling into a brief, private smile. "A problem for you, or for Him?"

Gershom shrugged. "Depends who you ask."

"Maybe He's reminded constantly of actions that keep Him from forgetting," the old man responded, his eyes locked on the passing water.

"Maybe he's right. Our people wandered this wilderness because we refused to listen," Gershom thought.

For a while, no words were exchanged. The Moabite took a knife from his belt and began to whittle at a twig, the shavings falling in tight curls onto the top of his boot. Gershom took in the even rhythm, each slice matching the one before it. He wondered if the man had learned this from his own father, or if it was simply something men did when their words had run out.

"You will cross," the Moabite said at last, not as a question but a certainty. "Sooner than anyone thinks." He looked at Gershom, eyes sharp and unblinking. "Do you believe it?"

Gershom considered. "I believe it will happen. I don't know what comes after."

The Moabite grunted. "After? There is always after. You take the land, you plant your crops, you build your houses. And then the river is only water again."

Gershom laughed, but the sound was thin. "Is that how it was for you?"

The Moabite nodded, not taking offense. "My father's father saw the first of your kind cross the desert. They said it would be the end, but it wasn't. Just another beginning, but with different men at the table." He paused, then added, "You will find the soil good. The grass grows twice as fast as on this side.

The goats are bigger, and their milk is sweet. Don't get me started on the grapes."

Gershom looked at the river. "Do you mind?"

The Moabite shrugged. "I mind, but what is the point? The river is older than either of us. It remembers every crossing. Men come, men go, the water stays." He gestured with the knife, an orator's flourish. "You have your God. The river has itself. But if your God is as powerful as the tales say, then you should have nothing to worry about."

They sat in the quiet that followed, the river's sound broken only by the occasional buzz of a cicada or the faint slap of water against root. Gershom found his gaze returning to the Moabite's hands, the way they never stopped moving. There was a grace in it, a patience he envied.

"Tell me about the other side," Gershom said, surprising himself with the request.

The Moabite regarded him for a moment, then obliged. "It's not all what they say. Some places are bitter. Some are empty. There are wolves, and men worse than wolves. But there are also gardens. Springs that never run dry, even in the worst season. And the sky—" he glanced up, as if confirming it was still there—"the sky is wide, and forgiving. You can walk for a day and never see another soul, if that's what you want."

Gershom closed his eyes, picturing it. He had spent so much time thinking of the other side as an enemy, a thing to be conquered or feared, that he had not considered it as a place simply to be. A landscape waiting to be impressed with the memory of those who would cross it.

The Moabite set aside his knife and flexed his fingers, then reached into a small pouch at his waist. He took out a strip of dried fig, broke it in half, and offered a piece to Gershom.

"Peace," he said, as if the word needed no further context.

Gershom took the offering, the sweetness blooming in his mouth in contrast to the dryness of the air and the salt of old sweat on his lips. He chewed, swallowing past a lump he had not known was there.

He stood, wiping his hands on his clothes. "Thank you," he said, and meant it.

The Moabite nodded, eyes crinkling at the corners. "Thank you for not pretending," he said, "like so many of your kind do."

Gershom smiled. "I'm glad I was able to represent my people well." He stepped toward the water, turning his back to the old man. "Thank you for the information. It will be valuable to my people." He steadied himself with a nearby branch.

He fell silent again, taking in the landscape.

He let go of the branch, feeling the texture imprinted on his palm, and stooped to examine the roots growing into the water. Some were exposed, pale and slick, a latticework of need in competition with the inevitable collapse. Others burrowed deep, invisible but persistent. He traced a single root-line with the tip of his finger, following it until it vanished into the brown opacity.

A movement upstream caught his attention—a shout, followed by the wet thud of someone slipping and then a curse, muffled but distinct. The men had finished their work and were calling for him, their voices more insistent now, impatient with his absence.

Gershom straightened and faced the Moabite. "I appreciate the—"

He stopped. No one stood there.

He turned in a quick circle, scanning the riverbank.

"There's no way that old man could've left that fast," he thought, his eyes sweeping the empty stretch again.

The scout party called for him once more. With no time to search for the old man, he turned back toward the group, his mind still turning over the question of where the Moabite could have gone.

He rejoined the others, his body marked by the residue of the water, his mind drawn tight as a bowstring. He offered nothing to the conversation as they prepared to double back, but he allowed himself a final, surreptitious glance over his shoulder, the old man was nowhere to be seen. The river continued, relentless, unmodified by human intention, and yet something in its ceaseless motion, for a moment, invited the thought of crossing. Not for free, and not without loss, but possible.

He walked away with the others, both the old man and river's voice receding but never quite vanishing from the back of his mind.

And that, somehow, was a comfort.

The boundary of the camp was marked by more than watch-fires and the dusty depressions of sentry feet; it was the change in air, in the density of voices, in the choreography of bodies moving with either intent or fatigue. Gershom crossed the threshold in the half-light of early evening, his own pace slow, deliberate, as if the few hours away required a reacclimation to the collective pulse. As in most evenings, the lanes between tents were crowded, women ladling out beans, children dragging sticks through the guttered dirt, old men propped on crates arguing over the proper timing of a barley harvest they might never see.

The scouts had spread out on return, some already peeled off to their own families, others taking detours to pass news or score a hunk of bread before the official report. Shammah and Elead, who bore the responsibility of the mission, went directly to Joshua's tent, their voices carried ahead of them in clipped, anticipatory debate.

Gershom slowed as he passed a tent near the center of the camp, its flap only half-lowered, the inside lit by a single guttering wick. From within came the noise of a family argument, the tones modulated for secrecy but stretched by panic and pain. He would have kept moving, but then a child's voice, high and brittle, cut through the thrum: "Please, do not let him die, not before we cross, not before he sees what's on the other side."

A scuffle came next, a vessel clattering over, and then a stillness filled by the soft, uneven sound of someone weeping into their hands.

Gershom stopped, his shadow stretching across the threshold. Inside the tent, the old man lay propped on cushions, his face waxy, his eyes flicking between the children and the ceiling. The woman, likely his daughter, held a bowl of broth, trembling so violently the liquid sloshed over the rim. Two children huddled at the foot of the cushions, clinging to each other with the desperate belief that if either one let go, the world would finish breaking.

The old man's lips moved. Gershom strained to hear.

"Don't cry for me, you blockheads," the patriarch rasped, his voice a gravelly parody of his own. "I'm not gone yet, am I? Did you see the sun set? So did I." He turned to the girl, his granddaughter maybe, whose cheeks glistened with anger and salt. "I will cross. Even if they drag me on a litter and throw me over like a sack of grain. I will see it. Even if I have to peer at the land from under this damned tent cloth."

The girl sobbed harder, the sound low and angry, as if resenting the man for not being immortal.

The woman with the bowl tried again to coax him to sip. "Please, Abba. Please just taste it." The old man jerked his face away, a gesture both childlike and absolute.

Gershom felt a hand rise halfway to the tent flap, as if he might enter, or maybe brush against it. But he let it fall, the gesture unfinished. There was nothing he could do that would not make the ache worse. He stood, listening as the voices inside modulated from argument to resignation, from grief to a worn, threadbare hope: the hope that the sun would rise again, that the old man would last another day, another night, long enough to see the waters part or the first stalk of wheat in the Promised Land.

A man's legacy, Gershom realized, was not the voice with which he once commanded the camp, or the inked decrees of a priest's hand, but the way his absence was felt in the weft and warp of the living. The quiet that filled the tent after the sounds ceased was, in its own way, more articulate than any speech.

He moved on, retracing his steps through the maze of canvas and cord, feeling the press of every conversation, every transaction of bread or water, every inconsequential act that, together, defined the present-tense of his people. By the time he reached the avenue leading to Joshua's tent, dusk had painted the upper edges of the encampment in a bruised blue. The command tent stood in the middle of the camp, illuminated from within, a lantern making a pale disk on the trampled ground outside.

As he approached, Gershom caught Shammah and Elead outside the tent, their words sharp but muted as they argued over the danger of the river crossing. Elead, always the pragmatist, insisted on waiting for a better season; Shammah, driven by a kind of fatalistic clarity, wanted to go as soon as possible, before the enemy noticed their preparations.

"You saw it yourself," said Shammah. "It's fast, but it's fordable. Wait too long and the channel will shift. We may not get another chance."

Elead shook his head, frustration sparking in his narrowed eyes. "We lose the first column, and we lose the crossing. Who's going in first, you? Or the High Priest in his robes?"

Gershom hung back, listening, the old habit of invisibility now a tool rather than a curse.

Shammah spat into the dirt, then said, "Joshua decides. But you heard the boy, he wants to move. He's not like the old man." Shammah glanced sideways, noticing Gershom for the first time. "You think the people are ready?"

Gershom shrugged. "No one's ready. But no one waits, either. It's the only way."

Shammah grinned, a quick, feral baring of teeth. "You got your father's taste for it, after all."

Gershom thought of the old man in the tent, refusing to sip, refusing to die on the wrong side of the water. He thought of the Moabite's words, the way the river was always high until someone crossed it. He thought of his own hands, empty but not unmade, and of the burden that might yet fall upon them.

He nodded once, then slipped past the arguing scouts and into the tent.

Inside, Joshua waited, alone at the table, a battered map spread before him and the lantern making his features appear both ageless and, for the first time, exhausted. He looked up, meeting Gershom's eyes with the stripped-down candor of a man who had given up on ceremony.

"What did you see?" Joshua asked.

Gershom described the river, its speed, its temperament, the way the light struck the surface in blind spots, and the reeds holding the silt. He told of the acacia groves along the bank, of the places where a crossing might be tried, and of the men's confidence, which was thinner than the ice that sometimes formed on the animal troughs at night. He left out the Moabite, the dying old man, the fig upon his tongue.

Joshua listened, nodding at each point, his fingers tracing the route on the parchment as if rehearsing the journey in his mind. When Gershom finished, Joshua sat back, exhaling in a steady, controlled vent of air.

"I'll have the tribes made aware. In two days," he said, "we send the Ark ahead. The priests will step in first. The rest will follow when they see the way."

Gershom nodded, accepting the plan as both inevitable and, in its own way, miraculous.

Joshua looked at him a long moment. "You'll be there, won't you?"

This time, Gershom did not hesitate. "Yes," he said. "I'll be there."

He left the tent, allowing the curtain to fall behind him. Night had fully taken the camp now, but the river's voice was still audible, threading through the dark with its unending monologue of distance and promise.

Gershom stood for a while in the stillness, then turned toward his own tent, feeling the pull of the camp and the river and the waiting dawn, all braided together in the logic of a story not yet finished.

He walked on, the lanes between tents narrowing and then

opening, the sound of a child's laughter—or was it weeping?—carrying from somewhere behind him. He did not look back.

For the first time in a long while, he understood what it meant to cross.

Tima's Truth

Dawn broke with the tremorless certainty of an axe through ripe fruit, splitting the last, brittle residue of night and laying bare the encampment's battered geometry. The horizon to the east burned white-gold, fierce and unsentimental, and each tent's shivering canvas reflected the first light with a fresh, pitiless clarity. By the time the second rooster had crowed, the entire plain was breathing: children's shouts broke open the hush, the thud of mallets hammered out a staccato of urgency, and a thousand hands had already turned to the first labor of the day.

Gershom found himself standing a pace back from the main thoroughfare, a coil of leather straps looped over one arm, three water skins bulging at his hip, and a parcel of spare cloth tucked like a question against his ribs. It was an awkward load, not one he had been assigned, but the compulsion to carry something, anything, had struck him as he took in the first stirrings of the Levite quarter. He hovered for a moment, shifting his weight from foot to foot, then threaded his way along the already-crowded avenue toward the circle of tents where Tima's family kept their station.

The camp had, overnight, transformed into an organism bent on self-evacuation: at every turn, families worked to dismantle the architecture of home with the muscle-memory of a people who knew never to settle. Poles clattered to the ground, boys dragged empty baskets in loud, zigzagging trails behind their elders, and everywhere the air was scored with the overlapping calls and instructions of women trying to impose order on a process that fundamentally resisted it. Even the livestock were drawn into the choreography; goats shuffled in tight, reluctant herds, the bells around their necks tolling a rude, discordant morning anthem.

Tima was easy to spot: she moved with a steadiness that, even now, remained unaffected by the surrounding maelstrom, her hair braided tight and practical against the wind. She knelt by the mouth of the family tent, wrists dusted with flour and arms sunk to the elbow in a sack of grain. Beside her, a younger sister strained to lift a bundle of kindling, while their mother hunched over a pile of stitched bags, double-checking every knot and seam for weakness. Tima's face was set in a line of intent concentration, but when she lifted her gaze, sweeping the horizon in a practiced arc, it landed on Gershom, and the line of her mouth softened briefly.

He made his way over, feeling the attention of the camp shift as he passed. A boy with a basket of dried figs eyed him sidelong, then hurried on; a man with a spear made a brief, dismissive noise in his throat and turned away. The judgment stung, but only faintly; Gershom had grown used to it, the way a man grows used to the splinter in his heel.

He knelt beside Tima, careful to keep his parcels contained and not invade her space. She acknowledged him with a slight, almost imperceptible nod, the kind reserved for confidants or, perhaps, those who had already proven their usefulness.

"What brings you to our tent," she asked playfully.

"I figured you, your family could use a little help today. Leather straps," he said, setting them down. "For the crates. And some skins, if you need them."

She wiped her forearm across her brow, leaving a pale streak of flour on her temple. "We sure do, and your help is more than welcomed. The new harvest sacks, they split if they're not bound tight."

He handed her a length of cord. Their fingers brushed, and he was surprised at the callus on her thumb, how it matched his own in miniature. She took it, looping the cord through the rough handles of the grain sack with a deftness that belied the effort.

Her mother shot him a single, measuring look, a quick up-and-down, the sort that could inventory a man's value with a blink, then returned to her task. Gershom's presence was not, he knew, either wholly welcomed or resented; in Tima's family ledger, he was neither asset nor liability, one more element to be managed before the hour of crossing.

They worked side by side, their silence unremarkable and, in its way, companionable. The job required no conversation: Gershom steadied the sack as Tima knotted the cords, he pressed down the lid as she tied off the corners, she ran her hands along the seam to check for leaks, then passed it to her sister, who dragged it off in a plume of dust. The beat of the task became its own language, each gesture a small act of trust or concession. Occasionally their hands met in the act of reaching for the same item, and neither withdrew first.

Sunlight filtered through the mesh of the tent wall, catching dust motes and transforming the air into a haze of gold. In that light, the sweat at Tima's brow gleamed like oil, her face radiant with the unadorned honesty of work. Gershom glanced at her once, then again, and felt an unexpected warmth rising behind his sternum, a sensation at once comforting and destabilizing.

They went on like this for several minutes, the clamor of the camp a distant, constant tide.

At last, as they cinched the last of the heavy bundles, Tima spoke, her voice pitched low. "You didn't sleep last night."

It wasn't a question, so he didn't bother denying it. He finished threading the last strap, pulling it tight with a small grunt of effort.

"I saw you sitting on the outcropping, looking out at the river," she said. "You were there before the watch changed."

He let his breath out slow. "Couldn't find the reason to stay in the tent. Not with everything moving."

She considered this, then nodded. "I understand. The river draws. It's the one thing that doesn't seem afraid to move forward."

He let the words settle, then found himself speaking before he could plan the shape of what he meant to say.

"I think I'm afraid of what happens when we get to the other side," he said, voice barely above a whisper.

She did not mock or dismiss him. Instead, she reached for another skin and began the same binding process, her hands moving in measured, careful loops.

"Most of us are," she said. "But we keep moving. Because to stay is to disappear."

He watched her, feeling the pulse in his neck slow for the first time since he'd awoken. The methodical repetition of the task, the cadence of her voice, the clarity in her eyes—they grounded him, brought the world back into a scale he could manage.

He worked alongside her in silence until there were no more sacks to bind.

Then, as she dusted the flour from her hands, she said, "You're always thinking. You hold everything in."

He shrugged. "Someone has to. Otherwise it leaks out and ruins everything."

She turned, facing him squarely, her face set in an expression equal parts challenge and curiosity.

"That's not always true," she said. "Sometimes it helps to let things spill."

He opened his mouth, then closed it again, unsure what to make of her directness.

But then he looked at her, really looked, and the set of her face carried his mother's defiance, her refusal to bend, her unflinching gaze.

The moment stretched, then resolved as Tima's mother called for her from inside the tent. Tima gathered up the last of the bundles and stood, waiting for him to do the same.

He rose, brushing the dust from his knees, and fell in step behind her.

As they moved toward the next task, he felt his body relax in increments, shoulders at ease but still sure , jaw unclenching, the thrum of anxiety replaced by the fatigue of honest labor. He caught himself humming under his breath, a tune without melody, but it startled him all the same.

Tima glanced back, the faintest curve of a smile at her mouth.

"See?" she said, her tone light, "It's not so bad. Not if you're willing to share the load."

They finished the job, and when the sun had fully risen, Gershom looked down at his hands, dusty, chafed, and streaked with flour. For the first time in weeks, he thought that maybe he had earned his place at someone's table after all.

The morning, having established its dominion, now baked the encampment in a thickening light. The business of departure swelled to a new register: voices overlapped, the trample of feet was constant, and the dust kicked by every movement caught and refracted the sun in jagged, shifting prisms. At the edge of Tima's family space, a cleared square bound by washing lines and upright casks, stood Eliezer, arms folded, his shadow covering the last of the grain bundles.

He had not announced his approach, but the perimeter of awareness in the small workgroup rippled as soon as he stopped moving. Even Tima's mother, intent on sorting dried figs from their stems, paused, her hands hovering over the bowl as if arrested by the presence of a weather front. Tima herself stilled, one hand on the handle of a water skin, the other braced on her knee. It was not fear, exactly; more the recognition of a coming storm, one whose shape was intimately familiar.

Eliezer let the moment hang, his gaze locked on his brother who had not noticed him, allowing the assembled to sense him fully before he spoke.

"So this is where you've been hiding," he said, his voice pitched just loud enough to carry. "Courting a wife to improve your standing among the Levites? If so, all you had to do was stand and take up what father had established."

A brief stillness followed, the words hitting with the flat certainty of a slap. Several nearby workers looked up from their own tasks, necks craning, a few going so far as to stand for a better view. The air sharpened, the familiar smell of dust and sweat now cut with the tang of pending humiliation.

Gershom, who had been kneeling by the last sack, did not

flinch or rise to the bait. Instead, he finished tying the final knot, smoothed the loose end with his palm, and only then stood up. He dusted his hands off on the thighs of his tunic, a slow, deliberate gesture, then faced his brother. The effect was that of a man adjusting his balance to receive a blow, but not intending to return it.

Eliezer stood firm, feet apart, his frame expanded, jaw locked in stubborn defiance. Even at rest, he looked like a man mid-confrontation, muscles perpetually engaged, eyes narrow and faintly contemptuous. By contrast, Gershom's stance was unadorned; arms loose at his sides, his gaze level and clear, no flicker of anger or the old, reflexive shame.

Gershom waited a long moment before replying, as if he were weighing not the words but the necessity of words at all.

"Your opinion of my intentions," he said, his tone even and almost gentle, "says more about you than me, brother."

The phrase was not a rebuke, but it hit with unexpected force. There was a subtle shifting among the onlookers; a young boy in a blue sash grinned, then quickly stifled it. An older woman, hunched over a crate of onions, muttered something to her neighbor and both kept their eyes fixed on the brothers.

Eliezer's brows climbed, the usual mask of irritation briefly slipping to reveal surprise. For a half-second he lost his place, as if the script had been tampered with and his next line misplaced.

He recovered, but without the same assurance. "We need you at the Levite quarter. The lists are wrong, and the order of march will be a disaster if the sacks aren't double-checked. Unless you've decided your future is to carry grain with the women."

The new challenge, delivered with a sharper bite, should

have drawn a retort. Instead, Gershom only nodded, as if accepting a valid correction, and turned to Tima.

"Thank you for letting me help," he said. He glanced at the older woman, who nodded in acknowledgment. "I'll return these," he added, gesturing to the few unused cords and straps.

Tima smiled, not with teeth but with the crinkle at the corners of her eyes, the approval silent but unmistakable. Her mother, for her part, shot a glance at Eliezer, then at her daughter, the unspoken conclusion passing between them as cleanly as a coin.

Eliezer, realizing he had lost the audience, tried to salvage a final word. "See that you do," he muttered, then pivoted and strode off, the soles of his sandals thudding out a frustrated tattoo against the earth. The onlookers, having witnessed the outcome, returned to their work with a sense of something resolved.

Gershom held for a moment, breathing in the stillness that followed. His hands no longer trembled; the skin around his knuckles, usually tight and pale from the effort of control, was loose and alive. The dust settled in the space where his brother had stood, and for the first time he sensed that he had not only endured the confrontation but come through it whole, maybe even altered.

He turned back to the bundles, checked each one with a quick, professional glance, then gathered the stray straps and headed toward the Levite quarter. Tima and her mother resumed their work, but as Gershom walked away, he caught the faint echo of their voices, soft, almost affectionate, threading the air behind him.

"Gershom! Gershom!" Tima called, hurrying up behind him.

He turned to face her. "What is it, Tima?"

She pressed a hand to her chest, trying to steady her breath. "My mother... she wants—" she paused again, collecting herself. "We want to know if you would honor us by joining us for dinner. It's our way of thanking you for your help. You saved us at least half a day's labor."

Gershom's expression softened. "It would be my honor to accept," he said, smiling.

Relief and excitement lit up Tima's face. "Good! I—I'm really glad. We'll see you at dinner then." She gave a small, happy nod before turning and practically skipping back toward where she'd been working, her steps lighter now that the invitation had been accepted.

She moved off, and after a moment Gershom continued on his path, the faint smile still lingering as he walked.

The morning noise returned, the rhythm of the camp resuming as though nothing had happened. Yet, for those who had been present, the day's story had shifted: the older brother had not only held his ground but had turned the confrontation into something altogether different. A new pattern, previously unimagined, now existed in the fabric of the camp. And Gershom, walking with an unaccustomed lightness, felt himself part of that pattern, no longer avoiding or advertising the change. He lived it, one step at a time.

Evening drew its slow blue curtain across the Plains of Moab, and the heat of the day receded with surprising gentleness, as if the dust and clamor had been a fever that finally broke. The camp, having expended its restlessness, now retracted into its thousand private circles. Tents that remained standing, glowed with oil lamps, the corridors between them populated by softer, slower movements.

Tima's family tent, when Gershom arrived, was illuminated by a single, resolute lamp hung from a hook in the central pole. Inside, the world shrank to a circle of warmth and the low table, flanked by three mats. He paused at the entrance, the membrane of canvas holding in a murmur of voices and the distinct clink of pottery. There was a moment, brief but real, where he considered retreating, inventing a reason to keep to his own company, but the memory of Tima's smile and the morning's dust still on his hands compelled him forward.

He ducked inside, the transition immediate and complete: the lamplight threw sharp shadows on the cloth walls, and the air was saturated with the aroma of simmering stew and something sweet he could not name. Three girls, Tima, her younger sister, and a cousin, lifted their eyes from their bowls, polished stones in the glow. At the head of the table sat Medad, the father, his frame tall and lean, the silver of his beard catching and magnifying the lamp's glow. His hands were large and deeply lined, one cradling a cup of water, the other resting, proprietary, on the knee of his robe.

Tima gestured Gershom to the mat beside her, and he settled there, careful not to press too close but near enough to sense the residual heat from her arm. The cousin slid a bowl toward him; it was filled with lentils, carrot, and shreds of onion, steam curling up to cloud the rim. There was also a plate of flatbread, torn unevenly, and a cluster of dried figs arranged with a precision that suggested ritual.

Medad regarded him for a heartbeat, then nodded once, a gesture at once formal and oddly intimate.

"Welcome," he said. "Eat while it's hot. The day was long."

The words were simple, but they carried a weight—an implicit challenge to bring his best self to the table, to not let the day's failures or grievances sour the bread.

Gershom tore off a corner of bread, dipped it into the stew, and took a bite. The texture was soft, almost creamy, and the taste was rich with cumin and something tart at the back of the tongue. He felt the food settle in his stomach with a warmth that surprised him; he had not realized until now how hungry he was.

The conversation, at first, followed the predictable lines: a brief accounting of the day's work, the tally of what had been packed and what remained, a gentle reprimand for the cousin who had lost a sandal in the commotion by the well. Medad asked about how the preparations for the Ark was going, and Gershom responded in measured phrases, reporting that the inventory was nearly complete and the Ark's coverings had been checked twice over by Phinehas himself.

Medad grunted approval, his eyes hooded but attentive. He broke a fig in half, handed one piece to Tima, and popped the other into his mouth.

"We have one more day until the beginning of something new," he said, more to the air than to anyone in particular. "We will wake in a place we have never seen, and the old stories will become the new law."

Tima's sister, emboldened by the comfort of home, asked, "Is it true that the river will part like the sea did for our fathers?"

Medad smiled, a slow unfolding that softened the angles of his face. "It is said so. But I think the lesson is not in the water, but in the willingness to step in, even when you do not know what the water will do." He looked at Gershom, the gaze direct but not unkind.

"And what do you think?" he asked.

Gershom hesitated, aware that this was not a trick, but a genuine inquiry.

"I think it is easier to believe in miracles for other people," he said at last. "Harder to imagine they could happen for you."

Medad nodded, as if confirming a private calculation.

"Your father used to say much the same, when he was young," he said.

The table fell quiet. Even the youngest cousin stilled, the spoon halfway to her mouth.

Medad set down his cup, interlaced his fingers, and leaned in. "May I tell a story?" he asked, the question clearly rhetorical.

"In the early days of the wandering, before your father had found his way to the confidence of the elders, he was a man very much afraid of mistakes. He thought, as many young men do, that the world would not forgive error. Once, when we were encamped at the edge of Sinai, he was tasked to deliver a message to the southern quarter, but instead became lost among the tents. For three hours, he wandered, too proud to ask for help, inventing reason after reason to keep moving forward. By the time he delivered the message, the hour had passed, and the men were already gone to the meeting."

He paused to let the story breathe.

"Your father was ashamed, and spent the next two days avoiding the eyes of anyone who might have heard. But when at last he confessed to his father-in-law, the old man only laughed and said, 'Better to be lost among your own than to never move at all.'"

Gershom let the story sink in, and for a moment he saw his father not as the granite prophet, but as a young man, shamed and human and desperate to avoid the disappointment of his elders.

Medad continued. "He was not born knowing the law. He had to learn it, word by word, mistake by mistake. And he learned, eventually, that the value of a man is not in how rarely he stumbles, but in how he recovers."

The girls, sensing the gravity of the moment, fell silent. Tima reached for another fig, split it, and set the other half on the rim of Gershom's bowl with the easy familiarity of someone who had always expected him to sit at their table.

Gershom found himself blinking, the heat of the tent stinging his eyes.

Medad, watching him, nodded. "You are your father's son. But you are also yourself. There is no inheritance more precious than that."

He broke off another piece of bread and passed it around the table, the gesture smooth and deliberate, "May our Lord guide our steps with strength and peace," he added.

Gershom took his share, hands sure, and ate, the food tasting now of something more than salt and spice.

The meal wound down in a calm of mutual contentment. The youngest cousin stood, stretching through a long yawn before slipping away to curl up on her mat, the day's fatigue finally overtaking her. Tima gathered the bowls, stacking them in a quiet pile, while her sister began clearing crumbs from the table with a scrap of cloth.

Medad stood, stretching his arms above his head, and said, "We pray now."

He moved to the corner of the tent, where a small, carved box held the family's prayer scroll. He unfurled it, the parchment unrolling with the easy intimacy of long habit, and began to recite the evening blessing, his voice deep and unyielding, the cadence clear of both rush and show. The others gathered around, Tima at his left hand, Gershom behind her, hands loosely folded, head bowed.

As Medad spoke, Gershom found the words coming more easily than they had in months. The old awkwardness, the sense of being a fraud or an interloper, had dissipated somewhere between the bread and the story of his father. He listened, then joined in, his voice weaving into the family's, indistinguishable and, for once, unquestioned.

When the prayer ended, Medad replaced the scroll, and turned to Gershom.

"You are welcome in our tent any night," he said, and this time there was no formality in it, only the plain truth of belonging.

Gershom smiled, and the muscles in his face, so long trained to stillness, remembered how to do it.

"Thank you all for this evening," he said, his voice steady yet warm. "It was a comfort to share supper with such good company."

Medad nodded in acknowledgment, and Tima, her mother and sister smiled, their features glowing in the soft lamplight. Tima walked with him to the entrance of the tent. The air outside was cool and fragrant, a gentle reminder of the night sky stretching above.

As they paused below the canvas flap, Gershom turned to Tima, their eyes meeting in a moment that felt suspended in time. "Thank you for this evening. It was nice to have supper with someone other than myself," he said, a hint of vulnerability threading through his words.

"Anytime," Tima replied, her voice light yet sincere. Her eyes sparkled in the lamplight, holding a mix of amusement and something deeper, a promise of shared moments yet to come.

Gershom gave a faint nod, a smile breaking across his face, warming the chill of the night. "I sure hope so," he said, stepping back into the darkness, the weight of solitude feeling a bit lighter as he left.

Walking, he inhaled the scent of lentil and lamp oil that still clung to his clothes, and felt, if only for a moment, that the world was not a place of exile but a place of return. He walked the avenue back toward his own tent to begin packing the belongings he'd put off tending to all day. Each step felt measured, each breathe a little easier than the last.

Brother against Brother

The midday sun arrived unannounced, glancing off the rim of the Levite quarter and rendering the lines of tents in a haze of oscillating heat. It was not the oppressive, suffocating heat of high summer, but the precise and surgical incandescence of a season nearing its end—every stone, every thread of canvas caught in merciless relief, shadows etched so hard that they looked like wounds. The camp was awake to the day's significance. Children were banished to the margins, dogs lashed to stakes in the rare shade; even the flies, too numerous to expel, hummed at a tentative remove. This was the day of assignments—the day the Law, so recently rehearsed by the full assembly, would be parsed out, enacted, incarnated in the trembling hands and hopeful throats of its inheritors.

At the quarter's nucleus, the elders had arranged themselves on a dais of stacked crates, the makeshift bench sagging under the ceremonial gravity of the moment. Scrolls were arrayed in bundles at their feet, each tied off in blue cord. The cords were tokens of legitimacy, but also, for those who remembered, a veiled nod to the old rebellion, when a fringe of blue marked the ones who refused to be forgotten. Phinehas, his face a lacquered mask of composure, stood at the right hand of the company, one finger snagged in the seam of his garment as though it might unravel into air. To his left, the scribe's held the wooden dowel of the Law, awaiting the cue to begin.

Levites clustered in loose ranks, their posture a blend of military drill and the anxious choreography of men about to be judged. There was laughter, forced and arrhythmic, and a smattering of low curses when a name was mispronounced or a status recounted with less luster than was owed. Yet, at the edges, beyond the magnetic pull of the dais, a solitary figure leaned against the tent pole, arms folded, gaze averted, a man occupying the space of an afterthought rather than a witness.

Gershom watched the proceedings with the half-lidded attention of a sick animal: alert, but prepared for pain. The skin under his outer tunic was still raw from yesterday's labor, and the joints of his fingers ached from the late-night packing he had undertaken after dinner. He regarded the gathering as one might regard a stranger's funeral; every gesture carried recognition, yet none invited his presence. There was no one to talk to, so he allowed himself the rare luxury of watching the world unmediated, letting the sound of the names, the arrangements of the tribes, the ritual call and response, wash over him.

Eliezer was in his element. The younger brother stood not with the massed bodies of the junior Levites, but at the very front, shoulders set, chin raised so that his face was the first to catch the sun. If the glare stung, he did not show it. Instead, he played to the crowd, pivoting slightly whenever a new list was unrolled, his jaw twitching with each announcement. The muscles in his forearm stood out like braided rope; the signet ring, which he had taken to wearing even in the field, flashed with every gesticulation. He exuded anticipation, no, entitlement, waiting for the hour when his name would be called, and he could stride forward to collect the mantle he had been denied at birth but had since convinced himself was his by merit.

The scribe called out the first grouping, the voices of the tribes echoing in uneven waves as each sub-clan was named and their appointed task revealed. "Sons of Kohath—bearers of the Ark, vanguard at the crossing—" A hush, almost reverent, though not without its share of envy. "Merarites—tenders of the altar, keepers of the fire—" A murmur of approval. "Gershonites—packers, porters, those who manage the lesser burdens—" A few groans, one outright laugh.

Gershom, predictably, was listed among the Gershonites, his name wedged between two cousins who had not spoken to him in months. His charge: the supply carts, a duty so menial that the scribe did not bother to specify which row he would be leading. The only embellishment was a phrase tacked on as if by afterthought: "See to it that all things arrive in order." It was not an insult, but neither was it a benediction.

He nodded, the gesture so small it was almost invisible, and stepped back a half-pace. The world continued. The names unspooled, the tasks distributed. He watched as Eliezer was finally summoned, and the air around the dais shifted—men craned their necks, the elders leaned in as if the next pronouncement would determine the shape of the future.

"Son of Moses," intoned Phinehas, "Eliezer ben Zipporah, you are to take position at the right hand of the Ark-bearers, with responsibility for the sacred shrouds and the trumpets of assembly. You will serve as witness and—" here, the pause was deliberate, the weight of it almost corporeal "—as voice."

For a moment, Eliezer was still, his mouth a hard line. Then, as if compelled by an external force, he stepped forward, dropping to one knee in the way of old warriors or those too theatrical to trust in the adequacy of standing. The elders murmured approval. Even Phinehas allowed a brief smile, though whether it was sincere or tactical, no one could say.

Gershom felt nothing. Not anger, not shame, not even the bristling resentment that had accompanied every public elevation of his brother for the last decade. He simply took the news as one might take news of the weather, unwelcome, but not avoidable, and certainly not worth a display. He looked at Eliezer; the stiff lines of his face twitched, a flash of victory surfacing, and he released it.

He did not see the next part coming. Neither did the assembly.

The session adjourned with a final blessing, the elders standing to stretch their legs and shake hands with the newly appointed. Levites jostled for position in the loose postlude, some congratulating the chosen, others lingering at the margin to compare notes or swap rumors. Gershom, in the habit of shadows, moved along the perimeter, intent on reaching the side-lane that would lead back to his tent. He made it three steps before he heard the slap of sandals behind him, a gait he knew without needing to turn.

Eliezer's hand caught him at the shoulder, the grip sharp and insistent. Gershom paused, but did not pivot.

"You took that well," Eliezer said, the words as taut as wire. "Almost like you expected it."

Gershom, facing away, kept his tone flat. "Why wouldn't I? You always wanted the show. Now you have it."

He expected a retort, a shove, maybe the old routine of words meant to wound but falling flat. Instead, he felt himself spun around by sheer force, the momentum catching him off-guard.

He braced for an argument, only to find Eliezer's fist already in motion. The punch landed square on the bone above his eyebrow, the shock of it white and then red, stars bursting at the periphery of his vision. He stumbled, not from pain but from the surprise of it, his knees buckled, and for a heartbeat he was on the ground, dust gritting into his cheek, the world at a thirty-degree tilt.

The Levite quarter went utterly still. Not the orderly calm of a crowd, but the tense quiet that falls when men see a line crossed and wait to know if they must act.

Eliezer stood over him, breath heaving, fists clenched at his sides. The sun caught the veins in his neck, the wildness in his eyes. His voice, when it came, was ragged and loud enough to carry to the furthest edge of the quarter.

"Come stand and fight, Gershom!" he shouted. "If you were unwilling to fight for our father's mantle, then at least fight for yourself. Show them you're not already a ghost!"

He waited, chest rising and falling, as the people adjusted to the new reality of the day.

Gershom, for his part, said nothing. He stood slowly, dust clinging to his robe, the left side of his face already swelling. He wiped the blood from his brow, smearing it in a diagonal across the bridge of his nose. The ache was sharp but distant, as if the body refused to process it in the moment. He looked at Eliezer, at the spectators, at the elders who now peered from their dais with the collective expression of men both appalled and excited by the prospect of scandal.

He did not advance, did not raise his fists. Instead, he squared his shoulders, rolled them once, and stood at full height. His arms hung at his sides, hands open, palms facing forward. He exhaled, a slow, deliberate venting of air, and then waited.

Eliezer, made clumsy by rage, lunged again. The second blow was meant for the mouth, but Gershom turned his head enough that the fist caught the corner of his jaw, the pain bright but manageable. This time, he did not stumble. He absorbed the force, let it travel through him, and remained upright.

A voice in the crowd: "Enough, Eliezer!" Another: "He's not fighting back." The ring of onlookers tightened, a living noose, every man present secretly grateful it was not his own brother's violence on display.

Gershom met his brother's eyes, and for the first time saw the terror underneath. Not fear of him, but fear of what might be left if the violence failed to produce the expected result.

The two men stood in the circle of judgment, blood on the one and sweat on the other, and the distance between them existed as both an endless gulf and no space at all. In that moment, the audience of Levites was irrelevant. The elders on the dais, the scribes, the clustered sons and nephews, all were reduced to the status of bystanders in a private apocalypse.

Gershom waited for a third strike, but it did not come. Instead, Eliezer's rage broke, not with a shout but with a shudder. He turned, spit into the dust, and then stalked away, those nearby parting before him as if he were a contagious disease. The onlookers dispersed more slowly, uncertain whether to applaud or mourn, the episode already fragmenting into a thousand whispered analyses.

Gershom stood alone for a moment, dust and blood congealing on his skin. He flexed his jaw, testing the new ache, and then, almost as an afterthought, walked back toward his tent, his head high, his back unbent.

It was not until he reached the shelter of his own threshold that he let his hands shake.

He did not remain undisturbed for long. The commotion in the Levite quarter had not, as Gershom had hoped, faded into the oblivion of forgotten insult. Instead, it had thickened, congealing into a presence outside his tent that would not be ignored. Within minutes, the air beyond his threshold prickled with the static of expectation, the crowd's hunger for a verdict, for an intervention, for the reimposition of order after such a spectacular breach.

The flap of his tent, stitched and patched by his own hand, shuddered as the presence at the entrance materialized into a figure. Without introduction, Phinehas entered, moving with the silent inevitability of a storm. He did not wait to be received. He did not bow, nor did he avert his eyes. He simply entered, the linen brushing aside the space between them, carrying the pungent aroma of crushed hyssop and the clean, coppery tang that marked a man who spent his days at the altar.

He regarded Gershom for a moment, the silence stretched taut between them. Phinehas was older than memory, but the veins in his forearms stood out like riverbeds in drought, and his gaze was as acute as any living thing in the camp.

"Come," he said, not as a request, but as the final word in a debate Gershom had not known he was losing.

They exited together, the sea of people outside parting with the nervous choreography of men who had been trained since youth to obey the man's every gesture. Eliezer had not gone far; he stood a few paces away, posture belligerent but already wilted at the edges. His eyes flickered between the faces before him and the ground at his feet, unwilling to meet the gaze of his judge.

Phinehas did not waste words nor his steps. He reached out,

not gently, and gripped Eliezer's upper arm, squeezing until the blood must surely have pooled beneath the skin. "You are finished here," he said, low enough that only the three of them could hear. "Attend to your duties, and be grateful your brother does not answer violence in kind." He held Eliezer in his grip until the younger man's body went slack, then released him with a push that was both dismissal and benediction.

Eliezer backed away, lips compressed to a colorless slit, and the crowd retracted with him, the drama of the moment already beginning to distill into legend.

Phinehas turned to Gershom, and the camp went still. He gestured for him to follow, then led the way along the avenue of tents, past the agora where the remains of the morning market steamed in the midday heat, past the cluster of elders who conferred in loud, performative tones but fell silent as the two approached. At the far boundary of the Levite sector, where the ground sloped down toward the dry gully that marked one of the edges of the encampment, Phinehas stopped.

For several seconds, he did nothing. but only stood, breathing through his nose, eyes on the sharp, white-hot horizon. Only when the last of the distant voices faded did he speak.

"I saw something in you today," he said. "Something I have not seen before."

Gershom tensed, expecting the words to be followed by rebuke—a lesson on dignity, or a recitation of the protocols for public conduct. Instead, Phinehas continued, his voice softer but no less precise.

"You could have fought. You could have ended it in the manner of most men. But you stood. You did not escalate. You did not degrade yourself, even when given every reason to do so." He paused. "You chose the more difficult path."

Gershom was silent, unaccustomed to this flavor of scrutiny. His face still throbbed where Eliezer had struck him, and the sweat that had dried on his skin now felt like a scab he dared not scratch.

Phinehas turned to look at him, the full force of his regard falling on Gershom's battered countenance. "Your father," he said, "was not always as he became. The Moses of legend, the one whose words are inked in every scroll and whose name is evoked in every convocation, was, for most of his life, a man at war with himself. He thought humility was weakness. He thought service was a slow kind of dying. It took years, even decades, before he understood that to lead is not to dominate, but to endure. To take the blow and remain standing."

Gershom, caught off guard by the unexpected turn, opened his mouth to reply, but nothing came out. His throat was thick with the residue of unshed tears, with dust lodged deep and a thousand unspoken grievances.

Phinehas took it in. He shifted his weight, and for the first time, a glimmer of weariness entered his voice. "You are not your father," he said. "But you are something I did not anticipate. I thought you would run from the Law. Instead, you have become its silent champion. Not by the letter, but by the act."

Gershom looked away, unwilling to let the words penetrate fully. They did, anyway, creeping in around the edges, settling into the soft tissue behind his breastbone.

"I don't know what you, the camp, wants from me," he managed, the words shaky.

Phinehas smiled, a rare and disarming gesture that transformed his face from a stern worker of the law, to something almost human. "Want? Nothing. Expect? That you will continue to surprise me." He reached into the folds of his robe and produced a strip of linen, which he pressed into Gershom's hand. "For the wound," he said. "Let it be a mark, not a memory."

With that, he turned and walked away, leaving Gershom alone on the slope, the camp stretching before him, the sounds of daily life already encroaching on the thin pocket of silence they had created.

Gershom stared at the linen strip, its fibers coarse but strong, and wondered if it was meant as a bandage or a reminder. He did not move for a long while, letting the words and the sun and the wind work at him, softening something he had thought was already dead.

When he finally returned to his tent, those who had waited had left. Only the outline of his own shadow remained, etched faintly on the ground where he had stood.

Night bled into the camp not as a velvet hush, but as a slow, relentless compression, the moon's light milky and raw, the air scraped clean by the wind's persistent fingering. Inside Gershom's tent, the darkness was nearly absolute. Eliezer lay across the far mat, body sprawled in the indelicate abandon of the truly spent. Even in sleep, he managed to snore with the rhythm of a man refusing to yield, the sound low and unlovely, but oddly reassuring in its regularity. His brother's chest rose and fell in a slow rhythm, each breath catching on a soft, unguarded snore slipping from his slightly open mouth. For a moment, Eliezer was as he had been, small, furious, determined to outpace the legend that hung over them both.

He wondered when it had soured, when the bond of blood had become a contest of scars. Perhaps it had always been this way, only the roles reversed: once, Gershom had been the favored, the delicate, the one spared the lash of discipline; now, he was the absence in the center of the narrative, the ghost who haunted his brother's dreams. He felt no anger, only a fatigue so deep it bordered on chemical.

He waited until the breathing in the tent slowed, then rose quietly, avoiding the creak of the mat, the catch of the canvas flap. He stepped outside into the chill, the world reduced to the muted geometry of tents, the intermittent glow of lanterns banked low to save oil, the scent of woodsmoke and animal funk sweetened by the night-blooming cress that grew wild along the gully.

The camp, viewed from the margin, was a collection of huddled shapes, each one a world of its own, each one giving off a faint, residual pulse of need and desire. Gershom walked the perimeter, keeping to the darker alleys, the places where no one would think to look for a Levite unless he was on watch or up to no good. He moved along the edge of the square, where the morning's violence still clung like an afterimage to stone and dust. At the boundary of the camp, where the ground lifted into a rocky bluff, he stopped, pulling the cold air deep into his lungs.

The sky above was unblemished, a vault of blue-black stippled with stars so numerous they made the dark seem crowded. He felt the urge to climb, to put space between himself and what had transpired, to inhabit a vantage point where the world and its injuries could be reduced to abstractions.

He climbed the incline, hands finding purchase in the rough-cut steps worn by a thousand feet before his own. At the crest, he expected solitude, but a figure was already there, silhouetted against the luminous horizon.

Joshua.

The leader of Israel was not standing in oratory, not walking the perimeter with the measured tread of command, but kneeling, his knees pressed into the rock, arms loose at his sides, head bowed in an attitude of utter submission. The image was at once unfamiliar and deeply intimate: the man who, by day, ruled the camp with the calm authority of one who had long ago made peace with his mission, now laid bare by the indifference of the cosmos, nothing but a supplicant like any other.

Gershom halted, unwilling to intrude on whatever negotiation transpired between a man and his god. He hovered at the rim of the outcropping, invisible save for the vapor of his own breath, watching as Joshua murmured words too soft to reach the ear but potent enough to ripple the air around him.

There was no performance in it, no audience to impress, no scribe to record the moment for later mythologizing. This was prayer stripped of posture, stripped of the theater of leadership. For a long time, Joshua stayed as he was, the only movement the gentle bob of his head, the fall and lift of his breath. Occasionally, he would lift his face to the stars, and in those moments the moon painted his features in strokes of bone and resolve.

Gershom felt a prickle at the back of his neck, a sensation he had not known since boyhood, wonder, maybe, or its lesser cousin, envy. He realized then that what he saw was not the burden of command, but its release: a man surrendering, if only for a moment, to the vastness that did not care about tribe or rank or the wounds of the day.

Joshua finished, making a gesture with his hands, something circular, something whole. He rose slowly, legs stiff, and stood for a while looking out over the plain. Gershom, still frozen in his shadowed niche, tried to absorb the image, to fix it somewhere permanent.

He did not approach, did not speak. Instead, he backed away, retracing his steps down the bluff, each footfall placed with the caution of a man determined not to shatter the spell.

The walk back to his tent felt different now, the air clearer, the bitterness drained from his limbs. He let his thoughts wander, unspooled and easy, to the memory of his mother, to the words of Phinehas, to the sight of Joshua at prayer. Somewhere in the night, a dog barked, then another; the camp shifted in its sleep, the fabric of the community knitting itself closer in the dark.

He ducked inside the tent, lay down, and closed his eyes. The ache in his jaw and brow had receded, replaced by a warmth that was not comfort, exactly, but the beginning of something like it.

Above him, the stars wheeled on in their fixed orbits, heedless of the struggles below.

Laying there, Gershom dreamed not of the camps wandering or his brother's anger, but of water, of the taste of it, of the wonders of crossing.

He woke before dawn, and for a moment, he felt ready to step into the river.

The Eve of Crossing

Before the horizon even considered the possibility of dawn, inside the brown tent that served as home, Gershom endured the night on a splintered stool, legs tucked close, arms wound across his ribs as if to keep the chest from shattering. A single oil lamp burned between him and the rolled mats where Eliezer slept, the flame fighting a losing battle against the cold and the inertia of old, unmended hurts. The tent, stripped of ornament and unburdened by sentiment, looked as if it were already halfway to desertion: two sleeping rolls, three water skins, and a shallow basin whose glaze had long ago surrendered to the fingers of sand and time.

The older brother watched the younger sleep with a vigilance at once predatory and pitiful, unable to say if he meant to guard or to condemn. Eliezer's face, even in sleep, wore the armor of contest, lips compressed, brow furrowed in anticipation of attack. Occasionally, the muscles in his jaw flexed, grinding through whatever fragments of dream demanded adjudication.

Gershom let his own breathing settle into the shallow trough between one anxious throb and the next. He knew how this would go. Had known, perhaps, from the hour Eliezer was born and began, at once, to cry out against the injustice of coming second.

He did not have to wait long. Sometime before the first rooster called out from the distant pens, Eliezer's eyes slit open, the pupils already hard and assessing. He did not flinch at the sight of his brother's silhouette, yet he avoided meeting it head-on.

"What are you staring at?" Eliezer's voice carried a pebble of derision, thrown before he was fully awake.

Gershom exhaled, a careful rationing of air, and placed the lamp on the dirt between them. "We need to talk," he said, shaping the words as if to make them unbreakable.

A groan, and Eliezer rolled upright on his mat, swinging his legs out so they formed a barrier. "Of course we do. Wouldn't be the morning of the crossing if you didn't want a confessional." His hand scrubbed at his face, fingers lingering on the scar under his left eye, a souvenir from a childhood accident neither would claim responsibility for.

Gershom ignored the bait, straightening on the stool. "I want this to be—" He hesitated, caught on the unfamiliarity of what he was about to attempt. "I want us to walk into today as brothers. Not as whatever it is we've become."

Eliezer laughed, a short, contemptuous burst. "You mean you don't want another public spectacle? Don't worry, the Levite quarter has already seen enough of your silent-martyr routine to last a generation."

The comment was a careful probe, searching for weakness. Gershom took the measure of it and pressed on.

"We don't have to agree on everything," he said, "but—"

Eliezer cut him off with a snort. "You're right, we don't. You made that clear when you gave up on Father's calling. Or did you forget how you used to recite the Law as if it would save you from being what you are?" He spat into the dirt beside the mat, a gesture half ritual, half reflex.

Gershom flinched, but only slightly. "I don't know what I am," he said, "but I know what I'm not. I'm not the man who stood before the Ark and pretended it meant nothing."

"Oh, so now you care about the Ark?" Eliezer's voice rose, the bite of mockery growing sharp. "The same Ark you avoided touching for months because you thought you'd defile it with your doubt?"

Gershom's hands went white on his knees, the tension radiating through his arms. He glanced at the tent's entrance, expecting at any moment to see a neighbor's shadow linger there, drawn by the argument. None appeared; either the world had finally lost interest in their private war, or it had simply decided to let them finish each other off without outside interference.

He tried again, forcing his tone to a lower register. "Look. We're about to cross. Today, or the next. All of this—" he gestured at the tent, at the emptiness around them, "—will be gone. I can't keep doing this with you. I don't want to."

Eliezer considered this, lips parting as if to deliver another rebuke, but for once he hesitated. His hands fidgeted with the hem of his tunic, twisting the coarse weave until it threatened to tear. "What do you want, then?"

"Peace," Gershom said, and though the word sounded pathetic to his own ears, he let it stand. "That's all."

Eliezer's head dropped, the crown of his hair catching the lamplight in a corona of copper and black. "You want peace now. Convenient, isn't it, when you've already abandoned every obligation that mattered to father."

Gershom's voice, when it came, was almost inaudible. "You don't get to decide what mattered to him."

"Like hell I don't," Eliezer shot back. "I watched him until the very moment he walked away, waiting for you to show some sign that you were worthy of his name. You didn't even come see him as he was commanded by the Lord to die. You didn't even say goodbye." His face contorted, the thought as fresh as the ache in his words.

Gershom bowed his head, the weight of the accusation pressing down until he threatened to fold in on himself. When he finally looked up, his eyes shone wet in the dim light. "You think I wanted that? You think I haven't spent every night since wishing I'd done it differently?"

The tent filled with a silence so dense it weighted the air itself, making each breath a labor. At length, Eliezer shifted on the mat, his posture deflating. "If you hated him so much, why do you care about this now?"

Gershom shook his head. "I never hated him. I hated that I could never be what he wanted."

"And what was that?" The challenge was softer now, almost desperate.

"A son who believed," Gershom said. "A son who could pick up where he left off. Who didn't look at the Law and see only the ways it failed us."

Eliezer's voice was thin, the old armor rattling loose around the edges. "You think it failed us?"

"I think it failed me," Gershom replied, honest for once. "And I think it's failing you, too."

The younger brother looked away, fixating on the pattern the lamp's shadow threw on the canvas wall. "I don't know how to stop fighting you," he admitted. "If I let go, I don't know what's left."

Gershom's mouth opened, closed, tried again. "We could

try."

The idea hung between them, fragile as the crust on a sleeping wound.

In the quiet, outside, the first horn sounded, the long, descending call that signaled the gathering of the assembly. Both men flinched at the intrusion, their argument swept aside by the greater summons of the nation's hour.

Eliezer stood first, rolling his mat with the efficiency of a soldier. He gathered his tunic, checked the straps on his sandals, then regarded Gershom with a look that was neither forgiveness nor acceptance, but something like possibility.

"You coming?" he asked, voice stripped of artifice.

Gershom nodded, slow but certain. He doused the lamp, letting the darkness have them both for a heartbeat before the dawn, and followed his brother out into the cold.

The air outside the tent was a bite of river-water, every inhalation laced with the metallic clarity that only comes before the day's first light. The avenue of tents, which by midday would pulse with the algorithmic madness of a nation on the march, now lay in peace, the cadence of footsteps suppressed beneath a shared, exhausted anticipation. Far off, the horns' echoes doubled themselves against the barren rock, urgent but not yet frantic.

All along the central axis of the camp, men emerged from their shelters in twos and threes, children sleep-dazed in their mothers' arms, elders propped between younger backs like creased, living scrolls. A few carried banners, stiff, weather-beaten flags marked with the emblems of clan and ancestor. Most carried whatever possession might bind them to the memory of a place, a time, a parent not already buried in the ground behind them.

Gershom followed Eliezer through the thinning gloom, the two not walking side by side but at an angle to one another, their paths close enough for a shadow to slip between. The calm that had smothered the tent now crackled with the aggregate sound of thousands assembling in obedience to a call older than language. They converged on the makeshift plaza at the camp's heart, where a platform of lashed timber jutted above the pressed-earth amphitheater. The rising buzz of those gathered called to mind not the chaos of a mob, but the focused, surgical hum of an instrument about to cut.

Joshua stood atop the platform, his silhouette backlit by the thinnest rim of gold bleeding from the eastern hills. He wore the mantle of his calling without flourish, no jeweled collar, no gleaming diadem, only the plain linen of a man who fully expected at any moment to be spattered with the dust and sweat of his own work. Beside him stood Phinehas, the priest's robes catching and magnifying the dawn, each stitch an annotation of the Law's authority. The rest of the elders gathered in a crescent behind, faces set, bodies hunched against the morning chill.

At the final blast of the horn, the people drew in on themselves, bodies tightening and voices fading until not a whisper remained. The transformation was instant: every child stilled, every side conversation wilted, even the goats that had been loosed for the crossing were suddenly mute, their heads canted as if waiting for a verdict.

Joshua's voice, when it came, rolled out over the multitude with a force that sounded drawn from the plain's depths, not from lungs and throat. "Sons and daughters of Jacob," he began, "the night has ended. This is the day we have awaited, these forty years and more. The Lord our God calls us to the water, and beyond the water, to the land of promise."

He paused, allowing the words to metabolize, and for a moment the silence threatened to thicken into something suffocating. Then, in a different tone, more intimate, as if speaking to each hearer in their own tent. He continued. "Today, we remember the promise, and the path by which we came. Today, we enter the river not as slaves, nor as wanderers, but as a nation chosen and kept."

A wave of reaction passed through the multitude: some hands lifted, others pressed flat against hearts, a few clutched at the arms of their neighbors as if to anchor themselves in the reality of the proclamation. Gershom felt the hairs on his forearm prickle, not with inspiration, but with a restless, involuntary awe.

Joshua outlined the order of the crossing with the precision of a man who had reviewed it in dream and in waking a thousand times. "First shall go the priests, who will carry the Ark of the Covenant into the waters. They will not falter, and the Lord will be with them. Behind them, the leaders of the tribes, and then the Levites, bearing what is sacred and what is necessary for the life of the people. After them, the rest: every household, every man, woman, and child. None shall lag behind. None shall be lost."

He turned to the priests, his voice cutting clean as flint. "Phinehas, gather your men. Prepare the Ark." The priest bowed, and with a series of gestures, dispatched runners into the crowd.

Joshua's gaze swept the company, and for a brief second, Gershom imagined the man's eyes locking with his own. The thought was absurd. He was one among tens of thousands, indistinguishable except for the inward twitch of shame at having failed every role expected of him. Still, the sensation persisted, as if Joshua were speaking not to the sea of faces but directly into the hollow behind his ribs.

Beside him, Eliezer stood straight as a blade, his arms at his sides, chin lifted so the early sun caught the geometry of his cheek. There was no trace now of the desperation from the tent, only a raw, almost hungry attentiveness. He looked, for the first time in years, exactly like their father, less the body, more the fire that burned behind the bones.

Joshua was not finished. He recited, in a voice as measured as the Law itself, the chronicles of their journey: the plagues and the flight, the bread that fell from the sky, the years of circling and the graves of generations left behind. With each item, the camp pulsed as if the entire nation shared a single, fevered heartbeat.

"We have wandered long enough," Joshua intoned, and the words came down like a decree. "Today, the Lord will show us that He is not only the God of promise, but the God of fulfillment. When you see the waters stand up, when you see the Ark in the midst, do not hesitate. Do not turn back. Walk, and let the Lord do as He said."

A murmur swept through the people, first like the shiver of wind on a wheatfield, then growing, cresting, breaking into a chant: "He will do as He said. He will do as He said." The cadence lifted, rolled, then faded into a lull again as Joshua raised his hand, palm open, signaling completion.

He dismissed the assembly not with a flourish, but with a final, practical directive: "Pack what you can bear. Leave what you must. In one hour, we move."

The horns sounded a second time, shorter, sharper, and the spell broke. All at once, the camp surged with kinetic purpose, families rushing to collect their remaining bundles, men running to secure the carts, children chasing after the goats that had scattered during the proceedings. Gershom watched as the order dissolved into managed chaos, every tribe and sub-clan executing its task with the efficiency of a people who had survived the constant risk of annihilation.

He stood rooted, the inertia of the moment anchoring him as the world swirled around. He could see Eliezer already several paces ahead, absorbed into a knot of Levite youth who would march nearest the Ark, their hands trembling in anticipation or terror, it was hard to tell which. Eliezer glanced back only once, the motion so brief that Gershom almost missed it, and then he was gone, a particle drawn into the gravity of a greater mass.

Gershom's feet would not move. The instructions, the order of march, the rationale for every placement, he knew it all, could recite it in his sleep, but still he hesitated, as if by standing still he could keep the coming hours from unspooling. He looked to the platform, now emptied of everyone but Joshua, who stood at its center, arms crossed, face unreadable.

The light had fully breached the hills now, washing the camp in gold and shadow. Gershom blinked against it, the glare sharpening every imperfection in the canvas of the tents, the stains on the sleeves of his garment, the calluses on his own hands. He felt the weight of his ancestors, not as inspiration, but as a kind of indictment: every one of them had crossed something. Everyone had borne the mantle of expectation.

Somewhere behind him, a woman's voice began to weave through the air, a haunting melody that echoed the spirit of their journey. "I will sing to the Lord, for He has triumphed gloriously," she sang, her voice rising and falling like the gentle sway of the Jordan's waters. The words flowed like a river, neither a lament nor a celebration, but a testament to the trials endured and the promises yet to unfold.

As she continued, "The horse and rider He has thrown into the sea," the camp seemed to fall silent, the constant serenity pulse of her song binding the hearts of the people together.

Gershom felt the weight of fear lift upon hearing the words of his father's words being sung. His fears being replaced by a fragile sense of unity. Each note stitched together the fabric of their shared history, intertwining threads of hope and resignation, transforming the moment into something almost sacred.

He took a step, then another, joining the tide of bodies as they funneled toward the river. His earlier resolve, the fleeting peace he'd found in the tent, now hung as fragile as the threadbare cloth of his tunic. The crowd pressed forward, relentless, and he let it carry him, the memory of his brother's face, their father's voice, and the impossible promise of dry land on the other side.

At the outskirts of the camp ground, Gershom paused, looking once over his shoulder at the city of tents he'd called home for every year he could remember. The sun, relentless, scoured the world clean behind him. There would be no returning, no pause, no way to unlive what the next hours would require.

He turned and walked on, the river's dull, endless roar already in his ears, the future unrolling before him like the path of a man who no longer belonged to himself, but to the story that demanded his crossing.

Divided Waters

By the time the last blue shadow retreated from the stones at the river's banks, the Israelite camp had already transformed into a single, collective act of expectation. The lanes between tents now gone, only to be replace by a mass of people marching along. Its domain of chaos and shouted orders, now pulsed with serenity—so that orders could be heard.

To the east, the river caught the early light, its surface alive with the convulsions of spring melt, the muddy current curling and uncurling in erratic, insistent flex. The air above it shimmered with gnats and anticipation. The reeds at the bank bent with the strain of the water, their roots clutching the mud as though they alone could resist the passage of a people whose patience had been rendered, over generations, into something both weapon and wound.

At the point where the camp met the water, Joshua stood, back straight, eyes fixed not on the people behind him but on the horizon beyond the far bank, where the Promised Land rose in uneven tiers, each one backlit and unreal. The leader's robe was stained with travel, the hem sodden with years of wandering. His hair, dusted silver at the temples, answered every stray current of wind; his jaw, immobile, marked time with the faint tic of a tendon. He did not fidget, did not consult the scrolls or the lieutenants at his flanks. Instead, he watched the river, as one might watch a serpent coiled across a threshold, aware that its violence was both obstacle and invitation.

The priests, four abreast, gathered behind him, their hands supporting the Ark of the Covenant on poles slick with the oil of preservation and the sweat of reverent terror. Each man's face was set in a mask of blank intent, the kind that covers terror with ritual, and ritual with the hope that the world will behave, at least today, according to its own rules. Their garments, white as raw bone, reflected the river-light in oblong flashes, making it difficult to distinguish the living from the mythic.

At the perimeter of the assembly, Gershom took his assigned position, halfway between the forward line of Levites and the families queued up in nervous increments. The role was absurdly ceremonial, his entire charge to serve as wayfinder for the slowest, the weakest, and the most easily trampled. He wore the blue sash of his line, the same one he had detested since boyhood, and tried not to let the fabric's scratch abrade the thin skin at the inside of his arm. His hands shook, but not in the expected manner; it was not the magnitude of the event that undid him, but the impossibility of ever, among so many, mattering at all.

Eliezer stood nearby, jaw set, his own sash knotted with the precision of a noose. He did not acknowledge Gershom, nor did Gershom expect him to. The moment was too large for petty hates.

A command passed from Joshua to Phinehas, from Phinehas to the priests, and then, with no further ceremony, the foremost of the Ark-bearers moved toward the water. The company breathed in as a single body. The first priest to reach the bank hesitated for a half-breath, then stepped in, the hem of his tunic immediately consumed by the brown, living water. The rest followed, their faces rigid, the Ark steady on their shoulders.

Nothing happened.

The priests waded forward, ankle to knee to thigh, each step slapping a fan of current in its wake. The Ark hovered, four cubits above the surface, as the men supporting it leaned into the drag. For a moment, all that changed was the sound: the mutter of the water, the strain of bodies, the whimper of a child too young to know why today mattered. Even the sun seemed reluctant, flattening behind a thin veil of mist and refusing to illuminate what might be the hour of either deliverance or farce.

Then, at the precise instant the last foot of the rearmost priest left the dry ground, the river stopped. Not gradually, not with a whimper, but with the ferocity of a butchered animal. The upstream water, charging down from the north, hit an invisible wall and recoiled, rising in a vertical sheet that flashed white in the sun, then crashed over, climbing rather than flowing The sound was not a roar but a drawn-out exhale, as if the river, at last, had tired of its own resistance. Here a gush of cool wind cascaded over the entire camp as if welcoming them in.

Downstream, the water vanished. One moment the channel was full, the next it was an exposed chute of slick, glistening stones, the remaining rivulets draining away as if embarrassed by their own inadequacy. The priests stood, suddenly dry to the shins, their sandals clinging to the raw riverbed. Behind them, the Ark hovered, inert and patient, the gold of its crown catching the first real light of the day.

The crowd, hundreds of thousands strong, stood agape. Somewhere in the back, a woman shrieked, the sound triumphant and terrified in equal measure. A ripple of murmurs spread, then fractured into shouts, then finally coalesced into a chant: "The stories are true. The stories are true." The phrase built, assembled out of disbelief and relief and a hunger for meaning, until even the skeptics at the margin took it up, unwilling or unable to remain outside the collective awe.

Gershom stared at the wall of water, its top curling with the weight of the current, mist rising in rainbow prisms that flickered and then dissipated in the sun. He tried to remember the first time he had heard the story of the Red Sea, how his mother had described the waters as walls "firm as the sides of a grave," but animated with a force that could choose, at any moment, to collapse. He had doubted then; he doubted now, even as his eyes beheld the evidence.

The air near the river's edge was thick with the smell of silt and wet vegetation, the metallic tang of ancient earth laid open for the first time in millennia. The wind, routed by the sudden verticality of the water, whipped back onto the camp, carrying with it the chill of a thousand springs and the shock of the new. The light, too, changed. What had been diffuse and uncertain now blazed with the crystalline clarity of a world remade.

At Joshua's signal, the Levites moved forward, forming a living corridor from the camp to the river's exposed floor. Gershom was swept up in the movement, his body following the mass even as his mind lagged, unready to step into a story so much larger than himself. The footing was treacherous at first, the mud sucking at the sandals, then firming to a packed surface studded with stones polished to a glassy sheen. To one side, the wall of water remained, rippling but unbroken, their height impossible to measure, their threat both implicit and absolute.

The families followed, mothers clutching children, elders leaning on staffs, the sick and the feeble carried in improvised litters. The sound of their footsteps echoed in the hollow, amplified by the tunnel of water and the certainty that nothing like this would ever happen again.

Gershom moved with the mass, eyes fixed ahead, senses assaulted by the newness of every detail. At one point he stumbled, a stone rolling underfoot, and for an instant he thought he would fall and be trampled by the press behind him. But a hand, he never knew whose, caught his elbow and righted him, the grip quick and impersonal, a gesture not of care but of necessity. He nodded in silent thanks and pressed on.

Overhead, the sun cleared the last remnant of mist and struck the water-walls at an oblique angle, sending shards of color arcing over the heads of the pilgrims. Children pointed, some laughed, others whimpered at the sight. The grown-ups did not speak, or if they did, their words were lost in the ambient roar of wonder.

The camp began to approach the halfway point where the river was at its narrowest, and here the pressure of the people increased, each person driven by the fear that the miracle might be rescinded at any moment. Gershom felt it, too—a pulse at the back of the neck, a certainty that he must not dawdle, must not question, must simply get across. He lengthened his stride, letting the company sweep him, his breath coming in short, hot gasps.

Ahead, the bank of the far side grew closer, the exposed mud there already trampled by the first arrivals. Beyond it, the fields and hills of Canaan undulated in the morning sun, their green so vivid it bordered on the impossible, even after a lifetime of desert eyes. Gershom slowed, not wanting the moment to end, but also not wanting to be left behind. He glanced into the wall of water, and saw in its trembling surface the distorted reflection of the multitude, his own face among them, indistinct but present.

At the deepest part of the riverbed, the banks sloped in and the light refracted through the lingering mist, the world collapsed into a corridor of raw, unprocessed motion. The wall of water, now towered over the heads of those crossing, its surface alive with eddies and the translucent passage of fish stranded in a medium neither river nor air. Occasionally, a whirlpool would snap into existence, a tight gyre of silver scales and vapor, then vanish as quickly, the surface returning to its fragile, vertical rest.

Gershom's duty was simple, at least on paper: walk the route ahead of the crowd, mark the places where the footing gave way, direct the elderly or the injured around the worst of the debris. It was the same work he'd done in the wilderness, only here the ground was made new with every passing second, the mosaic of stones shifting under the pressure of thousands of feet.

He moved ahead of a cluster of children, their hands locked in a daisy chain, eyes wide at the sight of the water wall. "Don't touch," he said, voice cracking with the strain of authority he did not feel. "It's not for us." They nodded, serious as acolytes, and steered clear of the roiling current, their sandals making wet, sticky sounds on the riverbed.

The press of people was relentless. They flowed past, some pausing to stare at the wall, others intent on the far shore.

And the further he walked, the more the world funneled down to this path, these stones, this gauntlet of attention. The grandeur of the moment, what the others experienced as triumph, sat in his mouth like a rotten seed.

He felt the pressure in his chest first, a tightening band that made the act of breathing an effort measured in increments. His pulse doubled, then doubled again. The sound of the crowd faded, replaced by a hiss, pale and unbroken, rising from within the wall. His hands shook, the tremor now violent, uncontrollable, and sweat burst from his skin in rivulets, cold despite the heat of the sun overhead.

He tried to slow his pace, to let himself be overtaken, but the flow of people pushed from behind and there was no place to hide. The walls of water blurred at the periphery, growing taller and more abstract with every step. His knees buckled, first one, then both, and he nearly pitched forward, arms windmilling for balance.

The thoughts came, jagged and humiliating:

You don't belong here. This is not your miracle. Your father parted the sea; you can barely stand upright on dry ground.

He wanted to scream, but could not trust his voice. His vision tunneled, black spots dancing at the edges. He could feel the blood in his ears, a drumbeat of shame that pulsed louder than the camp, louder even than the collapsing silence of the parted water.

Someone grabbed his arm. At first, the touch was nothing, a blur of sensation lost in the riot of nerves. But then it resolved: a hand, cool and strong, fingers digging into the meat of his elbow. The grip steadied him, stopped his forward collapse. He blinked hard, twice, and the world swam back into focus.

Tima.

She had come from nowhere—he could not remember having seen her in the line, or heard her approach—but now she was beside him, matching his stride with a calm he could not comprehend. She did not look at him, did not smile or chide, only said, low and fierce: "Breathe with me."

He tried to answer, but the air caught in his throat.

"Breathe with me," she repeated, softer this time, as if teaching a child. Her other hand moved to his shoulder, guiding him upright, her thumb pressing a steady pulse into his skin.

He inhaled, shallow at first, then deeper as her rhythm took hold. The hiss in his head receded. The sweat cooled. His vision widened, the wall of water retreating to its proper, terrifying distance.

They walked on, side by side, her presence an anchor against the undertow of his thoughts. She never let go, not once, her grip as constant as the force holding back the river. Around them, the throng had dwindled; most had already crossed to the far shore, their shouts carrying through the hollow with a tone half celebratory, half relieved.

Ahead, the corridor narrowed, the last section of riverbed rising in a slick ramp to the western bank. The wall of water, pushed further upstream by some unfathomable power, was now nearly out of sight, a long off shimmer, then nothing but mist and the roar of emptiness.

Gershom felt his feet moving again, the lock within him undone. He risked a glance at Tima, saw the set of her jaw, the curve of her mouth. There was nothing but resolve there, a stubbornness he recognized from the days when she would outwork every boy in the camp, even when her arms shook with fatigue.

"Thank you," he said, the words barely above a whisper.

She shrugged, but did not let go. "It's not for you," she said. "It's for all of us."

At the top of the ramp, the ground leveled, and the company spilled out onto the open plain, the air sharp and unfamiliar. Gershom slowed, then stopped, letting the others pass. Tima released his arm only when she was sure he would not fall.

He looked back once, at the place where the water had been, where the miracle had held for long enough. He thought of his father, of the stories, of all the times he had imagined himself the inheritor of something larger than fear.

He realized then that this was all there was. The trembling. The walking. The miracle, and the doubt that followed it.

He smiled, barely, and let the wonder in.

The far shore was nothing like Gershom had imagined in his childhood, when the stories of Canaan came packaged as a kind of fever: a land gorged on milk and honey, every stone replaced by a pomegranate, every hill slick with oil. In reality, the slope rose gentle, then more severe, a tiered expanse of grass pocked by the dark loam of winter's retreat. Beyond the margin of the river, a scatter of wild barley had already gone to seed, bending under the force of a wind unfiltered by tents or the expectant murmur of a waiting multitude. The air, sharp with the residue of the miracle, now layered in a new register: the green sweetness of wet growth, the bracing note of distant smoke, the faint, mineral aftertaste of the river's old bed exposed and then concealed again in a matter of hours.

For a while, the crowd did nothing. They simply stood, letting the truth of the crossing percolate through muscle and memory. Some fell to their knees, others sang, some only sat, staring at the bank behind as if expecting it to call them back.

The Ark remained in the riverbed, the priests arrayed in their formation, the wall of water rolling backwards upstream. At intervals, Joshua dispatched runners to count heads, to reassemble the tribes in their assigned order, to prepare the ground for the ceremonies that would begin even before the last of the Levites had reached the new shore. The voice of the leader, when it finally rose, cut through the confusion not with the bombast of a conquering king but with the blunt utility of a man intent on the next necessary thing.

"We will remember this day," Joshua said, his voice carrying across the width of the people. "Each tribe will take a stone from the river's heart, and we will build a monument here, so our children will know what was done."

A rustle of excitement, disbelief, and, beneath it all, the old, hard skepticism. But the runners moved through the ranks, selecting men by lot, each one to represent his people in the act of memory. Most were young, but not all. The oldest man to cross, a patriarch from the tribe of Reuben, protested that his knees would not survive another descent into the riverbed. When the time came, he went anyway, his steps slow but relentless, flanked by two grandsons who steadied him with the solemnity of men carrying a body and a lineage.

Gershom watched as the chosen made their way back down the bank, their shadows elongated in the late sun, their voices muffled by the distance and the persistent, uncanny blow of wind against the water. The riverbed, once a chaos of motion, now held only the Ark and its bearers, the selected eleven, and, at the very margin, a ring of priests maintaining the perimeter. Eleven went forward, each man stooping to lift a stone, not a pebble but a boulder, something that required the full body and the groan of effort to dislodge. The noise of the work was dull, but it reverberated through the dry channel and up onto the plain: the sound of the future being manufactured, one backbreaking gesture at a time.

When it was done, the eleven returned, each carrying his stone on the shoulder, sweat and mud streaking the robes that had been, minutes ago, ceremonial and pristine. They arranged the stones in a rough circle at the spot where the assembly had first reached the shore. Joshua stood at the center, arms raised, and began the incantation that would consecrate the place.

But before he could finish, he turned, as if struck by a thought, and called out: "Gershom, son of Moses."

The use of the patronymic—rare, and always loaded—sent a charge through the people. Heads turned. Eliezer, somewhere in the ranks of the Levites, froze mid-sentence, his mouth open as if to receive or reject the moment. Gershom felt his knees go loose, but did not move.

Again, Joshua: "Gershom, son of Moses, come forward and choose the stone for the tribe of Levi."

A pause hung between breaths, and the wind surged, sweeping the grass low and tossing a stray lock of hair into his eyes. For an instant, he considered refusing, pretending not to have heard. But the old habit of obedience, of being the one who is summoned and who answers, overrode everything else. He stepped out from the ranks, aware of every eye, every muttered speculation, every measure of his worth and the worth of the man whose shadow he carried.

The path to the riverbed was slick, but he did not stumble. The priests at the margin parted for him, their faces impassive but not unkind. The wall of water, now nowhere to be seen.

At the center, he stood before the Ark. The gold of its cover gleamed in the fading sun, the cherubim facing each other with an intensity that made the hair rise on his arms. The stones at his feet ranged from the size of a man's fist to the girth of a child's head. He reached for one, then another, each time feeling the texture, the cool weight, the irregularity of surface. At last, he settled on a blue-gray rock, smooth and oval, dense as a secret. He lifted it, heavier than he had expected but not impossible, and cradled it in both arms.

For a moment, he looked up, not at Joshua, but at the mist which caught the light, bending it into a fractured arc of color that hovered above the riverbed, then vanished as a cloud passed overhead. He felt the presence of the multitude behind him, the weight of their expectation, and the singular, hollow ache of knowing that, even in the midst of miracle, he was alone in the act of choosing.

He turned and walked back up the slope, the stone pressing into his ribs, his arms trembling with the strain. When he reached the summit, he placed the stone in the center of the monument, flanked by the others but distinct in its color and shape.

Joshua approached, resting a hand on his shoulder. The gesture was simple, but it carried with it the charge of a benediction, or a release.

"For the Levi, and for the sons of Moses," Joshua said, voice pitched for only the two of them. "So that your children will know it was not by accident, but by faith."

Gershom nodded, unsure if the emotion in his throat was relief or dread.

Behind them, the people cheered, the voices building in a wave that rolled up the hill and out across the plain. The priests, seeing their charge complete, lifted the Ark and turned to leave the riverbed. As the last foot cleared the bank, a sound that could have been mistaken for thunder rolled down from upstream as the wall of water came rushing back. The ground shuddered, as the river surged forward, filling the channel in seconds, the surface boiling and churning as it reasserted its claim on the land.

In the aftermath, the monument of stones stood alone at the margin, a memory encoded in earth and sweat. Gershom stood before it, hands numb, breath shallow, the words of the blessing still echoing in his ears.

Those of the company began to disperse and begin moving once more, while a few children ran for the water, daring each other to dip a toe in the resumed current. The land ahead beckoned, its fields and hills a challenge and a promise, a world waiting to be claimed by those who had, at last, crossed.

Like always, Tima locate him on the outskirts of the camp, her eyes bright in the evening light. She said nothing, only stood with him, her presence a rebuke to the idea that any journey was ever completed alone.

He looked out over the land, unsure what to make of it, or of himself.

But the stone remained, blue-gray and solid, a testament that, for one moment at least, he had chosen and had been chosen to bear witness.

And the world, miraculous and unfinished, waited for what would come next.

Shadows in Gilgal

Night layered the camp at Gilgal in descending veils of blue and black, the calm at its margin a living membrane that defined the difference between inside and out. Here, at the raw edge where the last tent staked its claim against the shapeless dark, Gershom sat on an overturned crate, legs splayed, palms resting flat against the brittle surface as if to hold himself down in the new world's gravity. The river, a memory now, lay two bowshots behind, its current replaced by the arrhythmic lull of wind over packed earth. Nothing about the ground underfoot suggested miracle; it had the hard, anonymous texture of any other place, scraped by recent migration and irreparably marked by the thousand small deaths required to make a people move.

He had chosen his site with precision. The nearest fire belonged to a family three rows inward; their laughter, when it came, was muffled by the intervening canvas, a sound like water percolating through stone. Further on, the Levite quarter exhaled its own distinct signature: the deep-voiced rumble of men arguing Law in the darkness, the quicksilver laughter of their wives, and the intermittent, high-pitched shrieks of children who had not yet learned that the night was no longer dangerous. Every so often, a gust of wind would catch the breath of the central fires and sling it outward, the aroma of roasting grain and lamb infiltrating Gershom's isolation with the quiet authority of home.

He watched the camp without looking directly at it, his gaze trained on the horizon but tuned to the periphery, alert for any detail that might require the fraction of a response. It was better, he had learned, to exist as a rumor on the periphery of other people's lives. Observation required little of him, participation demanded everything, and tonight he was rich with the former and bankrupt in the latter.

Inside the camp, life had already been rewritten into legend. The first hours after the crossing were a feast of retelling: each man, woman, and child rehearsed their own version of how the river had split, what they had seen, what it had felt like to stand on the old side and then the new. By the time the sun set, there were a dozen songs circulating, their melodies cribbed from older miracles, but the lyrics crafted to serve this generation's hunger for memory. Gershom heard the drums first, then the low strings and flutes. The music gathered force, swelled to fill the hollow at the center of the camp, and spilled out along the avenues in rivulets, the sound refracted by tent walls and bodies until the whole world was pulsing with the cadence of arrival.

He felt none of it. Not the pride, not the relief, not even the tiredness. His mind moved instead along the farthest perimeters, calculating the distance to the nearest olive grove, the speed with which the grass at the riverbank would recover from a hundred thousand trampling feet, the amount of time it would take for the camp's waste to poison the upper layer of soil. These thoughts were a comfort, a barrier against the encroaching warmth of belonging.

He wondered what his mother would have made of this place. She had hated the desert for its monotony, but had respected the logic of its emptiness. Here, there was no logic, only the violent imposition of newness, of rules unanchored by familiarity. He imagined her moving through the lanes, taking inventory of the edible weeds, cataloguing the scents in the morning air, recording the names of the birds that nested in the tamarisk groves. She would have found a way to make it home, no matter how much it resembled an enemy's land.

A blast of laughter erupted from the family fire nearest him—a sudden, sustained whoop that resolved into the off-key ululation of an old man already deep into the night's wine. Gershom watched as the old man's shadow, thrown grotesque and elongated by the fire, lurched upright, swayed in the direction of the dark, and then collapsed in a heap. For a moment, the fire's glow caught the man's face, a webwork of lines, mouth open in what might have been joy or pain. The others gathered around, propping him up, pouring more wine, and soon the music drowned out the moment entirely.

It was possible, Gershom supposed, to imagine a world in which he would have gone over, offered to help, accepted a bowl or a seat by the flame. It was also possible to imagine a world where he had never left the far bank, never shouldered the burden of a legacy he could not articulate and did not deserve. Neither fantasy held any traction tonight. He was, in every meaningful way, an observer.

He let his eyes slip closed, the darkness behind his lids richer and less complicated than the one outside. For a moment, he drifted, weightless and unrooted, ears ringing with the white noise of celebration. He might have fallen asleep, or entered the deeper trance of men who have nothing left to lose, had it not been for the sound of footsteps approaching from the direction of the main avenue.

They were not stealthy. The walker moved with the unself-consciousness of one whose presence required no introduction. The stride was heavy but measured, the footfalls cushioned by the grass but audible in the empty interval between songs. Gershom remained motionless, waiting to see if the figure would pass by or stop at his threshold. When the steps halted short of the circle of lamplight that marked his camp, he knew it was the latter.

He opened his eyes. The figure was a silhouette, broad at the shoulders and hooded against the chill. The face was in shadow, but the stance betrayed none of the hesitation common to men with business among strangers.

"Gershom ben Moses?" The voice was uninflected, the accent of a man trained to speak at assemblies, not at tables. Not Levite, yet not wholly apart, a voice that bore the echo of the altar without sanctity's claim.

He stood, brushing the dust from his tunic. "I'm here," he said. The effort to keep his tone neutral cost him more than he would have liked.

The visitor remained at the margin. "I have a message," he said. "From Joshua."

Gershom waited, arms folded, not bothering to invite the man closer.

"It is required that every male of fighting age, born in the desert, be circumcised at Gilgal before the Passover. The elders have selected men to carry out the command. You are among them."

A thin smile, almost involuntary, flickered at the corner of Gershom's mouth. "Of course," he said, "because the priests are too busy, or too precious, to do the bloody work themselves."

The messenger did not rise to the bait. "You are chosen because you have skill," he said. "It is known that you have practiced the art, and that your hands do not fail."

He blinked, once. "What else is known?"

"That you are the son of Zipporah," the visitor said, as if reciting from a ledger. "And that she learned from her father the arts of wound care and healing. We will need such skill, in the coming days. There are many to attend."

Gershom stepped into the full light of his own lantern, so that the man could see his face. "You realize the irony of this, I hope."

"I do not presume to judge what is or is not ironic," said the messenger. "Only to deliver instruction. The first gathering will be at dawn. The site is marked with a banner. Bring your knives, and your ointments."

"Who else?" Gershom asked.

The visitor's head tilted, as if considering whether the answer was classified. "Phinehas will preside. There will be assistants. You are not to concern yourself with hierarchy."

Gershom smiled again, this time with more teeth. "I never do," he said.

The messenger inclined his head, then turned to leave. After a few steps, he paused. "It is a good thing you do," he said, without looking back. "For the people."

He waited until the footsteps receded, then sat down heavily on the crate, the exhaustion settling into his bones like the first frost of the season. He stared at his hands, at the nicks and calluses accumulated over years of tending livestock, mending, or the chores scorned as undignified, given to those who would never be priest or prince. His mother had always said that the hand is a second brain, that it remembers things the mind is too proud to record. He had never believed her, but tonight, the hands moved independently, flexing, curling, uncurling, rehearsing the necessary motions before the need arose.

Inside the camp, the music had shifted from exuberant to melancholy. The voices were softer now, the flutes drawing out the long, minor notes of a song that must have come from Egypt or earlier. It was a song for the dead, or for the things left behind. Gershom listened to it, letting the sadness work its way into the cracks of his armor.

He wondered, not for the first time, if his father had ever felt this way: not the despair, but the relentless, remorseless sense of being assigned a task that was both too small and too large, too menial for the weight of expectation, too consequential to be refused.

He reached for the pouch that held his mother's knives, the blades wrapped in linen and sealed with a twist of wax. He passed the outskirts of the square, where the memory of the morning's violence lingered like an afterimage.

Tomorrow would be pain, and the day after, and the day after that. Tonight, there was only the silence, the margin, and the invisible wall that held him at the outskirts of a story that was no longer his.

He sat in the dark, eyes open, and waited for the night to end.

Dawn broke silver over the camp, the aftermath of last night's riotous celebration written in every slackened shoulder and dragging foot. The energy had drained, leaving only the twitch of expectation and the slow, reluctant shuffle of men summoned to a duty none would willingly claim. The site selected for the ceremony lay a half furlong from the main avenue, on a flat, packed terrace bordered by stakes wound with fresh cord—a makeshift hospital as much as a holy precinct. There was a lean-to for shade, but most of the ground was open, and already the dew had been trampled into mud by the procession of initiates.

Gershom arrived before the first light breached the valley. He set his mother's kit on a low table, unwrapped the linen from the blades, and arranged the salves and unguents in a neat line. The bandages were strips of cotton, boiled and dried, rolled tight as scrolls—he counted out and placed within reach. The care in his preparation was not lost on the two Levite boys assigned to assist; they watched him with the wary interest of men who had seen enough wounds to know that neatness mattered.

He could sense Phinehas before he saw him, the air in the immediate radius growing charged, even at this hour. The priest moved among the early arrivals, offering a word, a touch, a reassurance. He did not linger, but the weight of his presence reshaped the morning, as if each blade of grass stood a fraction taller in his wake. When he reached Gershom, he said nothing, only nodded once, his eyes tracking the arrangement of tools with the practiced scrutiny of a man who had learned to trust only what he could verify.

The initiates began to arrive in clusters, first the older boys, then the young men, and finally the handful of fathers who had, by some accident of birth or fate, avoided the ritual until now. They were a motley lot, some with faces set in grim lines, others with the bravado of men determined to outlast their own bodies. A few wore their best tunics, as if the ceremonial element outweighed the prospect of blood and pain. Gershom noted the variety but withheld judgment; he had seen, more than once, the sudden collapse of confidence at the first sight of a blade.

Phinehas stepped forward, his presence commanding as he raised his hands to the heavens. "O Lord of Hosts," he began, his voice a deep rumble, sharp with urgency. "We gather today beneath Your watchful gaze, bound by the covenant made with our father Abraham. We come, not as mere men, but as vessels of Your promise." He paused, letting the burden of his words settle in the still air, those gathered holding their breath.

"Let each initiate stand firm," he continued, his tone unwavering, "for this rite is not merely flesh but a passage into Your grace. Each one must pass through the gate of the flesh, shedding the bonds of childhood to take their rightful place at Your table." His eyes swept over the figures before him; shoulders tightened, jaws locked, and hands clenched at their sides. Some stared wide, their breath caught, while others held their gaze, a flicker of determination burning through the strain.

"May they find strength in this moment, O God," he implored, "and may their hearts be open to Your will. As we perform this sacred duty, let us remember the legacy of our ancestors, who walked through trials to reach the land You promised."

There was no softness in his words, only the stark clarity of the Law, unyielding and resolute. The air crackled with a sense of purpose, the gravity of his invocation echoing against the backdrop of a morning that felt both monumental and solemn.

The work began.

The first was a boy of thirteen, tall for his age, with the bowed legs of someone raised in a camp and not a city. He lay on the mat, hands at his sides, eyes fixed on the sky above.

Gershom knelt, washed his hands in the basin provided, and spoke the necessary words: "It will be quick."

He placed the blade to flesh, made the cut, pressed the cloth, and applied the salve. The boy did not cry out, only winced, the tendons in his neck standing out like ropes. Gershom worked with speed, not out of indifference but from a knowledge that time was the true enemy in such things. He wrapped the wound, checked for bleeding, and nodded to the assistant to help the boy to the shade.

The next was older, almost a man, and he had the look of someone who had never submitted to anything in his life. He glared at Gershom with open hostility, daring him to make a mistake. Gershom met his gaze, let the hostility pass through him, and did the work. This time, the man yelped, then cursed, then bit his tongue and bled into the cloth. Gershom applied the paste, bound the wound, and turned away before the next word could be uttered.

By the tenth, the cycle had taken hold: cut, press, salve, bind. Each wound was unique, each reaction the same: pain, surprise, then a kind of numb relief. The air grew thick with the smell of blood and antiseptic, with the guttural animal groans of men trying not to shame themselves. Gershom worked without comment, his mind narrowed to the space between hand and knife, to the heat of the wound and the pressure required to stop the flow.

At intervals, Phinehas would drift by, sometimes pausing to adjust a bandage, sometimes speaking to the men as they waited for their turn. Once, he stopped beside Gershom, placed a hand on his shoulder, and held it there for a second too long. The touch was not paternal, but neither was it perfunctory. It was the gesture of a man who understood what it meant to be both healer and outcast, both necessary and unwelcome.

The worst cases came at midday: men whose fear had delayed them until the sun was at its peak, whose bravado had evaporated in the wait. One fainted before Gershom even touched him; another soiled himself and wept openly. The assistants, initially amused, grew solemn as the day wore on, their jokes dying in the heat and the mounting tally of bandaged bodies.

At the boundary of the field, a pile of soiled linens grew higher, the crimson stains blooming into dark, vegetal shapes as they dried in the sun. Gershom paused only once, to drink water, hands trembling as he lifted the cup to his mouth. He looked around at the men reclining in the shade, some speaking in hushed tones, others silent, eyes closed against the pain or the shame or both.

In the afternoon, as the last wave of initiates shuffled in, Gershom noticed Phinehas standing apart from the others, his gaze fixed not on the ceremony, but on the sky above. The priest's lips moved, but no sound carried. In that moment, he appeared neither fierce nor holy, but deeply tired, a man who had spent his entire life trying to convince himself that the pain of the flesh could be made meaningful by the Law.

The final procedure was a boy of eleven, small and shivering in the heat. Gershom knelt, wiped the tears from the boy's cheek, and whispered, "It will be over soon." The cut was clean, the bleeding minimal, but the boy still clung to his arm as Gershom finished the wrapping.

When it was done, Gershom sat back on his heels, sweat pooling at the base of his spine. He stared at his hands, so steady, so precise, so alien to him now. He flexed his fingers, watched the dried blood crack along the lines of his palm. The work was finished, but the noise of it, the groans, the prayers, the faint drumbeat of feet as the injured tried to stand—echoed in his head, crowding out every other thought.

Phinehas approached, stopping at a respectful distance. He looked at Gershom, not with pity, but with a kind of understanding. He nodded, once, then again, as if affirming a contract neither had signed but both were bound to.

Gershom wiped his hands on a clean cloth, folded the knives back into their linen, and stood. He surveyed the field of wounded, the assistants weaving through them with water and food, the gradual, stubborn return of life to bodies bent but not broken.

He should have felt something: pride, perhaps, or a grim satisfaction at having done what was required. Instead, he felt only the echo of the cut: the knowledge that every act of entry into a people came at the price of pain, and that for some, the wound never healed.

He walked away from the field, the weight of the day pressing down with every step, and wondered what the covenant would require of him next.

The days that followed blurred into a single, gray slab of pain and repetition. The field of the wounded, once bounded by stakes and cord, blended into the camp, a territory marked not by conquest but by convalescence. Gershom made his station on a lichen-patched rock at the periphery, overlooking the mats where the young men sprawled, wrapped in clean linen and the narcotic haze of pain's aftermath. By noon, each day the sun seared the ground to a dazzling white, and the air around the infirmary shimmered with the scent of old blood and the acrid tang of medicinal herbs.

He worked without saying a word, tending the wounds with the same meticulousness as before. His hands moved with a stubborn autonomy, cleaning, binding, unbinding, applying salves in the precise ratios his mother had drilled into him years ago. The young men came to him one by one, or sometimes in pairs, limping, cursing, or stifling their discomfort behind the bravado of forced jokes. He acknowledged them, but only barely, his attention fixed on the flesh and the task and the gradual, uncooperative business of healing.

A peculiar camaraderie enveloped the injured, a language of shared suffering that Gershom could not penetrate but recognized, nonetheless. As dusk settled over the camp, the wounded men congregated around the water jars or nestled in the shade, their voices weaving through the evening air like a familiar melody.

"Did you hear about the cities?" one young man said, his voice tinged with excitement. "They say the gates are made of iron, real iron!"

"Pah! Iron gates? I'll believe it when I see it!" scoffed another, flicking a pebble at him. "I'm just hoping for a roof over my head. I'll build a house so grand that my whole tribe can feast inside!" His gaunt frame rose with pride as he spoke.

Laughter erupted from the group, a sound mingled with pain yet buoyed by hope. "Three wives, huh?" an older man chimed in, his tone teasing. "You think you can keep them from tearing each other apart before the year's out?"

The younger man grinned, undeterred. "I'll make it work! Watch me!"

The others joined in, their words rising with playful banter, then spiraling into light-hearted arguments, each trying to outdo the last with tales of ambition and dreams for the new land.

Gershom listened, at first with indifference, then with a creeping, prickling envy. The confidence in their words, the unguarded certainty that the world ahead would open to them, he could not recall ever having possessed such a thing. Even as a child, he had viewed the future as a riddle meant to be solved, not a promise waiting to be unwrapped.

One evening, as he changed the dressing on a particularly stubborn wound, the boy attached to it, a mop-haired teenager with fever-bright eyes, looked up and fixed him with a stare that was both accusing and awestruck.

"You're really Moses' son, aren't you," he said. It wasn't a question.

Gershom finished tying the bandage, then wiped his hands on a rag. "I am."

The boy hesitated, then asked, "What do you think he'd say about all this?" He gestured vaguely at the field, at the camp, at the sprawling, wounded collective.

Gershom blinked, caught off guard by the directness. He had an answer, several in fact, words rehearsed in the dark, arguments assembled for debates that would never take place, but none fit the occasion.

"I don't know," he said. "He's not here to ask. But to be honest, I would like to know myself."

Disappointment crossed the boy's face, then was gone. "I think he'd want to see what happens next," he said. "He'd want to know if it was worth it."

Gershom made no reply. He cleaned the wound, gave the boy's shoulder a gentle tap that told him he'd done well. Then he rose and drifted toward the next child waiting in line.

That night, as the last of the injured dozed under the moon or huddled in muted conversation, Gershom lingered on his stone, letting the chill of the air seep through his garbs and into his bones. The sky above was black and bottomless, the stars so numerous they rose beyond counting, more than the grains of earth beneath his feet.

The events of the past days had emptied him out, scraped away the last of whatever faith or hope might have been clinging to the inside of his chest. What was left was a clean, dry hollowness, the kind his mother used to describe when talking about the bones of animals left to bleach in the desert sun. Nothing left but the structure, the shape of what had once been alive.

He pushed to his feet, rolling the stiffness from his back, and scanned the camp. Smoke curled lazily from dim-burning fires, and most of the tents were drawn tight, their flaps snapping in the night breeze. The world, for the moment, was as close to peace as it had ever been.

He began to walk, not toward his own tent, but away from the camp, where the laughter and chatter faded into a distant murmur. The grass thinned, yielding to rough scrub, and the first stones of the new land jutted out like forgotten memories. With each stride, he felt the fatigue accumulate in his legs, a heaviness that dragged him down, while the ache in his shoulders blossomed into an even burn.

"What am I doing?" he wondered. *"Why do I feel so discon-nected from this moment of triumph? The air tasted different here, less of smoke and more of mineral, as if the ground were exhaling in anticipation of the world being remade. But what about me? Am I meant to be part of this new beginning, or am I just a shadow of my father's legacy?"*

Gershom halted, allowing the questions to swirl in his mind like the grit kicked up by his feet. The stars above twinkled with an indifferent brilliance, mocking his uncertainty. He had always imagined he would find clarity in this promised land, yet here he was, adrift in a sea of doubt. Every breath came laden with expectation, his own and that of those who regarded him as Moses' son. What did they see when they looked at him? A leader? A failure?

He resumed his walk, the uneven ground under him reflecting the turmoil within. As he moved further from the camp, he yearned for something, answers perhaps, or a sense of belonging. Would he ever feel worthy of this land, or was he destined to wander forever in the shadows of his father's greatness?

He walked until the last sounds of the camp were gone, until the glow of the fires was no more than a rumor on the horizon. He found a narrow ridge, crouched there, and lifted his gaze to the sky. The stars loomed closer, almost within reach, but remained utterly indifferent to the struggles below.

He knelt, not to pray, but because his legs refused to carry him any further. He let his head fall forward, his hands pressed to the cool, unfamiliar earth. He breathed in the night, the sharp clarity of it, and let himself, want something.

Not certainty. Not even hope.

The chance to keep moving. To see what happened next.

The Midnight Voice

Gershom continued to kneel at the margin of darkness, where the stillness of the desert lay close to the farthest boundary of the Israelite camp, and no sound from the world of men could reach him. He had not slept; sleep was an indulgence for men at peace within, or at least unburdened by the kind of questions that gnawed the root of the soul.

He folded there, body doubled over the way a seed curls inward beneath the press of its own possibility, forehead resting against the chilled rock. The cold was a living thing, crept in through the ragged hem of his tunic, made a home of his flesh and drove his thoughts into a tighter, more brutal focus. The air, unchecked by even a single acacia or scrub, licked at his cheeks, and the granules that swept against him stung the corners of his eyes until he no longer knew if it was the night, or the pain, or the utter failure of hope that made them wet.

He placed his palms on the stone, felt the microtopography of the world's surface scored into his skin, the brittle ridges and the pockets where time had chewed away the softer bits, the sharp edges that would never heal because no one ever walked here. This was not the riverbank where the world had been remade; it was the in-between, the unclaimed margin, a space that existed precisely because it was too unwanted for even the tribal boundaries to covet. It was, he supposed, the natural home of men like him.

He had not brought a lamp; he did not need one. The moon was full and raw above, and each time a cloud scraped past, it cast the landscape in a different register, now bone, now blue, now a colorless ash that suggested not illumination but exposure, as if all the secret shame of the world had been laid out for audit. In the distance, the camp shimmered with its own life, the specks of firelight diffusing through the canvas like gold through dirty water. The sound did not travel, but the smell did: the echo of smoke and the faint, impossible sweetness of roasted grain. It caught in the wind's teeth, bit at him every few minutes, a reminder that somewhere, people were eating, talking, preparing for something he wanted no part in.

He stayed that way for a long time, unmoving but never at rest, waiting for the darkness to change him or at least convince him to change himself. But the darkness had never been interested in him, and so the change, when it came, was not external but a turning inward so abrupt it nearly made him retch.

He did not expect the recollection. It arrived with the precision of a spear, bypassed the tired fortress of his will and rooted in the most unguarded quarter of his mind. It was his mother's tent, not as it had been in the last frail days, but in the years when she had commanded the space with a dignity that could not be confused for pride. She was there, backlit by the lamplight and the woolen walls of home, her hands wrapped around a spindle, the fibers collecting between her fingers in a rhythm so sure the whole world felt as if it depended on her motions.

The detail was exquisite. He could smell the lanolin of the fleece, feel the subtle vibration of the reed mat under his bare feet. He could see, through the haze of lamp smoke, the way her brow pinched when she concentrated, her right eyebrow always a hair higher than the left, as if she was forever skeptical of the world and its promises. She hummed as she worked, a tune with no melody but an unyielding undercurrent of order.

He watched her for a time, was it a second or the better part of a night, and then the scene shifted, as memories do, to the moment that had hurt the most.

He was a boy, wracked with fever, sweating through a blanket so sodden it might have drowned him if left another hour. She knelt at his side, the same spindle now set aside, her hands cool on his brow. She pressed the backs of her fingers against his cheek, then dipped a rag into a clay bowl of river water and wrung it out with the precision of a ritual. When she spoke, the words came as a blessing, though he only understood that later.

"You are not your father's son," she said, "until you have seen God for yourself."

At the time, he thought it was a rebuke. Now, sitting in the dust on the brink of the new world, he wondered if it had always been a comfort.

In the memory, she lingered with him through the worst of the night, her presence a bulwark against the twin tyrannies of pain and time. When the fever broke, and he awoke hours later to the gray serenity before dawn, she had already retreated to her work. But her words had hung in the tent like the scent of spun wool: invisible, but inescapable.

He tried to summon the next moment, to will the memory

forward, but the mind, like the moon, offers no guarantee of continuity. Instead, he was left with the echo of her voice, and the feel of the cool cloth on his brow, and the bone-deep conviction that the only inheritance that mattered was not what had been left to him, but what he could claim for himself.

The memory was so strong that, when he blinked, he half-expected to find himself in the tent again, the world reduced to the manageable proportions of a mother's care and a child's need. Instead, he opened his eyes onto the same barren patch of stone, the horizon bleached by moonlight, the future as uncertain as the sky's refusal to yield even a single drop of rain.

He laughed, a sound so small it barely registered against the immensity of the silence. "You are not your father's son, until you have seen God for yourself."

It was a riddle and a release. For years, he had carried the weight of expectation, the notion that, in order to be worthy, he must somehow reconstitute the essence of Moses in a body and soul so ill-suited to prophecy that even the priests had learned not to ask him to recite the Law.

He looked up at the moon, and for the first time, it did not seem accusatory. It was the moon, old and indifferent, witness to the folly of men and the slow, grinding persistence of the world. He thought of his father, not the myth, but the man whose hands had trembled when angered, who had once dropped a scroll in the sand and cursed it, thinking no one was listening. He wondered if Moses, in the last hours on Nebo, had ever stopped measuring the distance between himself and the God he had served.

He wondered, and for the first time in months, he let himself want something. Not forgiveness. Not greatness. Only the chance to look back, years from now, and know that he had walked into the wilderness with his eyes open, and that it was enough.

He sat there a bit longer, letting the cold burn through him, until he finally stood, knees stiff, the ache in his bones a comfort rather than a curse. He brushed the dust from his hands, then from his tunic, and stepped away from the stone, leaving the stillness behind him. The walk back to camp was far from triumphant, nothing so crude, but it was steady, and the ground, if not softer, showed a faint willingness to give way beneath him.

The dawn, when it arrived, was neither gentle nor triumphant. It bled up from the horizon in incremental hemorrhages of light, staining the undersides of clouds and painting the valley with the kind of raw honesty that left no shadow unexamined. Gershom walked the avenue toward the tent cluster, the cold still lodged deep in his bones, the muscles in his legs groaning protest with every step. The camp was waking: the distant murmur of voices, the smell of baking flatbread, the lowing of goats unsettled by the promise of another day.

He saw her before she saw him. Tima stood at the camp's edge, arms crossed firm, chin set in a line of worry that looked chiseled in stone. Her hair was down, falling wild over her shoulders, and she paced the margin with a tempo that bespoke either impatience or rage or a hybrid of both. She scanned the horizon at intervals, her gaze skipping over each detail as if inventorying every possible threat the new world could conjure.

He tried, for a moment, to slip past her, to melt into the comfort of routine before she could intercept. But the attempt was hopeless: she spotted him before he had cleared the final row of tents, and with a sudden, explosive pivot, she was moving toward him, not running but walking with a velocity that made running look like a stalling tactic.

"Gershom!" Her voice was pitched low to keep from waking the children, but the urgency in it cut through the dawn like a horn.

He stopped, shoulders braced, not because he expected a blow but because he was no longer sure what he deserved.

She closed the distance in four strides, and before he could manufacture a greeting or a defense, her arms were around him, tight and inescapable, the kind of embrace that speaks more of restraint than of welcome. He stood rigid for a beat, then let himself sag into the warmth, the top of her head tucked under his chin as if designed for the purpose.

"You shouldn't do that," she said into his chest, the words muffled by the fabric.

He blinked, uncertain. "Walk outside the camp? People do it all the time."

She pulled back just far enough to look him in the face. Her eyes were red at the corners, but the rest of her was resolute, unsparing. "No, you donkey. You shouldn't have me worried that you died out there. Or worse, that you decided not to come back."

He tried to laugh, but the sound collapsed in his throat. "I know it's not safe. Everyone tells me that. But I needed—"

She cut him off with a sharp punch to the upper arm, not enough to hurt but enough to reset the terms of the conversation. "You always need," she said. "Maybe someday you try wanting instead."

He looked at her, really looked, and saw for the first time the shadow his absence had thrown over her night. The fatigue, the irritation, but beneath it all a filament of care so thin it barely survived the air, yet so strong it had pulled her to the edge of the world to wait for him.

Without thinking, he leaned down and kissed her. It was not a question; it was the answer to every fear she had not voiced. Her lips, cracked by the wind, carried salt. When she kissed him back, it was hard, unyielding, more possession than tenderness.

They stood like that for a breath or two, then separated, the moment preserved in the white-hot catalog of things neither would ever admit aloud.

She was the first to recover. "Come," she said, grabbing his hand. "If you're going to give me a heart attack, you can at least help me carry water for the old ones."

He followed, the throb in his arm where she had punched him outmatched only by the heat still radiating from his mouth. They walked to the nearest well, hand in hand, and the world gathered around their movement, the rhythm of the morning syncing with the pulse that carried him forward.

They worked in silence at first. The buckets were heavier than usual—either the well had grown lazy, or his muscles were still soured by yesterday's labor. Tima did not offer to lighten his load; she expected him to carry his share, and he did, grateful for the normalcy of work, for the way it forced his mind into the present.

It was only after the last pail had been delivered, and the old men had muttered their thanks, that she allowed herself to pause.

They sat together in the shade of a tree beyond the tents, and gaze out at the distance, the hills of Canaan, sharp-edged and impossible in the slant of sun's light. The chill was gone from the air, but she still pressed against him anyway, shoulder to shoulder, her warmth more comfort than necessity.

He stared at the hills, searching for the right words. "Tima," he started, then stopped. He tried again. "I think I understand now what I was missing. What Father always meant."

She waited, saying nothing, her profile as still as the horizon.

"I kept thinking I had to be him," he said, the words coming slow and uneven, as if he were learning to speak all over again. "That if I just followed the Law, or did everything right, I'd get what he got. I'd get God. But that's not how it works. The Law is—" He paused, struggling. "It's a language, not a destination. It tells you how to walk, not where you're supposed to end up."

She nodded once, as if she had known this all along.

He went on, not trusting himself to stop. "Last night, I remembered my mother. Not only her face, but the way she made everything matter, even the smallest thing. She told me once that God makes worthy those He chooses, not chooses those who are already worthy." He glanced sideways, afraid to see her reaction, but Tima's expression was unchanged, focused, patient as rain.

"For the first time," he said, "I think I want to find out what it's like to be chosen for something. Not because of my name. Because I want it."

She reached over, took his hand, and squeezed. "Welcome to the world," she said, and there was no mockery in it.

They sat together as the air became full of noise, cries, calls, the metallic clash of pots and the laughter of children—but here, at the margin, there was space enough for the two of them.

Gershom glanced down at Tima, a soft smile breaking through the weight of his thoughts. "That's enough about me," he said, his voice gentle yet curious. "What is it you truly want from the Promised Land?"

Tima looked out toward the horizon where the hills of Canaan rose sharply against the sky, her brow furrowing in contemplation. "I want... I want to feel like I belong," she replied slowly, her eyes reflecting the distant peaks. "Not just in the camp or among our people, but in the land itself. I want to walk through the fields and know that this is home, that it's ours to nurture and cherish."

Gershom could see the fire igniting in her gaze, a spark of determination that made his heart swell. "And what does belonging feel like to you?" he asked, intrigued.

She turned her head slightly, meeting his gaze with a thoughtful intensity. "It feels like the warmth of the sun on my face when I'm planting seeds, like the laughter of children echoing in the air as they play. It's knowing that my hands can shape the earth, that I can weave a life here, full of stories and love."

He nodded, absorbing her words, each one resonating deep within him. "You want to create something lasting," he said, a realization dawning upon him. "Something that connects you to the generations before us."

"Exactly," she said, her voice brightening. "I want to build a life where we can gather together, where families can grow and thrive. A place where the stories of our ancestors are not simply memories but living traditions that we pass down."

Gershom felt a warmth spread through him, a sense of camaraderie that transcended their individual struggles. "It's beautiful, Tima. You carry a vision that reaches past the land,

and you're dreaming of community."

She smiled at him, a mixture of gratitude and hope dancing in her eyes. "And what about you? What else do you want, Gershom? Now that you're beginning to find your own path?"

He hesitated, his own desires tangled in the remnants of his past. "Besides becoming my own person. I want this," as he looked at their interlocking fingers.

Tima squeezed his hand tighter, grounding him in the moment. "Then let's carve our paths together," she said, her tone resolute. "We'll help each other find our way, whatever that may look like."

Gershom smiled, feeling a flicker of hope ignite within him. "Together," he echoed, the word hanging in the air like a promise.

They stayed that way, with the comfortable morning breeze and the hum of camp behind them, until the sun climbed high enough to demand the next thing.

By midday, the camp was an engine of anticipation, every cog and lever engaged in the steady grind of preparation for the night's Passover. The air, already heavy with the promise of heat, hung dense with the twin perfumes of sweat and the bright, animal tang of blood. From the central avenue to the farthest cordon, every family seemed to be at work: grinding, kneading, scouring out old bitterness from bowls and hearts alike, rethreading the old rituals with the nervous, hungry thread of a people on the verge of something unrepeatable.

Gershom found himself drawn, almost magnetized, to the area reserved for the lambs. The pens sprawled in an uneven rectangle at the outskirts of the camp, a labyrinth of rickety fencing and trodden hay, where the selected animals bleated with a noise that was at once plaintive and exultant, as if they too sensed the importance of the coming hour. Levites milled around the pens, some with knives, others with buckets, all carrying an air of resigned efficiency. The ground was already slick with the residue of earlier sacrifices, and the flies attended in their own, black-clouded quorum, darting from wound to mouth and back with the abandon of creatures who knew their place in the order of things.

He stood at the edge for a moment, watching the choreography of slaughter and cleaning, the bodies carried in one direction, the blood in another, the skins peeled and stacked in a heap destined for the tanners. The logic of it all, the sequence, the economy, the refusal to waste, had always appealed to him. There was dignity in it, even for the animals, a kind of closing of the circle that made sense in a world otherwise intent on fraying at the edges.

He scanned for Joshua and found him near the main gate, conferring with a knot of elders, his arms folded across his chest in a posture of unwilling patience. The leader's raiment was immaculate, but his sandals were spattered with the same blood as everyone else's, and his eyes moved with the wary precision of a man who expected, at any moment, to be called upon for something only he could do.

Gershom approached, keeping his pace measured. He waited until the conversation paused, then inclined his head, a gesture of respect but not submission.

"May I have a word?" he said.

Joshua dismissed the others with a flick of his hand, the gesture as clean and final as a blade.

"You look like a man with unfinished business," Joshua said, his voice pitched low.

Gershom nodded. "I'd like to help," he said, and was

surprised to find that he meant it in the simplest way possible. "With the lambs, with whatever needs doing."

Joshua regarded him, the pause uncomfortably long. For a moment, Gershom feared he had overplayed his hand, or that the night in the desert had left something visible on his skin that marked him as unfit.

"Not many would volunteer for that work," Joshua said.

Gershom shrugged. "Maybe not," he said, "but I don't mind it."

Another long look, then Joshua smiled, a real smile, brief but unclouded. "The Levite in you runs deeper than you let on," he said. "Go. They'll put you to use."

He turned away, and Gershom felt, in the subtlest way, the weight of something old and impossible slide off his shoulders.

He walked to the nearest pen, where a line of young men, already up to their elbows in the day's business, shuffled lambs through a sequence of tasks: inspection, dispatch, cleaning, quartering. One of the overseers, a bony man with the permanent squint of a pessimist, handed him a short knife and pointed to a pair of animals in the holding corral.

"These two next," the man said. "Don't cut too deep, or you'll spoil the meat."

Gershom nodded and set to work. The first lamb trembled in his grip, but he held it firm, murmured the old words of comfort, and then did the necessary thing with a precision that left nothing to chance. The second was smaller, but fought harder, and he found himself admiring its stubbornness even as he subdued it. When both animals lay still, he cleaned the blade on a scrap of cloth and moved to the cleaning table, where a pair of assistants stripped the carcasses with a speed that bordered on artistry.

The cycle asserted its presence: lamb, knife, blood, water, flesh, salt, repeat. Each action erased the hesitations of the one before it, until the work became a kind of meditation, a way of inhabiting the moment so fully that the rest of the world, the rest of his life, receded into mere background noise.

He worked alongside the other Levites, and in their faces he saw neither curiosity nor judgment, only the recognition of a fellow laborer. They did not speak much, but their silences were companionable, punctuated only by the occasional instruction or warning, or a dry joke about the quality of this year's crop.

At one point, during a lull, one of the younger Levites passed him a cup of water and grinned. "You do this before?" the boy asked.

"Not like this," Gershom said, "but I've seen my share of cuts."

The boy laughed, wiped his hands on his garment, and said, "Good. We need men who can finish what they start."

The words, unremarkable in themselves, lodged in a place deep inside Gershom. He took the water, drank, and returned to the line.

The afternoon wore on. The sun, once sharp, turned viscous in the west, casting everything in a gold so thick it threatened to slow the world's rotation. By the time the last lamb had been processed, the pens were empty, the ground tamped flat by the passage of a hundred pairs of feet. The air was quieter now, and the only sounds were the distant shouts of children and the softer, almost reverent murmur of women preparing the meal.

Gershom cleaned his knife, handed it back to the overseer, and flexed his fingers, surprised at how little they hurt.

He stood for a while at the edge of the pen, watching the camp as the first torches were lit and the shadows drew long and ambiguous across the ground. Somewhere behind him, a family was singing, a slow, winding melody that wrapped around and refused to resolve. He listened, and did not try to remember the words.

He felt no pride, exactly, but the absence of shame was a kind of triumph. He felt he had begun to finally understand what it was to serve not out of fear or expectation, but because the work was good and necessary and, in the end, shared.

He wiped his hands clean, squared his shoulders, and turned toward the avenue, where Tima and the others would be waiting.

It was enough.

The First Passover

In the courtyard designated for the Levites' work, Gershom slipped into the rhythm of preparation. The dough-pile before him was a squat mountain, fourfold what his mother had ever set upon a slab, the flour sifted in frantic increments by a trio of girls whose giggles, at first nervous, soon rejoined the hymn of the crowd. The bowl was clay, chipped, and the surface of the kneading table already veined with white. Yet the act of mixing, adding water and folding in the first crystals of salt, was a comfort so primitive it asked for no thought and no doubt.

He worked the mass with the heel of his palm, pushing down and away, then letting it rise and slap back with a squelch. The Levite to his left, a sour-faced man with the posture of an unstrung bow, moved methodically, wordless. To his right, a youth with elbows as sharp as grasshoppers tried to mimic Gershom's technique, missing the table with half his swings and sending the rest scattering into a corona of flour at their feet.

"Not like that," the elder Levite muttered, never raising his eyes.

The youth ignored him, face set with the wild optimism of the untrained. Gershom kept working, noting with private satisfaction how the ball in his hands began, by degrees, to submit: first resisting, then yielding, then finally taking the shape of something it had not known was possible. He remembered, without quite meaning to, the precise way Zipporah's knuckles had dimpled the surface of her dough, her jaw set to the work even when her mind had long since traveled ahead to the next day's meal.

By midday, the air in the camp had thickened. The avenue of tents had become a grid of humans and livestock, each tribe elbowing for space, each household determined to prove its readiness for the coming night. From the platform at the camp's center, the sound of drums signaled each new hour, the beat so regular that after a while it faded into the pulse of the work.

Gershom shaped the dough into rounds, flattening each with the heel of his hand, then passing it to the boy, who whisked it to the fire-side where the women took over. In return, the boy ferried back a stack of reed mats, still dewy from last night's soaking.

"Arranged in circles," the boy said, beaming, "as they did in Egypt. My mother says the angels look down and see only the pattern."

He set the mats down with a flourish, the implied order of their placement so urgent that Gershom, against all logic, felt compelled to check his own work: the rounds of dough were near-perfect, almost uniform, their pale surfaces already beginning to dry in the unkind wind.

Across the courtyard, several Levites stood at attention, their robes hitched above the knee to keep them out of the red mud. Beyond them, the day's first lambs turned lazily on their spits, the motion so languorous it read as a quiet mockery of the urgency of everything else. The men assigned to tend the fire kept up a quiet but unending commentary, disputing the correct angle of the skewer or the sequence in which the animals should be rotated for even browning.

"There is a science to it," one insisted, pinching the spit between two thick fingers. "If you turn too soon, you lose the juices. If you wait, the outer flesh blackens before the bone has even considered heat. Timing is everything."

Gershom found the remark oddly comforting. He watched as the man adjusted the spit, his hands sure but gentle, the motion oddly reminiscent of his father's care with the tablets of the Law—never hurried, never careless, as if the smallest deviation might topple the order of the universe.

A sudden voice broke his reverie. "Which do you think is harder—crossing the river, or parting the sea?"

He turned. The speaker was a boy, maybe ten, stick-thin, with a mop of curls and a face freckled raw by the sun. He hovered at the edge of the mat array, shifting his weight with the restlessness of someone not quite invited but unable to stay away.

"I beg your pardon?" Gershom said, keeping his tone neutral.

The boy planted his feet. "My father says the sea was easier, because the wind did all the work. The river, he says, took more courage, because you had to trust it would stop when you stepped in. But the wind—" here he made a gusting motion with his hands, "—the wind, you could see it, and you could feel it in your bones before you moved."

The logic was exquisite, unassailable. Gershom nodded. "I suppose it depends on who you are. Some men trust what they see. Others trust what they remember."

The boy grinned, revealing a line of teeth so ragged they looked like the tines of a comb. "But you, your father did both! He made the sea obey, and trusted what the almighty said. Didn't he?"

Gershom felt, as he always did, the small contraction in his chest, the squeeze of legacy, the reflex to duck and run. But today, for reasons he did not bother to interrogate, he stayed put.

"He did what he was told," Gershom said, breaking a strip from the finished round and offering it to the boy. "The wind, the water, they belonged to Someone else."

The boy chewed, considering. "Do you think He talks to people now?"

Gershom glanced up, searching the sky for any sign of a reply. "If He does, He prefers not to say so out loud."

A new round of laughter rippled from the fire-pit. The roasting lambs had begun to shed their first layer of fat, the hissing punctuated by small pops as the drippings hit the stone below. The aroma doubled, tripled, braided with the sharpness of fermenting dough and the faint bitterness of the herbs stacked in baskets behind the kneading table.

The boy edged closer. "Do you remember Egypt?" he asked, voice low. "Were you there?"

Gershom shook his head. "No. I was born in the wilderness. Egypt is simply a story to me."

"That's what my father says," the boy whispered. "He says some stories are truer than the things that actually happen." He looked up, daring. "Is that what your father taught you?"

The question, unanswerable, hung in the air like the after smell of smoke. Gershom studied the boy. His eyes were too large, and his hands knotted a corner of the mat with nervous energy.

"My father taught me that stories are the only way to make sense of fear," he said finally. "If you want to know what happened, you ask the old men. If you want to know why, you listen to the stories."

The boy nodded, as if this confirmed some private hypothesis. "Would you tell me one?" he said.

Gershom felt the eyes of the dough-boy, the mat-boy, the sour Levite and the youth with the elbows, all of them now pivoted to him. For a moment he thought to refuse, but the words came, slow and unhurried, as if summoned by the logic of the morning.

"There was a night," he began, "when the world waited for a sign. The old men say you could taste the tension in the air, the way you taste iron in a bleeding mouth. My mother told me that every family huddled around their tables, listening for the sound of death passing overhead, hoping their doorways would hold. The bread was flat, the lamb was bitter, but the real meal was fear, and the portion was enough for every living soul."

He broke the narrative, checking the boy's face for boredom, for mockery, for the impatience of children. Instead, he saw only hunger.

"When the sign came, it was not in thunder, or fire, or the sudden end of night," he continued. "It was in the hush, the moment when even the crickets stopped, when the wind folded its wings, and every man heard the sound of his own breathing as if it belonged to someone else."

The dough-boy blinked, awestruck. The Levite's hands stilled on the rolling pin.

"My mother said that was the moment the people were

born," Gershom said. "Not when they crossed, not when they received the Law, but that first silence, when they knew they had survived, and that the world would never again be what it had been."

The courtyard was silent now, save for the low, desultory murmur of the lamb-tenders and the occasional clink of wood on clay. The boy stared at Gershom, mouth open.

"Did it hurt to leave?" he whispered.

The question, so raw, so surgical, made Gershom laugh a real laugh, pulled from the place somewhere behind the ribs. "Everything hurts, at first. But what comes after is the real test."

The boy nodded, said nothing more, but resumed his place at the mat, smoothing its surface with deliberate, almost reverent care. The other boys set in to help, each one now invested in the arrangement, as if the geometry of their work might be a bulwark against the fears to come.

Gershom wiped his hands, the skin dusted with flour and streaked with a line of dough so thin it read as part of him. He looked up, startled to see how the sun had shifted, the light now hard and unyielding, the shadows grown short and severe.

In the distance, the women's chorus had begun to practice the night's songs, their voices rising in a three-note pattern that repeated, then twisted, then repeated again. The lambs rotated on their spits, their skin now a glossy brown that crackled when the wind shifted. The Levite at the table resumed his work, but his movements had lost their edge; the elbows-boy, once hopeless, now shaped his dough with something like pride.

The moment was brief, but it lodged, unmistakable. He knew he had held their attention, and that the words of his father, so often a burden and a freight of expectation, had become, for these minutes, a bridge.

He flexed his hands, testing for the old tremor. There was none.

He stacked the last of the dough rounds, set them on the mat, and looked to the fire-pit, where the boy who'd challenged him now stood, watching the lambs, face illuminated by the first dance of evening flames.

The camp was a crucible, a world mid-transformation. And for the first time in a long while, Gershom found himself looking forward to the night.

***

Night arrived not as a gentle veil but as a swift, decisive force, folding the camp into a series of luminous islands ringed by darkness. At the heart of Gilgal, the Levite courtyard, earlier a factory of hands and voices, was transformed. Its hard earth was swept and retiled with low mats, each concentric circle measuring the social geometry of tribe, clan, household, guest. At the center, a ring of fire-pits and the coals of the day's labor cast up a breathing glow that rendered all faces at once ancient and newborn.

From the perimeter, the approach of the tribes was not a march but a convergence: single bodies, pairs, then families in brief, charged procession. The children, already scrubbed and bundled, walked in an order far above their station, and the old men, their eyes hollowed by the newness of it all, shuffled into place with a gravity that made the air feel denser by the minute.

Gershom took his seat at the far side of the first circle, the mat to his left occupied by Tima, her hair plaited and wound above her nape in a spiral so severe it stood as a challenge to anyone who might contest her presence. To his right, the boy Shem, no longer the nervous questioner of the morning but now invested with the solemnity of a newly minted witness, sat cross-legged, hands folded atop his knees. Behind them, a wedge of Levites formed a living boundary between the ceremonial center and the restless ocean of bodies crowding the avenue beyond.

The smoke from the firepits crawled low, curling around the first platters of roasted lamb and the bowls of bruised herbs arrayed on reed baskets. Flatbread, still warm from the afternoon's baking, steamed gently in the night air, each round stacked so as to provide easy passage from hand to hand. At intervals, the baskets of bitter greens moved with the grace of prayer, each man or woman taking a pinch and chewing. Once the worst of the bitterness struck, they closed their eyes and bowed their heads for a breath or two.

At the appointed hour, Joshua rose from his mat in the innermost circle. The firelight caught the furrows of his face, making a topography of every scar, every sun-etched crease, and every old grief. He waited for silence, which, this night, arrived without struggle.

"My brothers and sisters," he began, the voice as measured as ever, but with a current underneath, something slow and seismic. "Tonight we remember the night of the first passing, the night when death came near but did not take us. We eat this meal not in the shadow of Egypt, but in the promise of Canaan, with our feet set upon a land we call our own."

A ripple moved through the crowd, not a sound, but a tightening, a collective exhale as the words landed. Joshua lifted his head, scanned the rows, and continued.

"Long ago, the Lord made a difference between His people and the people of Egypt. He asked only that we mark our doors, that we eat in haste, that we trust in the promise of tomorrow. For forty years we have kept this memory in the wilderness. Now, we keep it here, on ground we have crossed by miracle, in a place He said would be ours."

He paused, then added, in a softer tone: "We do not forget those who led us. We do not forget the words that carried us when food and water failed. Tonight, we honor not only the crossing, but the Law itself, for it is the Law that makes this house a house, and this people a people."

At the phrase, several elders exchanged glances, the way men do when the past refuses to stay buried. Joshua let the moment linger, then, as if acting on a sudden memory, he turned his gaze to Gershom.

"In the days of our mourning," Joshua said, "there was one among us who recited the Law with a voice not his own, but with the spirit of his father. Gershom, son of Moses, would you stand and give us the words?"

The camp fell completely still. The crackle of wood, the low cough of an elder, even the creak of the mats faded, leaving only a taut, expectant lull.

Gershom felt the blood rush to his face, then to the soles of his feet. He imagined himself being thirteen again, summoned to the center of a tent to recite a passage he had learned not for pride, but for the pleasure of seeing his mother's eyebrow rise a fraction in approval. He looked to his left, where Tima gave him the smallest nod, her hand hidden from all but him, giving a brief, urgent squeeze at his knee.

He stood, smoothing the hem of his tunic, and let his gaze

travel the circle. The faces were unfamiliar, but the posture, the tilt of chin, the narrowing of eyes, the faint pinch at the corner of the mouth, was one he recognized: every person in the camp waiting to see what the Law, re-embodied in flesh, would sound like in a world with no more wilderness.

He began, not with the Shema, as he might have in youth, but with the words that prefigured the meal: "When your children ask you in time to come, 'What does this ceremony mean to you?' you shall say—"

He paused, letting the words settle in the air.

"—It is the sacrifice of the Lord's passing over, for He spared the homes of our ancestors when He struck down the Egyptians, but delivered us from slavery with a strong hand and an outstretched arm."

The cadence was slow, but not labored. With each phrase, he felt the weight of memory pressing in, the voices of a hundred old men and women layering his own. He continued, shifting to the words his father had spoken on the first night after Sinai, when the Law was still warm in the mind, uncurdled by years of disappointment:

"'This is the bread of affliction that our fathers ate in Egypt; let all who are hungry come and eat; let all who are needy come and celebrate Passover with us.' Tonight, we are here— hungry, but filled; needy, but together."

His voice, at first brittle, found its register. The phrases rolled out, each one echoed by the firelight on the faces around him. When he glanced sideways, he saw Tima's eyes fixed on him, not with the sharpness of correction but with a quiet, delighted awe.

He finished with the closing: "You shall remember that you were slaves in Egypt, and the Lord your God brought you out from there with a mighty hand; therefore, keep this commandment."

He lowered himself onto the mat, his heart hammering like a drum in the quiet that wrapped around him. An eternity opened before him, the air dense with anticipation and unspoken words. Just as he began to wonder if anyone had heard, a voice cut through, a woman behind him, her tone rising like a lark at dawn.

"Blessed be the Lord who has delivered us!" she sang, her pitch clear and unwavering.

One by one, others joined in, their voices rising and intertwining like the threads of a tapestry, each note a testament to shared faith and resilience. Gershom felt the swell of sound wrap around him, lifting him from the weight of doubt.

"Together, we remember!" an elder called, his voice mingling with the melody, urging others to join.

With each passing moment, the camp transformed into a chorus of hope, the vibrant harmonies echoing across the plains. Gershom closed his eyes, allowing the music to wash over him, binding him to the community that surrounded him.

The meal commenced. Gershom broke the first round of bread, handing it to Shem, who tore off a piece and, with exaggerated solemnity, passed it to the next mat. The bowls of bitter herbs made their circuit, each new taster suppressing a shudder, a grimace, a watery-eyed laugh. The lamb, having roasted to perfection, was sliced and distributed by the Levites, the meat so tender it fell away from the bone at a touch.

At intervals, Joshua led the assembly in the raising of the cups, each time with a different blessing, each time with a different flavor of hope or memory. By the second cup, the edge had come off the night; by the third, even the most rigid of the elders had allowed themselves a sliver of contentment, a moment in which the Law was not a trial but a feast.

Across the circle, Gershom caught the eye of Joshua. The leader inclined his head, not as a master to a servant, but as a man acknowledging another's place at the table. Nearby, the elder Levite, earlier so severe, was smiling, and the boy with the elbows was already slumped against his neighbor, sleep having conquered ritual.

Gershom let himself relax, the unfamiliar ease settling into his bones. He turned to Tima, who still held his hand under the cover of the mat, and saw in her face not the shadow of the camp, or the memory of what he'd lost, but the simple, undeniable joy of the present.

He raised his cup, as Joshua did, and drank.

Outside the circle, the stars burned brighter than the fire. The Law, recited and consumed, was more a river than a monument, alive, in motion, part of a world which, despite everything, refused to end in silence.

When the meal's last fragments had been consumed and the wine reduced to its sediment, the camp exhaled its collective fatigue into the open night. Groups split off, drifting in slow counterpoint back to their shelters; children were bundled under blankets and carried, half-asleep, through the avenue of tents; a few determined voices lingered, trading last rounds of jokes or memories before the ritual quiet of sleep took hold. Gershom found himself alone at the edge of the fire circle, the warmth of the coals clinging to his shins and the brightness of the stars above falling, for once, without the interference of lamp or smoke.

He leaned back, propped on his elbows, and watched the night unspool. It was a sky he had never known in the desert, an expanse sharp and crowded, unblunted by the haze of sand or the omnipresent sense of waiting. Here, each star was a thing of violence: a burn, a collision, an act of birth or destruction witnessed from a safe remove. He tried to pick out the old constellations, the ones Zipporah had mapped for him when he was small, but the patterns would not hold; this was a new sky, for a new world, and if it contained augury or promise, he was content to let it go unsolved.

Tima sat beside him, knees drawn to her body, hands wrapped around her legs. For a while they said nothing, letting the night fill the space between their bodies.

Her voice came first, slicing through the waiting hush. "You surprised everyone tonight," she said, her voice pitched low, as if afraid to disturb the stars. "Most of all yourself."

He considered pretending otherwise, but the old impulse to evade or deflect seemed pointless now. "I suppose I did," he admitted. "It felt like standing on the edge of a cliff and discovering you could swim."

She smiled, then reached beside her to produce a clay cup. "I brought you this," she said, passing it to him. "It's the last of the wine. I thought you might need it."

He took the cup, noting the gentle warmth where her fingers had been. He drank, then set it between them, the unspoken invitation hanging in the air.

Tima rubbed her hands together, then, as if the gesture had reminded her of something, took his left hand in hers and began, gently, to knead the knuckles. "Your hands aren't trembling," she said. "That's new."

He flexed his fingers, marveling at their steadiness. "Maybe it's the bread," he offered, half-joking. "Maybe it's the Law."

She shook her head. "It's you. You spoke the words as if they belonged to you, not to your father."

The observation, so plainly true, struck him harder than any compliment. He looked at her, seeing the woman who had chosen, again and again, to witness his unbecoming and his return.

He wanted to say something that would capture the fullness of the moment, but the words would not coalesce. Instead, he reached across the fire-lit space and took her hand in his, holding it until the pulse at her wrist aligned with his own.

They might have stayed that way all night, content in the silence, had it not been for the sound of heavy, deliberate footsteps approaching from the direction of the main avenue. Gershom felt the old tension snap back, the possibility of conflict or disappointment reasserting in the bones.

Eliezer emerged from the gloom, his face half-shadowed by the tilt of his head, the rest lit in profile by the embers. He paused at the margin, as if waiting to be acknowledged.

"Sit," Gershom said, not as a command but as an offering.

Eliezer hesitated, then lowered himself to the ground opposite them. His posture was less combative than before, the lines of his body slumped with exhaustion or, perhaps, a kind of tentative peace.

The three sat in a triangle, the coals at the center. For a time, the only sound was the pop and sigh of burning wood.

It was Eliezer who broke the silence. "I didn't know you remembered the liturgy so well," he said, the words flat but not hostile. "Father always said you were his slowest student."

Gershom smiled, allowing the barb its due. "He said the same about you. Especially when you tried to read father's song with your mouth full of pomegranate."

A brief, unwilling smile flickered at Eliezer's lips, then

vanished. He looked past Gershom, past Tima, to the dying fire. "I used to think it would be different, when we crossed over," he said. "That the minute we set foot here, everything would make sense."

"It never does," Tima said, her voice gentle.

Eliezer nodded, staring into the embers. "I'm glad you spoke," he said, not looking up. "It was...good to hear it from you." He shrugged, a gesture so small it might have gone unnoticed, then stood, dusted his hands, and walked off into the dark.

The quiet that followed was gentle, no longer heavy with fear or hope, only the plain fact of three lives touching for a moment before drifting apart again.

Gershom watched his brother's retreating shape, felt the wound and the healing at the same time. He looked to Tima, who watched him with the patience of someone who had never needed a miracle, only the slow, stubborn work of living.

They sat as one, as the last stars burned their way to the western horizon. Around them, the camp had quieted, the only sound the distant, rhythmic breathing of a people finally at rest.

He picked up the clay cup, drained the last drop, and set it beside the coals, where the fire would dry it clean.

"You know what I want?" he said, the question surprising even himself.

Tima arched an eyebrow, inviting.

"I want to see what it's like tomorrow," he said. "To wake up and find out the world still makes room for people like me."

She reached for his hand, squeezed once, then let go. "It will," she said. "I promise."

They watched the darkness together, a little longer, until

the embers completely died away.

Walls of Jericho

At dawn, the Jericho plain gathered into a single, collective breath. The valley that only weeks before had been the unclaimed threshold of possibility now pressed the Israelite camp against the foot of the city, a cord of tension stretching from the highest ramparts to the last row of Levite tents. Gershom awoke to the silence, the sound of an entire people braced in readiness, an expectation so acute it threatened to crystallize the air.

The day's light revealed the city in full: Jericho's walls, double and thick, stacked in the geometry of defiance, crowned with watchtowers and banners that snapped red in the harsh air. From the vantage of the Israelite camp, the city was more verdict than dwelling, the sum of all the years spent wandering, now fixed and finite at the horizon. It was not beautiful. It was simply there, implacable, impregnable, the obstacle that rendered every other detail of the morning irrelevant.

They assembled at Joshua's order, the call passed from tribe to tribe, tent to tent, until the entire camp had shifted inwards, closing around the makeshift plaza at the heart of Gilgal. It was a different congregation than any that had come before. The loose discipline of the crossing, the euphoric confusion of the first night, had calcified into a new shape. It was ranked, rehearsed, each clan in its appointed place: the old men and the infants at the rear, the warriors at the front, the Levites circling the Ark in a band of white.

Gershom stood with the Levites, his own attire still bearing the faint creases of last night's feast. The boy Shem hovered nearby, face scrubbed and hair still wet from the morning's ablutions, as if cleanliness might serve as armor against whatever lunacy the day would require. To his left, the elder Levite from yesterday's baking session stood with arms folded, mouth pursed in the permanent skepticism of the bureaucrat. To his right, a knot of priests conferred in hushed, urgent tones. Their eyes flicked between the gathering and the ramparts of Jericho, as if measuring, with each glance, the shrinking distance between faith and failure.

At the platform's center, Joshua stood alone, his silhouette dark against the lambent blue of the morning. He wore none of the regalia of kingship, not even the jeweled collar that had marked Moses' final assemblies. Yet he held himself with a stillness so complete it drew the eye, silencing even the stray coughs and mutters at the periphery. He waited until the last body had stilled, until the air had carried away the final wisp of woodsmoke, and then he gave his words.

"Children of Jacob," he said, the voice stripped of ornament, "you have crossed over, and now the promise is before you. But the land does not yield to those who merely stand and look. It must be taken, and it must be taken by the means the Lord provides."

He paused, eyes traveling the host of people, landing for a heartbeat on each tribal banner before moving on. "Jericho is shut up, within and without. No man enters, and no man leaves. Its walls are high and its gates iron. But the Lord has said: I have given it into your hands, and you shall take it by obedience, not by the arm."

A wave of uncertainty rippled through the ranks. There was a subtle shifting of feet, a tightening of jaws. Some in the front rows, the zealots and the young, nodded with the fury of men who could not imagine failure. Others, the old, the twice-wounded, the mothers with infants bound to their backs, exchanged glances weighted with the memory of too many years and too many graves. The city watched, impassive, the sunlight sparking along the parapets.

Joshua raised a hand, and the hush returned. "Here is the command from the Lord your God," he said. "For six days, you will march around the city, all the men of war, circling it once. You will not shout. You will not raise a sword. The priests will bear the Ark, and before them, seven priests will carry seven rams' horns. The rest will follow, in silence, each in their place."

The plan, so nearly absurd in its precision, settled on the ranks with the heaviness of prophecy. There were no murmurs now, only the soft, collective contraction of a people realizing that their hopes would be wagered on a spectacle designed to confuse both themselves and the enemy.

"On the seventh day," Joshua continued, "you will march around the city seven times. Then, when the priests blow a long blast on the rams' horns, all the people shall shout with a great shout, and the wall of the city will fall down flat. Then you will go up, every man straight before him. This is the word of the Lord."

The stillness that followed was complete, the kind that pressed against the ears. Gershom felt the blood in his fingers and the pulse behind his eyes. For a moment, he wanted to laugh, to shout out the incredulity that surely gripped half the gathering, but the bearing of Joshua's face, without a trace of doubt or performance, held him back.

Instead, he studied the mass of people. Some, the sons of Reuben and Gad, squared their shoulders, eager to trade ritual for blood. Others, the Benjaminites, whispered to one another, calculating the odds. The priests were inscrutable; the Levites, by contrast, looked as if they'd been asked to perform a pantomime for the enemy's amusement. Only Shem, at Gershom's side, stood undisturbed. He looked up at Gershom and mouthed, with the solemnity of an oath, "Do you think it will work?"

Gershom shrugged, then, seeing the question deserved better, said, "It's not our part to know. Only to walk and see."

At the platform, Joshua beckoned to the inner circle, the priests, the elders, and a handful of men selected by lot. Gershom felt the tug of obligation and moved forward, the crowd parting enough to let him pass. At the steps, Phinehas waited, face impassive, but his eyes flickered with the faintest residue of humor.

"You are needed in the preparation," he said, voice pitched for Gershom alone. "The horns, the water for the march, the garments for the priests. It must all be ready. No errors." The last word was not a warning, but a certainty: any mistake would ripple outwards, contaminating the entire enterprise.

Gershom nodded, then climbed to where Joshua stood. Up close, the man's face showed none of the strain or exhaustion that had so often marked Moses in his final years. But there was something else, a density, a layering of will upon will, as if the only way to withstand the absurdity of the command was to become, oneself, more improbable than the thing required.

"Son of Moses," Joshua said, and the phrase, rather than a benediction or a goad, landed with the force of a diagnosis. "You are to serve with the priests today. Make sure nothing is overlooked. The Law must follow us, even in the shadow of war."

Gershom inclined his head, then waited, unsure if more would be said.

Joshua's attention bore down on him with such intensity the world behind him dissolved: the background, the city, every other presence. "It was never the Law that failed your father," he said, quietly. "It was the people who would not obey it, all the way to the end. Do you understand?"

Gershom started to reply, found he had no words, and simply nodded.

"Good," Joshua said. "Let us not dishonor him. Or the Lord." With that, he dismissed Gershom to the work.

At the margin of the platform, Gershom lingered, watching as Joshua conferred with Phinehas, then with the captains of the tribes. Each man left the conversation with the same look, some variation of resolved, defeated, or terrified, but Joshua remained unmoved, his presence a constant in a morning designed to dislodge all certainty.

The people dispersed, not in disorder, but in a series of concentric ripples, each man or woman returning to their role: sharpening swords, mending sandals, soothing infants, repacking the bundles that would be carried on the march. Gershom walked through them, feeling the expectation clinging to every face. At intervals, fragments of conversation drifted to him: the old men recalling Egypt, the younger ones rehearsing the logic of the plan, the mothers asking what would happen if the city did not fall as promised.

He entered the supply tent, where the horns were arrayed in a careful line, each wrapped at the grip with new leather, each tested for sound by an assistant Levite. The garments, too, were ready: white for the priests, blue for the Ark-bearers, the latter stiff with the ceremonial dye that had bled so many hands in its making. Gershom checked the lists, cross-referenced the names, made sure every bucket of water and basket of bread was accounted for. He did it all with the ruthless competence his mother had instilled, and with none of the longing for transcendence that had haunted his youth.

From outside, the sounds of the camp had shifted, no longer the clamor of a nation preparing for war, now the hushed choreography of a people steeling themselves for something they could neither imagine or refuse.

Gershom halted at the entrance, letting the morning light strike him full in the face. He looked out at the city, then at the Ark, then at Joshua, now a solitary figure atop the platform, his outline so sharp against the sky it seemed he might shatter with the next rush of air.

He wondered, not for the first time, what it would have been like to stand on that platform, to carry a people's hope and to listen for a voice that sometimes offered nothing in reply. He thought of his father, the way the old man's shoulders had narrowed under the burden of forty years. His eyes had scanned the horizon as if expecting, at any moment, a new and more punishing test.

He wondered what failure would look like, if it came.

He wondered if the Law, or the Lord, or even history would allow for such a thing.

He stood in the doorway, feeling the tension coil tightly within him, and watched as the camp prepared to march into the unknown.

It was, he supposed, the only way forward.

The air in the supply tent was equal parts wool, dust, and the oily scent of cured animal horn. Gershom worked at the long table near the entrance, his fingers dividing the rams' horns by size, sorting them into bundles tied with strips of linen. Each horn was a minor history, scars from old skirmishes, the subtle twist that marked one tribe's herd from another, and Gershom would stop now and again to trace the lineage of a particularly well-crafted specimen.

At the far end of the tent, two Levites wrestled with a tangled length of blue sashes, the fabric having fused together in last night's dew. Every so often, one would curse under his breath, then shoot a glance over his shoulder to make sure the profanity had not been witnessed by anyone likely to care. Near the center pole, a trio of younger men measured and repacked the water skins, their hands moving with the exaggerated care of those who would rather talk than labor. The conversation, as always, orbited around the latest command from Joshua.

"I heard," said one, "that on the seventh day, we're to march seven times around the city. Seven! In this heat?"

"Maybe the walls are supposed to die of boredom," said the second, voice pitched for effect.

The third, whose name Gershom did not know but who had the gaunt look of a professional skeptic, muttered, "If the Lord wants to hand us Jericho, why not just bring down the walls now, spare us the exercise?"

The first shot back: "Maybe we're supposed to get in shape before we take on the next city. What's after Jericho, again?"

The second answered, "I heard whispers of the city Ai. It's even smaller. Maybe we'll blow on it and save ourselves the walk."

They laughed, but the sound was brittle, a defense against the uncertainty that saturated the camp. Gershom kept his focus on the horns, aligning each bundle, making sure the binding was tight but not so tight as to crush the delicate inner structure. When he finished, he placed them to one side, then turned his attention to the folded garments: white linen for the priests, blue for those who would carry the Ark, and the rougher, undyed tunics for the rest.

His hands moved with an economy born of practiced muscle. For all the noise inside his skull, the rest of him operated on a plane untouched by anxiety. He liked the order of it: the way each piece fit the next, the predictability of the pattern. Here, at least, nothing was left to chance.

He was halfway through the last bundle when Phinehas entered. The priest's presence changed the room immediately. Laughter faded, the young men straightened into something closer to diligence, and the two at the end of the tent worked together wordlessly to untangle the sashes. Phinehas moved the length of the table, eyes scanning each item, checking every horn, garment, and cask of oil.

He stopped opposite Gershom, picked up a horn, examined the cut, and then placed it back down. "You do good work," he said, voice neutral. "You pay attention."

Gershom nodded, unsure if a reply was expected.

Phinehas ran his palm along the seam of a folded tunic. "The plan is not for us to understand," he said, more to the room than to Gershom, "but it is ours to enact, without error. To believe and trust the words given to our leader."

The words hung in the air, a challenge and a warning both. One of the younger Levites, emboldened by the group's earlier banter, said, "But will it work, sir? The walls, I mean. Will they really fall?"

Phinehas stared at the boy with a glare that would have peeled the skin from a more pliant soul. "If they do not, we will be the first to bleed for it," he said. "And perhaps that, too, is the will of the Lord."

The tent fell still.

Phinehas turned back to Gershom, as if inviting him to offer a counterpoint, a fragment of the old skepticism. Gershom felt the pressure of it, the expectation that he would say what the others would not. But instead, he simply kept folding, his hands flattening each garment with careful, deliberate strokes.

After a moment, Phinehas nodded, not in approval exactly, but in recognition that the lack of words was an answer.

He moved on, inspecting the rest of the work, offering a word here, a correction there. When he left, the tent exhaled; the noise returned, but at a lower register, the jokes now sharpened by the knowledge that the day would not yield to complaint.

When the last horn was packed, the last raiment folded, Gershom straightened his back, wiped his hands on his tunic, and joined the procession of Levites moving toward the tent flap. As he stepped outside, the heat slammed into him, carrying with it the smell of sunbaked earth and the faint, metallic tang of distant fear.

He scanned the camp, saw the lines of men already forming, the Ark being lifted onto its poles, the elders marshaling the children and the infirm to the shade of the nearest tents.

He wondered, briefly, what would happen if the horns were blown and nothing happened, if the walls of Jericho held fast, unmoved by all the marching and all the faith in the world.

He wondered, and then pushed the thought aside.

There was work to do, and a city to walk around.

He squared his shoulders, checked the line of his garment, and stepped into the daylight, the others falling in behind him, the rhythm of their movement almost enough to drown out the questions he no longer bothered to voice.

At the trumpet's first mournful moan, the camp fell into its prescribed order, a living helix unfurling, tribe by tribe, across the hard ground at Jericho's foot. Gershom took his place with the Levites, the Ark and its bearers ahead, the ram's horns forming a bristling, uneven halo at the front. No word passed, no chant rose, not even the usual shuffle or murmur of a military procession. In its place, a tension so thick it seemed to press the very air, each footfall of tens of thousands.

The city's defenders appeared at the ramparts before the procession had even begun to move, drawn by the impossible mass of bodies and the shimmer of gold from the Ark's crown. At first, the men on the wall simply watched, no arrows loosed, no shouts, simply a line of hard expressions squinting against the sun hanging near the horizon. Gershom, ever the observer, noted the pattern of their presence: the way some leaned out, eager for a closer look, while others hung back, reluctant to believe that such a strange, mute force could constitute a threat.

With the second trumpet, the column advanced. The pace was deliberate, not the charge of an army but the measured tread of a funeral cortege. They skirted the city at a distance just out of bowshot, the Ark at the center point, the rest of the tribes rippling out behind. To Gershom, the scale of it was both exhilarating and absurd: a parade designed for the humiliation of the enemy, or perhaps to keep the terror at bay for another day.

He watched the men to either side. The zealots marched with heads high, eyes locked on the horizon as if daring the city to withstand their faith. Others hunched their shoulders, eyes on the ground, each step an act of submission rather than conquest. The youngest, the ones who had only ever known the desert, moved with a kind of animal curiosity, taking in every detail: the sharp tang of the city's garbage pits, the mocking laughter that sometimes floated down from the walls.

The calm was oppressive. The only sounds were the crunch of sand underfoot, the labored breathing of the old men, and the intermittent cry of the rams' horns. Their irregular intervals punctuated the march in a way that unnerved both the Israelites and their adversaries. The Ark bearers, sweat already staining their tunics, kept their eyes locked dead ahead and posture straight, even with the strain of the poles digging grooves into their shoulders. Gershom followed, keeping count of each completed circuit in his head, even though there would be only one today.

As they rounded the far side of the city, the defenders broke into speech. It started as a muted chorus of derision, words that Gershom could not catch but whose tone was unmistakable. By the time the procession neared the main gate, the mockery had grown bold, with shouts and gestures that left no doubt as to the city's appraisal of its besiegers. Several guards pantomimed sleep, heads bowed forward, as if to say: "Come wake us when you're ready to fight." Others flung handfuls of sand or loose stone over the battlements, a rain of impotent defiance.

Gershom saw a line of archers ready their bows, but the city's captains held them back. There was nothing to fear from a people who would not speak, would not run, would not even look up to return the insult. The men on the wall laughed, spat, then, as the column passed, took to hurling scraps of dried meat or animal dung at the rear ranks.

None of it mattered. The march went on, steady and unbroken, the Israelites circling the city as if measuring it for a garment that would someday be their own.

By midday, the sun was a hammer, flattening the city and the valley into a single, glaring plane. The pace of the column never faltered, but by the final stretch Gershom saw the toll it took: men beet-red and sweating, children slumped against their mothers' backs, even the Ark bearers' steps growing ragged at the edges. They completed the circuit and returned to camp, not in triumph, but in exhaustion.

The throng thinned, leaving Gershom to slip into the shade of his tent. He peeled the tunic from his back and sank to the packed earth, knees drawn inward, staring at the ground as the sweat dried into a thin, salty crust on his skin.

Evening fell with a suddenness; in another mood, it might have offered something like mercy. Gershom sat outside his shelter, a wooden bowl of stewed barley cooling in his hands. The day's hush persisted, stretching out into the dusk, broken only by the distant clatter of women gathering children, or the sharp report of a tent pole driven home.

He became aware, after a time, of a small commotion near the margin of the camp. At first he thought it was the tail-end of some domestic quarrel, but as the light faded, the shape of it resolved: a boy, not much older than Shem, had gathered a circle of younger children and was leading them in a pantomime of the day's events. They marched in uneven ranks, each with a stick or a makeshift banner, circling a mound of stones arranged to represent Jericho. The boy at the front wore a strip of blue cloth tied around his brow and carried a reed flute, which he blew with all the sincerity of a priest.

The others followed, heads high, their words stifled by the day's discipline. They made a single, lopsided lap, then collapsed into laughter, rolling on the ground until one of the women scolded them back to order.

Gershom watched, suspended between amusement and something sharper. He remembered, without quite meaning to, the stories his mother had told. The children of Israel had never lost a war when they remembered who they were. Even the stillness, properly kept, could be an act of worship.

He was still watching when Tima appeared, slipping through the rows of tents with a stealth that made him wonder how many times she'd done the same without him noticing. She sat close beside him, looping her arm over his, her hair loose and unbraided, the lines of her face softened by the day's fatigue.

He offered her the bowl; she declined with a wave.

"You're thinking too much," she said.

He laughed, or tried to. "Hard not to, with the city right there. Every time I look up, it feels like it's watching me."

She glanced at the wall, then back at the mock battle playing out between the children. "I saw you in the march today. You looked like you wanted to disappear."

He shrugged. "It's an odd thing, to walk in an unimaginable circle for hours and call it progress."

"Doesn't matter what you call it," she said, her eyes trained on the city. "It only matters that you do it."

They sat, the question lingering in the air between them.

After a while, Gershom said, "Some of the men think it's a trick. That Joshua is only stalling, hoping for a miracle."

Tima considered this. "Do you think that?"

He took his time, watching the sky shift from gold to indigo. "I think he's heard from the Lord," he said at last. "And that's enough for him."

She smiled, the curve of her mouth like a crescent moon. "Well, then. Let it be enough for you."

He wanted to argue, to raise all the objections that had haunted him since the day his father died. Instead, he simply nodded. Together they watched as the boy with the flute led a new round of recruits in a deliberate circle around the city of stones.

When the last light left the sky, Tima kissed him on the cheek and stood, pressed a hand to his shoulder. "I have to help my family make preparations for tomorrow," she said.

"I will see you later," Gershom said, letting his hand linger around hers until she finally slipped away and started down the avenue.

Gershom sat alone a little longer, allowing the calm to settle deep within him.

Tomorrow would come, with its march and its stillness and all the questions that trailed behind.

But for tonight, he let the stillness be a comfort.

Walls Collapse

Each morning, the sun rose a fraction earlier, as if racing the clock ordained by Joshua's command. The days blurred together in a rhythm of grit, footfalls, and the heavy hush that pressed in from all sides. Gershom marched each circuit without deviation, the Ark always ahead, the wall of Jericho always on his right, its bulk looming over the relentless column.

On the second day, the city's defenders had rearmed them-selves with mockery. They painted their faces in grotesque masks, beat drums on the ramparts, and at one point sent a score of goats streaming through the main gate, hooves and horns tumbling down the slope before the Israelites. The gathering behind Gershom rippled with laughter. Some men hooted, others called out mock blessings for the goats' safe passage. Not a single Israelite broke ranks, the only sounds those of the rams' horns and the shuffling of sandals over dry ground.

By the third day, the humor on the wall had thinned, replaced by something rawer. The guards still jeered, but their cries rose higher, sharpened with the urgency of men who sensed a test they did not know how to pass. Gershom noticed their glances, furtive now, not always directed outward. It seemed the very refusal to fight had begun to gnaw at the city's resolve. He felt it too, in his bones: the sense that to walk in wordless restraint, to obey without comprehension, was a weapon, sharper than the blade at his hip.

The Israelites sensed it as well. By the fourth circuit, the men who had grumbled on the first day now squared their steps, shoulders back, eyes focused not on the enemy, but on the Ark, or the horizon, or the back of the man in front of them. Even the children, who could not possibly have understood the reason for the ritual, fell in with their mothers, their games and squabbles replaced by a grave imitation of the march.

At night, the camp filled with a different energy. The boundaries between tent rows grew porous, as families swapped stories, speculations, and, increasingly, rumors of miracles. Some said they had seen the wall shudder at the sound of the horns. Others claimed that the priests' footprints never left a mark on the ground, or that the bread in the tents did not diminish, no matter how much was eaten. Gershom listened without judgment, content to let the stories fill the spaces where doubt might have otherwise taken root.

On the fifth day, it rained: a brief, cold burst, almost violent against the earth. The march was not cancelled; instead, the column splashed its way through puddles and mud, the rams' horns sounding softer under the muffling of water. The city's guards huddled under tarps, their features masked and unreadable. Gershom saw, for the first time, a banner of white hung at the highest point on the wall. Some in the ranks whispered that it was a sign of surrender, but Gershom knew better. It was not a flag, but a wound dressing: the city was bleeding, and the best it could do was bandage the place where the pressure hurt most.

By the sixth day, the column moved as a single organism, all the old friction worn away by repetition. Even the Levites, notorious for their petty disputes, fell into a cycle of mutual assistance, passing water skins, balancing the load of the Ark's poles, correcting the wayward stride of a tired priest without a word of rebuke. Gershom found himself part of this, his body doing what was needed, his mind no longer split between skepticism and the need for proof. He simply walked, and the walking was enough.

That evening, the camp was electric with anticipation. The air held a static charge, as if the very ground were waiting to be told what to become. Gershom lingered at the margin of the street, watching as men sharpened blades, oiled shields, checked and rechecked the bindings on their sandals. None expected to use the weapons tomorrow, but the ritual of readiness was a comfort, an assertion of normalcy in a week designed to upend every expectation.

He wandered between the tents, pausing to listen when the mood of a gathering was worth the time. At one fire, two men, veterans of the desert wars, argued the tactics of the coming day, each convinced that the walls would fall but debating how best to exploit the breach.

"At first light, we rush the gate," said the first, a scar running from jaw to ear. "It's the weakest point, and the people inside will panic."

"You're a fool," said the second. "The breach will be at the corner, where the wall is new. The Lord never strikes the obvious target."

They traded insults, but underneath it was the shared confidence of men who had seen too many miracles to doubt the next one.

At another fire, a group of mothers sat with their children, plaiting hair and singing a song so old it likely predated the language. The melody was haunting, full of minor turns, but the children listened, wide-eyed, as if the song alone might keep the coming violence at bay.

Further on, two elders argued theology, their tones hushed and intense.

"It is not our obedience that brings the victory," said the first, "but the favor of the Lord."

"The two are the same," replied the second, shaking his head. "We obey because we have favor; we are favored because we obey."

Gershom drifted through these scenes like a ghost, taking in the spectrum of belief and uncertainty. It struck him, not for the first time, that faith was not a binary, not simply on or off, present or absent, but a scale, a shifting burden that changed from moment to moment. Some men lived at the far end of certainty, others hovered near the middle, always seeking the sign that would allow them to shift a little closer to conviction. Most, he thought, lived in the oscillation, never truly at rest.

He found Shem, as always, at the tent flap, hands busy with a coil of rope, eyes on the darkening wall of Jericho.

"Are you ready?" Gershom asked, settling beside him.

The boy nodded. "I think the wall will fall," he said, voice calm. "But I don't think that's the hard part."

"Oh?"

Shem glanced up, eyes wise for his years. "Afterwards, we'll have to live with it. With what we do next."

Gershom said nothing, but the truth of it lingered, heavy as the dew that would settle on the camp come midnight.

As the night drew in, Gershom returned to his own shelter.

He sat cross-legged, hands idle, the sounds of the camp drifting in on the wind. Somewhere, a woman laughed; somewhere else, a man wept.

He realized, with a clarity that surprised him, that he was not an unbeliever, not really. He did not need to lead, and he did not crave the certainty animating Joshua or Phinehas. It was enough, for tonight, to exist in the tension between.

He lay down, the ground cool and forgiving against his back, and waited for sleep.

Above him, the stars sharpened to points, as if the world were about to be drawn and quartered by the hand of God.

He did not fear the morning.

* * *

The morning of the seventh day broke with a brittle clarity, every detail of the camp rendered in hard-edged relief. There was no dew on the ground and no haze in the sky. Only a peace that settled like mist.

The command to march came before sunrise. Gershom joined the ranks as the sky shifted from black to gray, the column forming with an urgency that bordered on panic. He saw it in those around him: the pale lips, the eyes flickering with dread and hope. No one spoke, but the stillness was no longer empty; it was a presence that pressed against every chest, threatening to steal the breath away.

The Ark was lifted, the poles trembling in the hands of the bearers. The priests took their places at the fore, the rams' horns gleaming in the faint light. Joshua stood at the head of the procession, his posture so rigid it seemed he might snap under the strain. He raised his hand, and the march began.

The first circuit was fast, the pace closer to a jog than a walk. Gershom felt his heart hammering inside, each beat louder than the ground beneath his feet. The city's defenders watched without a word, their features caught in the glow of torches, their weapons ready but unused.

At the completion of the first lap, the column did not stop. Instead, it swung around and began anew, the second circuit even faster than the first. By the third, Gershom's robe was damp with sweat, his legs quivering with the effort. The city remained impassive, but a tremor had entered the line of guards at the top of the wall. A ripple of uncertainty moved through them, as if they sensed that something irreversible had begun.

Fourth, fifth, sixth time around. The sun climbed, flattening the shadows, rendering every figure in the procession a moving, sweating blur. Gershom's head spun; the wall shrank, then towered, then shrank again, as though their circling was stripping away the space between the people and their prize.

On the seventh circuit, Joshua raised his hand, a silent command that rippled through the ranks like a sudden gust of force. The priests responded instantly, lifting the rams' horns high, their polished surfaces gleaming in the harsh light of dawn. Gershom felt a jolt of electricity course through the men beside him, their bodies tensing as if they were coiled springs, ready to unleash all the pent-up energy of their faith and fear.

At the gate, Joshua turned to the gathering. His voice, when it came, was not a shout but a command so pure it cut like a knife.

"Now!"

The priests blew the horns. The blast was deafening, a sound breaking the week's calm in an instant no one could believe.

Then the people shouted, all at once, a roar that rolled across the plain and slammed against the city walls with the force of a physical blow.

Gershom felt the ground stutter beneath his feet, a shudder, then a faint, grinding vibration that traveled up his legs and into his core. For a heartbeat, nothing else happened. Then, from the far side of the city, a plume of ash rose into the air, followed by the unmistakable groan of stone shearing against stone.

The walls buckled. First a crack, then a fissure, then entire sections collapsing in on themselves, the towers tilting and falling, the ramparts disintegrating into avalanches of brick and debris. In under a minute, Jericho ceased to be a fortress; it became a ruin, the outer shell sloughed away by the invisible hand that had always belonged to someone else.

The Israelites froze, stunned by the miracle of their own cry. For a breathless interval, no one moved, not even the children, not even the animals. Gershom stood rooted, his mouth open, grit and shock grinding against his tongue.

Then the army surged forward, a tidal wave of bodies pouring into the city, scrambling over the rubble, the first of them already at the breached gates. Gershom did not follow immediately. He lingered, watching the aftermath, the stunned expressions of the men beside him, the shell-shocked wonder that radiated from every pair of eyes.

He realized, with a jolt, that he was not a bystander, not today. He was part of the sound that had brought the wall down. He was, in his small, inconsequential way, a piece of the miracle.

He stood there, awash in the roar of victory and the distant keening of the conquered, and let the moment break over him like a wave.

* * *

Hours later, the city was gutted.

What the trumpet had begun, the men finished with fire and blade. The gates, already splintered by the force of collapse, now hung from their hinges like broken arms. The streets, once ordered and swept, ran with a slurry of ash and the pulped flesh of those who'd tried to make a stand.

Gershom stepped through the breach, the heat of the destroyed houses already radiating outwards in waves that made his eyes water. Every sense was assaulted: the char of resinous timbers, the iron tang of blood, the high sweet smoke of scorched barley.

He had seen aftermath before, in the villages of Midian, in the sand-choked hollows where raiders had done their work. But there was something different here, a density to the destruction, as if every blow delivered by the Israelites was a verdict long withheld and now rendered in the hardest possible currency. It should have felt like justice. Instead, it felt like hunger.

He moved with the first group of Levites, their charge to gather all that was "consecrated," gold, silver, vessels of iron and bronze, to be placed in the treasury. The rest was to be burned. Joshua's instructions had been explicit: nothing living to be spared except Rahab's house, nothing of value to be hoarded by any private hand. Gershom found it strangely calming, this clarity of purpose. There was no room for interpretation, no margin for self-delusion. Only the work, and the calm that followed it.

In the courtyards, women were herded together, their features streaked with smoke and terror, their hands clutching children whose eyes were too wide for their skulls. The men, the ones not already dead, were hauled into the street, some struggling, most slack with disbelief. Gershom saw a group of his own age, wrists bound, eyes darting from the Levites to the sky to the ruined towers behind them. He wondered, with a detachment that surprised him, what stories they had been told about the invaders. What rumors, what prophecies, what lies.

He paused at the threshold of a merchant's house, its doorway still marked with a faded blessing in the language of Jericho. Inside, the rooms were already being stripped by Israelite hands, the shelves cleared of anything that could be melted down or carried. A child's toy, a carved ibex painted in colors that had survived the fire, lay amid the wreckage. Gershom picked it up, turned it over, and placed it on the sill. The action felt both absurd and necessary.

He spent the day this way, moving from house to house, warehouse to temple, cataloguing the spoils and overseeing their removal to the growing mound at the city's boundaries. At noon, the sun reached its apex, baking the rubble and turning the air into a shimmering lens. The heat drove even the most zealous warriors to the shade, where they slumped in clusters, drinking from shared jars and boasting in hushed, exhausted tones about the treasures they had uncovered.

By mid-afternoon, the only resistance left was from the city, the refuse and remnants of thousands of lives, ground into the dirt or baked into the walls. Gershom found himself in the central courtyard, where the largest altar had stood. Here, the Levites were already stacking valuables for inventory, while a group of soldiers debated whether the altar stones themselves should be kept or smashed.

He bent to lift a battered silver chalice, its surface scored with the marks of hasty engraving. As he turned it in his hand, a voice behind him said, "Careful with that. The priests will want it unblemished."

He glanced up. Phinehas stood a few paces off, his white linen streaked with ash, the lines of his face deeper than Gershom remembered.

"I thought you would be at the front," Gershom said, straightening.

Phinehas snorted. "The front is everywhere today."

They watched, frozen, as the last of the soldiers hauled a protesting merchant across the square.

"Does this trouble you, son of Moses?" Phinehas asked, his voice soft.

Gershom weighed the chalice in his palm. "Not the victory. But its cost."

Phinehas nodded, as if this were the only answer worth hearing. "The Law is clear," he said. "But clarity is not the same as comfort."

Gershom place the chalice on the table with more care than was necessary. "Do you think this is what the Lord wanted? All of it?"

"I think," said Phinehas, "that the Lord's ways are not like ours. He does not tally grief the way we do."

Gershom thought of the women in the courtyard, the children pressed against their skirts, the mute horror in the eyes of the bound men. "If the Law is only justice, then it isn't enough. There has to be room for mercy."

"Mercy is for the living," said Phinehas. "Justice is for the dead."

The answer, cold as it was, struck Gershom as honest.

He asked himself, then, why the honesty made him feel so empty.

They worked in tandem for a while, sorting the last of the silver and bronze. Occasionally, Phinehas would pause to wipe sweat from his brow, or to shout a correction at the soldiers who had begun to grow careless with the loot. When the pile was sorted, he turned back to Gershom.

"You ask hard questions," he said, almost as a compliment.

"If we don't," Gershom replied, "we're just slaves to the unknown."

Phinehas considered this. "slaves don't make mistakes," he said. "They don't have to live with doubt."

"But they don't get to choose, either."

Phinehas smiled, the expression tight but not unkind. "Is that what troubles you? That you have a choice?"

Gershom started to answer, then stopped. He realized, with a clarity that startled him, that he did not know.

"It's what kept my father awake at night," he said, finally. "That he might choose wrong, and not find out until it was too late to fix it."

Phinehas put a hand on Gershom's shoulder, the touch heavy, almost paternal. "These questions do not weaken faith. They deepen it."

Gershom nodded, the words both a comfort and a challenge.

As dusk settled over the city, the Levites gathered the last of the consecrated things and began the long walk back to camp. Gershom lingered a moment, staring at the altar, now empty except for the scorched outline of where the fire had once been.

He felt the absence of God, and then, slowly, almost imperceptibly, the return of Him, not in thunder or flame, but in the cool hush that followed the day's violence.

He turned and walked away, the ruined city behind him, the road ahead uncertain but not without purpose.

***

Night bled slowly across the hills, the horizon simmering red where the last of the city's fires met the dark. The soldiers had ordered torches along the breached wall, their silhouettes moving in antlike procession as they secured the ruins and rounded up the last of the captives. From afar, it looked almost orderly, a people settling in, arranging the terms of victory. Up close, it was all sharp edges and unfinished business.

Gershom climbed the slight rise to the west of camp, the slope still littered with stones dislodged by the day's tremors. He picked his way to the top, then stood for a while, letting the breeze dry the sweat from his neck. Below, Jericho sprawled in a geometry of disaster: the grid of its old streets now fractured by heaps of rubble, the proud towers leveled to crude cairns, the temple a blackened carcass open to the sky. In a few places, the blue of Levite robes reflected the firelight, men still at work, collecting what was to be spared, or what was too valuable to burn.

He sank to his haunches and let the night settle around him. He thought of Phinehas, of their conversation at the altar, of the way even certainty could twist under the pressure of what it demanded from the living. He thought of Joshua, and the burden of obedience, how it could forge a man into something greater, or leave him hollowed by the weight. He thought of his father, and the price of never being able to rest in a victory, no matter how complete.

He felt, for the first time in days, almost at peace. Not because anything had been resolved, but because nothing was pretending to be simple.

A crunch of loose gravel made him turn. Eliezer stood a dozen paces off, hands thrust deep in the pockets of his cloak, shoulders hunched as if against a cold only he could feel. The lines of his face were longer than Gershom remembered; the boyish anger, which used to vibrate through every limb, had faded to something more diffused, like smoke after a fire.

They regarded each other for a moment, neither eager to be the first to speak.

"Mind if I join?" Eliezer said at last, his voice stripped of irony or challenge.

Gershom shook his head. "It's a big hill."

Eliezer sat, leaving a careful gap between them. He stared at the ruins, his mouth working as if to shape words that refused to form.

They remained like that, the pause forming around them like a scaffold, constructed carefully, piece by piece.

Finally, Eliezer said, "I need your counsel on something."

Gershom blinked, not sure he'd heard correctly. "You do?"

Eliezer nodded, still facing the city. "You're the only one who will tell me the truth. Even if it's not what I want to hear."

A long calm. Then:

"Was it worth it?" Eliezer's words emerged raw, unfinished. "The whole thing. Do you think... do you really think this is what we're meant to become?"

Gershom let the question hang. He considered the day, the sounds, the smoke, the expressions of the women and children as they were led from the burning houses. He thought of the

Law, and its demand for purity, and the strange, circular way it forced men to become both judge and executioner.

"I don't know," Gershom said, the words as much for himself as for his brother. "I think maybe it isn't about what we're meant to become. Maybe it's about what we refuse to stop becoming, no matter the cost."

Eliezer drew a shaky breath. "I used to be sure. That if I followed every rule, did everything Father would have done, it would all just... fit together. But it never does."

"It didn't for him, either," Gershom said. "He just got better at living with the gaps."

Eliezer laughed, a short, bitter exhale. "He never said that."

"He didn't have to."

The torches down below flickered in the rising breeze. They watched the last of the defenders marched into the main square, heads bowed, hands bound with strips of torn linen, the solemn gravity settling over the scene.

"I was scared today," Eliezer admitted, voice barely above a whisper. "Not of the fighting. Of what comes after."

Gershom nodded, the confession not needing an answer.

After a while, Eliezer stood and dusted off his robe. He offered a hand; Gershom took it, surprised by the steadiness of his brother's grip.

As they started down the hill together, Eliezer said, "What do we do tomorrow?"

Gershom thought for a moment. "We keep walking. One foot in front of the other."

"And after that?"

Gershom shrugged, a small smile breaking through the fatigue. "We figure it out. Like fathers always taught us."

The Sin of Achan

In the days that followed Jericho's unmaking, the Israelite camp had settled near Ai like a colony of shell-shocked ants: industrious by day, but restless, subtractive, the sense of forward momentum replaced with an atmosphere of anxious, unresolved self-surveillance. Where once the morning air hummed with the certainty of conquest, now the sky seemed to hang heavy and uncertain, every sunrise a dull reiteration of the same unanswerable questions.

Gershom woke to such a morning: a blue-edged pause, the air balanced between heat and cold, the tents around him cocooned in an indifference that stood as a kind of statement. He took his meal standing, bread and a hard-dried strip of lamb, then stepped outside and let the nothingness of the moment weigh on him. His shadow was a precise, unsparing blade on the ground. He watched as men gathered water at the cisterns, their exchanges brief and transactional, as if words themselves had become a luxury the camp could no longer afford.

A summons came: not the shofar, not the insistent drum that called warriors to readiness, but a deliberate relay of messengers, each one moving from cluster to cluster with the measured gravity of a coroner. The effect was immediate.

Within an hour, the elders of each tribe had arrayed themselves in a broad semi-circle at the camp's stone-strewn amphitheater. Not two weeks prior, they had stood in that same place and watched the smoke of Jericho's walls declare the victory of the Lord.

Gershom arrived near the end of the processional, his eyes finding at once the patterns of the seating: Reuben and Gad anchored the leftmost tier, Judah and Ephraim opposite, the Levites given their usual interstitial wedge near the front, close to the fire but a safe remove from the center. Eliezer was already present, his posture the blueprint of contained rage, hands locked at the wrists, jaw so tight the muscle looked on the verge of splitting the skin. Gershom met his brother's eye and gave him a nod, which Eliezer returned. They now slept in smaller tents of their own, ever since they had taken down the larger family tent before crossing the Jordan.

Joshua ascended the dais. He had never looked so unlike a conqueror; his tunic hung uneven, hair damp at the temples, the hollows under his eyes scored deep enough to draw sympathy even from his detractors. He did not bother with preamble.

"Men of Israel," he said, voice pitched low and even. "You know what has happened. You know that, when we set ourselves against Ai, the city did not fall. You know the cost—thirty-six of our own, struck down not by sword, but by the wrath that comes from disobedience." He paused, letting the number hang, the loss made more personal by its being neither round nor symbolic but stubbornly, sickeningly specific.

"There is a trespass among us," Joshua continued, "a violation of the herem. The Lord has withheld His hand until it is found and dealt with." His eyes moved slowly across the rows, landing for a fraction of a second on each tribal cluster. "So we will do as the Law commands. Tribe by tribe, clan by clan, household by household, we will draw out the offense."

He turned, signaling to the high priest, who approached with solemnity, carrying the urim and thummim: two small lots, sacred, shimmering with muted brilliance. Crafted from precious stones, one was dark as night while the other gleamed like the sun, their surfaces etched with ancient symbols of divine will. With reverence, he placed them upon the battered altar stone at Joshua's right hand, the worn surface bearing witness to countless judgments rendered in the name of the Lord.

The priest's hands were clean, the linen of his sleeves immaculate, as if the act of judgment required a visual counterpoint to the underlying ugliness. The urim and thummim served as instruments of divine communication, their casting a plea for guidance from God. When invoked, they would reveal truth or deception. The tension in the air thickened, for the outcome of this sacred inquiry would determine the fate of the camp, each question poised to unearth the hidden sin that had led to their suffering.

Gershom felt a hand on his elbow. It was the Levite overseer, an older man whose name he had never learned, but who exuded the air of someone who rarely wasted time on pleasantries.

"You and your brother," the man said, "will represent the tribe." The statement left no room for negotiation; Gershom merely nodded, then took his place next to Eliezer at the rim of the platform.

The process began: methodical, exhausting, the urim and thummim invoked in turn as each tribe was called. Benjamin,

Asher, Naphtali, all passed over without event. The atmosphere in the amphitheater grew brittle, each failed accusation heightening not the relief but the sense of impending doom, the knowledge that the error, whatever it was, was still in motion, still alive.

At the calling of Judah, the urim flashed. The priest announced the selection, his voice stripped of inflection. A ripple passed through the Judahnites, a tension not of guilt but of offended pride. Gershom recognized the body language: men squared their shoulders, raised their chins, as if to suggest that, whatever the crime, they would meet it standing.

Next came the clan of Zerahites. Again, the selection was confirmed by the casting. The gathering held its breath; even the children at the perimeter stilled, the air thick with the charged anticipation of public blame.

It continued: household by household, until at last it landed on the house of Carmi. Gershom watched as the ring of suspects contracted inward, each narrowing accompanied by a brief, involuntary scan of faces. Everyone in the gathering recalibrated their sense of risk, their proximity to the condemned. The final selection: Achan, son of Carmi, son of Zabdi, of the house of Zerah, of the tribe of Judah.

He stood, a man neither tall nor distinctive, but whose calm was almost preternatural. He walked to the center, eyes never leaving the ground, then knelt at the base of the altar stone. The priest gestured to Joshua, who now stood more as a somber executor of a duty forced upon him than as a leader.

"Achan," Joshua said, the words deliberate, "my son, give glory to the Lord, and make confession to Him. Tell us what you have done; do not hide it from us."

A hush. The amphitheater held its breath.

Achan spoke, and his voice was not the ragged, wavering admission Gershom had expected. It was clear, deliberate, a tone of recitation, as if he had always known this was the end toward which his story pointed.

"Indeed, I have sinned against the Lord God of Israel. This is what I have done: When I saw in the spoils a beautiful cloak from Babylon, and two hundred shekels of silver, and a wedge of gold weighing fifty shekels, I coveted them and took them. They are hidden in the earth inside my tent, with the silver under it."

He finished, and the gathering exhaled as one. The confession was so specific, so unadorned, that it left no margin for pity, no escape route through ambiguity. For a moment, there was a sense, not of triumph, but of the grim satisfaction that comes when the source of a sickness is at last exposed.

Joshua turned to face the people. "You have heard. The Law must now be fulfilled."

As the meeting dissolved into a series of barked orders and the shuffle of feet, Gershom and Eliezer found themselves standing side by side at the lip of the platform. For the first time in recollection, there was no contest between them for authority, no posturing or rehearsal of old wounds. They simply stood, watching as the men of Judah escorted Achan from the ring, the still air of the gathering more damning than any jeer or curse could have been.

It was, Gershom thought, a kind of justice. But whether it was enough, or whether it would heal anything at all, he could not say.

He looked to Eliezer, who was already watching him, the rawness in his brother's face a mirror for the wound in his own.

They led Achan and his family to a distant valley, softened by a golden morning light. The valley stretched stark and open, flanked by rugged hills that loomed like silent sentinels, their shadows long across the dew-damp grass. The air was crisp and still, broken only by the occasional rustle of leaves stirred by a gentle breeze. There was little ceremony, no wailing or ritual keening as might have accompanied a more ambiguous loss. The men of Judah, Achan's own kin, carried the implements: cords of hemp for binding, baskets of river stones chosen for heft and symmetry, torches in case the morning failed to provide enough spectacle.

Gershom walked at the tail of the procession, his feet uncertain on the chalky incline, every step forward a referendum on what it meant to be party to justice that neither persuaded nor absolved. Eliezer was ahead, his shoulders squared, his posture a study in the physics of containment. If he felt the horror of what was coming, he did not betray it, save for the tremor that sometimes moved through his hands when he thought no one was watching.

At the valley's rim, a ring of bodies had already drawn together. Women and children lingered apart, arms cinched tight across their chests or fingers clutching tunic hems as though bracing against the pull of the pit below. The elders stood closest, their faces carved into hard lines, the kind worn by men who long ago chose clarity over ambiguity.

Joshua waited at the bottom, flanked by the priest and a handful of guards whose expressions betrayed the mixture of dread and righteousness that attended such acts. When Achan was brought forward, he knelt without being told, his head bowed not in submission but in a kind of practical humility, as if to minimize the surface area available for injury.

Joshua made no speech. He nodded to the priest, who raised his hands and spoke a single, unadorned sentence: "The Law is clear." There was no invocation of mercy, no appeal to the Lord's capacity for forgiveness. The words were meant to be an ending, not an opening.

The stones came in a broken, uneven rhythm at first, sailing through the air before striking their mark. The men at the edges threw lightly, almost uncertain, their stones wobbling as if they hoped the wind might spare them from landing. But the circle tightened. Arms lifted higher. The thuds grew heavier, more deliberate. Each impact sent a ripple through Achan's frame as he slumped over with the force. Dirt clung to the sweat on his skin, turning him the color of the earth. His body hitched once, then again, a thin rasp of air squeezing past his lips. After a final blow, even that small sound fell away, swallowed by the settling quiet.

When it ended, Achan's wife and children were brought forward. The woman's face was drained of color, yet she held her spine straight, as if her body refused to collapse before her captors. The two boys clung to either side of her, shoulders trembling beneath their thin tunics. The little girl, no more than six, kept her eyes fixed on the ground, her small fingers knotted in the folds of her mother's garment.

At the priest's repeated command, the men lifted their stones again. The first strikes landed with dull, sickening knocks. The woman jerked with each blow, still trying to angle her arms toward her children. One of the boys toppled sideways, scrambling upright only to be struck again, his breath punching out in short, panicked bursts. The older boy tried to shield his sister, but a glancing stone struck her cheek, snapping her head back and sending her sprawling to the ground.

Gershom watched because the law dictated that he must, as turning away felt like a kind of betrayal he would not be able to name. But the scene blurred even as he forced his eyes open. His mind refused to give the violence a clean outline, smearing the motion of arms and stones into something shapeless. Already the details were slipping, eroding into fragments that would cling to him later, indistinct but heavy, impossible to forget.

At last, the priest signaled, and the guards dragged what remained of the bodies into a crude pile. Oil darkened the heap, and when the torch touched, flames leapt instantly, fat spitting and bone collapsing into a black, hissing smoke that climbed straight into the morning sky.

Gershom looked to Eliezer, who was standing ramrod-straight, his eyes fixed not on the spectacle but on the far horizon, as if searching for a version of the day that did not require such an ending.

The crowd dispersed quickly, leaving behind the place that would come to be known as the Valley of Achor, for it was there that Achan and his family were stoned. The men and women of Israel returning to their tasks with the deliberate efficiency of people who could not afford to be undone by the violence of their own rules. Gershom lingered at the valley's rim, his knees locked and his mouth dry, unwilling or unable to move until the last wisp of smoke had been blown to nothing.

Eliezer came to him, his voice soft, but shaped with unyielding clarity. "Our father upheld the Law," he said. There was no accusation in it, no attempt to justify or explain. It was a statement of fact, as clear and as damning as the sentence handed down.

Gershom nodded, but the motion felt hollow, incomplete. He wanted to speak, to find words that might bridge the gap between what was justified and what was right. Instead, he held back, the two of them bound together by what they had witnessed and what could never be spoken aloud.

Eventually, Gershom made his way back to the camp, the muscles in his legs refusing to cooperate, each step a negotiation with the echo of today's event. He bypassed the mess lines, the clusters of men sharpening weapons and reworking their ration logs, and headed instead to the water cisterns, where he knew Tima would be.

She was there, as always, her hair tied back in a knot that managed to convey both defiance and practicality. She drew water in slow, even strokes, her face turned away from the line of women waiting their turn. Gershom approached, but she did not look up until he was nearly upon her.

He stood awkwardly, waiting for her to break the quiet.

"You look like a man who's just come from a funeral," she said, not unkindly.

"Worse," Gershom replied, surprised by the bitterness in his own voice. "A slaughter."

Tima place the jar down, wiped her hands on her tunic, and regarded him with an intensity that made him want to flinch. "You did what was required," she said.

"Did I?" Gershom asked, and there was no irony in it. He searched her face for the certainty that had always steadied him, the quiet conviction that their choices, however costly, would one day make sense.

She closed the gap between them, and cupped his hands in hers. "You carry the Law," she said, "but you don't have to become it."

He let her hold him, if it was only for a moment, the warmth of her skin grounding him in the present, reminding him that not every act of judgment was a prelude to loss.

But Tima was distracted, her eyes darting now and then toward the border of the camp, where the foothills cast a long shadow over the tents. Gershom felt the shift, the way her attention flickered, and when he drew back, he saw the tension in the line of her jaw.

"What is it?" he asked, suddenly alert.

She hesitated, holding his hand, and led him away from the cisterns, past the mess of tents to a place where the ground dipped and the air guarded secrets of its own. Only when they were alone did she speak.

"There are strangers in the valley," she said, her voice barely above a whisper. "They came two moon ago, after the execution. They're Gibeonites. They want to make a covenant, they want peace, in exchange for servitude."

Gershom stiffened. "Did you tell Joshua?"

Tima shook her head. "They came to me. One of their women, she was trying to get water at the well, yesterday night while the camp slept. I think she's the one who sent them."

He tried to process this, the weight of it nearly as suffocating as the smoke from the funeral pyre. "Why you?"

Tima looked away. "Because I showed her kindness. Because she saw that I..." She stopped, then started again. "They're not like us, but they're not enemies, either. They're afraid."

The revelation left Gershom reeling. The Law was clear on the matter: no covenants with the inhabitants of the land. Still, the reality was knottier than the text.

"This is not good, Tima. You know what the law requires," he said in a harsh whisper. "I just came from one judgment."

"I know," she replied, her voice tight. "That is exactly why I'm telling you."

"You should've come to me first."

"It happened so fast. And mercy should not be something we hesitate over," she said. "Does not the law command us to love our neighbors?" Her face held no trace of doubt.

Her statement was something he could not deny, for he had remembered the ten sayings since his childhood.

"You know I can't argue against the law. But the camp is on edge, taking Jericho, losing soldiers at Ai, and Anchan's—" he paused, as to not let the images return. "The point is, you met with inhabitants of this land without telling Joshua?" Gershom said, his voice barely above a whisper, but charged with a vibration that made it feel larger, more dangerous.

Tima folded her arms, eyes locked on a fissure in the rock at their feet. "Like I said, I met with them because they asked for mercy," she replied. "And because they're not soldiers, not spies, but people, like us, who want to survive."

Gershom paced, his sandals grinding chalk to dust. "That's not your decision. The Law—"

"—is written by men who have never watched a child die of thirst," Tima snapped. "You think the Lord is only justice? What about kindness? What about..." She hesitated, then forced the word out. "What about love?"

The syllable landed with a gravity no one was prepared to carry. Gershom stopped, arms limp at his sides, his anger suddenly directionless.

"They tricked you," he said, but the conviction had already begun to leak away.

Tima turned to him, her eyes hot and wet. "They trusted me," she said. "Because I showed one of them kindness at the well. Because I listened. They could have gone to the elders, or tried to bribe the guards. They came to me because I am nothing—because no one would believe me, or care what I said."

Gershom pressed his fingers to his temples, as though he could dam the restless surge behind his eyes. He wanted to tell her she was wrong, that her voice mattered, but the hollow certainty of the Law stifled every impulse.

"The Law is clear about covenants with the people of the land," he said. "We're commanded—"

"Commanded," she interrupted, "not to show mercy, not to think, not to feel. Is that what you want, Gershom? To be a blade with no hand to guide it?"

He was silent, the image cutting too close to what he feared he was becoming.

She took a step closer, her hand reaching for his. "If we can't decide who we are, what's the point of surviving? What's the point of all this sacrifice, if it only makes us less than human?"

He looked at her, really looked: the lines of fatigue at the corners of her eyes, the wind-burnt cracks in her lips, the way her hand trembled even as she tried to be the still point in his chaos. He wanted to fold her into himself, to take her pain and hold it until it became his own. But he could not.

"I need to think," he said, and the words felt cowardly even as they left his lips.

Tima drew back, her face closing. "Then think," she said. "But remember what it is you're trying to save."

They stood a minute longer, a gust nudging the hem of Tima's robe, the air thickening, heavy and medicinal. Then she turned and walked away, not looking back.

That night, Gershom lay in his tent, the darkness around

him like a womb of uncertainty. He could not sleep. He replayed every word, every gesture, every possible outcome. He thought of Achan, reduced to ash in the valley; he thought of the Gibeonites, waiting in the hills with their faces wrapped against the cold, the terror of annihilation gnawing at their sleep. He thought of Tima, the warmth of her hand, the last brittle look in her eyes.

By dawn, he had made his decision.

He dressed and went to the tent of Joshua, who received him with the gravity of a man who knew the world was always about to end. Gershom laid out everything: the approach, the plea for mercy, the details of the meeting. He spoke plainly, without embroidery, arranging the facts as though they might redeem him.

At the end, he added, "She believes them. She believes their desire for peace is genuine. I ask that she be allowed to speak before any judgment is passed."

Joshua listened, as he always did, his eyes offering no warmth and no cold. When Gershom finished, he nodded once.

"The Law is clear," he said, "but the Lord's will is sometimes a mystery to men. Bring her, and we will hear what she has to say. But be warned: if this is a trick, it will cost more than your own life."

Gershom bowed, and left.

He did not eat with the others that day, nor did he seek Tima out. He went instead to the furthest reach of the camp, where the land dropped away into a dry riverbed, the stones there worn smooth by centuries of water that no longer flowed. He sat in the quiet, letting her words echo inside him.

"If we can't decide who we are, what's the point of surviving?"

He had no answer, but for the first time he understood the

shape of the question, and the necessity of asking.

He stayed that way until the sun was high, the heat baking every doubt into something hard enough to hold. When he finally returned to the camp, he did not seek forgiveness, or even certainty. He walked upright, his shadow clear on the ground, and waited for whatever judgment would come.

The Gibeonite Deception

The assembly hall had been rebuilt to the same state it once held before the crossing of the Jordan. Here it was carved from the raw skin of the earth. Circular in form, it was ringed with blocks of limestone. At its heart lay a platform worn smooth by years of bare feet and heavier reckonings. Tonight, the firelight was an encampment apart, casting the gathered faces into hard relief. The air tasted of lamp oil and anticipation, every draft coiling with the promise of spectacle or judgment.

The Gibeonite delegation had been stationed near the entrance, five of them, their faces striped with fatigue and what might have passed for humility. Upon closer inspection, the robes they wore were a deliberate parody of wilderness distress: hems frayed, dust smeared in the precise geometry of the desperate. They stood at attention, each a different angle of fear, their hands against their thigh. Behind them, a half-circle of elders filled the benches, their eyes bright with the carnivorous curiosity that always preceded an act of discipline.

In the faint hum before the proceedings began, a Levite functionary moved through the benches. His vestments were outshone only by the stiffness of his beard. He handed out slates for note-taking, as if tonight's verdict might one day demand documentation greater than the recollection of the defeated. Joshua, for his part, sat at the apex of the ring, above the level of the Ark. The Ark had been placed with priestly precision on a dais draped in a cloth so densely embroidered it seemed to have captured the very substance of night. To the right of the Ark, on a smaller but equally reverent table, lay the urim and thummim: the sacred lots, each resting on its own square of silk, poised to deliver verdicts too sharp for mere human tongues.

Gershom did not sleep that night after his meeting with Joshua, but he still managed to slip into the back, flattening himself against a tent pole where the shadow was deepest. The amphitheater's acoustics made every cough, every shifting limb, an act of public confession. He could see the full circumference of the event from here: the Gibeonites in their self-constructed misery, the elders with their chins tucked like birds, the Levites arrayed in rows of white, their hands folded so uniformly it might have been a single body multiplied by necessity. Gershom's own hands, felt out of place; he flexed them behind his back, as if to bleed off whatever guilt had come with him.

Joshua waited until the moon had centered above the opening in the roof, its borrowed light triangulating perfectly with the torches that ringed the room. Then he rose. The movement carried no flourish of dominance, only the warning of order about to be imposed by something sterner than courtesy.

"People of Israel," he began, the vowels flat and unhurried, "you have been summoned to witness the matter of the sojourners from Gibeon." His eyes did not leave the Gibeonite spokesman, whose face registered every syllable as a fresh cut. "These men claimed to come from a land beyond the reach of our swords, to make covenant with us in good faith. But this afternoon, by the evidence of their own feet and the crumbs in their pouches, it was revealed that they dwell among us, within the very lands the Lord has given."

A soft susurration moved through the onlookers; some clucked their tongues, others simply leaned in, the architecture of the moment making it impossible to pretend disinterest. Joshua let the sound pass before continuing.

"The Law is explicit," he said, his voice gaining heft. "Covenant is forbidden with the peoples of Canaan. Yet it is also written: 'Do not pervert justice. Do not show partiality. Judge your neighbor fairly.'" He paused, scanning the benches. "Tonight, we weigh both."

Joshua lifted a hand, and the head of the Gibeonite delegation eased forward. His knees knocked together, refusing to hold steady. Medium in stature, his skin carried the burnished cracks of sun and labor. The robe he wore, once ochre, sagged in faded folds, its edges frayed to threads that exposed the stark plainness of the tunic below. When he began to speak, the sound wavered, each word thickened by an accent worn thin from possible years of pleading before those who ruled the land, the cadence a confession rehearsed too many times.

"It is true," the man said. "We feared for our lives, for we saw what was done to Jericho. We dressed ourselves in rags, brought old bread, so you would think us far away. We beg for mercy—not for our own sake, but for our children's."

The effect was immediate. The benches stiffened, some elders exchanged pointed glances, others scribbled notes as if transcribing the exact phrasing of the plea would inoculate them against the charge of sentimentality. Joshua inclined his head, then raised a hand for quiet.

"There is another who must speak," he said. "Bring forth

Tima, daughter of Medad."

For a moment, the name clung to the air, heavier than any insult. Tima entered through the north passage, her spine drawn so straight it rebuked the ground beneath her. She moved to the center, each step deliberate, as if dignity might slip into defiance. Her tunic carried no adornment, sleeves pushed to the elbow. No jewelry marked her, not even the thread bracelet she'd once used to mark her days. From his post, Gershom watched, his heart battering against his ribs. He was certain every eye in the room caught the tremor in her hand, the instant she drew breath to still it.

Joshua motioned for her to speak.

Tima's eyes lifted to a point above the Gibeonites' heads. She did not meet their faces. Her focus hovered in the air, as though she spoke to the gap between their bowed posture and the judgment pressing down from above.

"I am summoned for judgment," she said, "because I gave ear to these men before the matter was brought to the council. I listened to them in secret, and I did not report it. That was my transgression."

A Levite elder, his voice pinched and nasal, interrupted. "Do you deny that you advised them on how to approach the assembly? That you taught them the words to use?"

Tima did not flinch. "I did not teach them how to lie. I only told them that the Law is most merciful to those who seek covenant, not by trickery, but by truth. It was not my counsel that led them to this ruse."

A mutter of approval, or perhaps disappointment, rumbled through the benches.

Joshua raised his palm, and the murmur in the hall thinned to nothing. "Why, then, did you not speak of this to the council, or to me?"

Tima's eyes flicked, just once, in Gershom's direction, but she did not linger. "Because I was ashamed," she said. "Ashamed that I wanted to believe them. That I, too, wished for a way out that did not end in more death."

There was a pause, not of relief, but of recalibration. Gershom watched as the faces of the elders shifted: some softening, others hardening, the calculus of justice and mercy running its numbers in real time.

Phinehas, who had until now remained a silent sentinel by the Ark, rose to his full height. "The Law forbids treachery," he said, "but it also commands: 'If a foreigner sojourns with you, you shall not do him wrong. The foreigner who sojourns with you shall be to you as the native among you, and you shall love him as yourself.' Do you believe these men seek peace, or are they spies, awaiting a chance to betray us?"

Tima answered without hesitation. "They are afraid. They wish only to live. If we make them slaves, they will serve. If we make them outcasts, they will perish. But they will not fight."

A murmur swelled through the benches, low voices quickened with urgency. Joshua bent toward the priests, their foreheads nearly touching, a cluster of heads pressed close like birds bracing against the wind.

At length, Joshua turned back to the Gibeonite spokesman. "You have heard the witness," he said. "You have deceived us, but you have also thrown yourself on the mercy of the Law. Do you submit to its judgment?"

The man bowed so deeply his forehead brushed the ground. "We submit."

Joshua gestured to the priests. "Remove them from the hall. They will await the council's decision."

The Gibeonites filed out, their gait a study in the mathematics of relief and dread. When the last had gone, Joshua turned to the those present.

"We must judge not only the sojourners, but also our own. Tima, you are accused of withholding information from the council, and of aiding foreigners in circumventing the Law. What say you in your defense?"

Tima squared her shoulders, her voice clear despite the tremor that threatened to undermine it. "I broke the letter of the Law, but not its spirit. I preserved life where life could have been taken. If there is punishment, let it be justified, but remember this: even the Law was written so that men might live, not die."

The room stilled, every breath held back, every whisper cut short. Gershom's skin prickled as though the air had solidify to press down on them.

The elders withdrew to deliberate. Their departure was a choreography of starched linen and hollow footsteps, the echo of sandals shuffling on dirt, setting the pace for the waiting. The rest of the assembly remained motionless, as if the outcome might be altered by the fidgeting of a single hand.

Gershom watched as Tima stood alone in the center, her arms folded, her jaw betraying nothing. She glanced once in his direction, not accusatory but distant, already withdrawing to a place where forgiveness was measured not by verdict but by survival.

The elders came back sooner than anyone thought. Joshua stepped forward to speak.

"Tima," he said, the voice stripped of both ceremony and sympathy, "your offense is clear. But so is your intent. For the sake of mercy shown to the sojourners, and for the confession you have made, your punishment is commuted. In the future, you will bring such matters to the council at once. No judgment is yours alone to make."

He paused, letting the words hang like smoke in a windless room.

"You are dismissed."

Tima bowed, once, then turned and left by the same passage she had entered. She did not look back. Gershom, still rooted to his place, traced the line of her back, the way her hands, once composed in the gathering, now trembled with each step. The company breathed out as one, and the torches, waning, flickered in their sockets.

The Gibeonites would live. Tima would bear the knowledge of what she had done, and what she had not. Gershom lingered at the fringe, certain that what he had won was nothing, and what he had lost had no name.

He did not follow her out. Though he wish he did.

The Gibeonites were brought in again. The head of the delegation knelt with all the artistry of a professional supplicant, but his eyes tracked every movement in the room, cataloguing each gesture for later use.

Joshua inclined his head toward Phinehas. The priest stepped forward, and when he spoke, the hall tightened. Even in its gentlest register, his voice struck with the bite of iron, each word ringing as if forged.

"We are bound by our word," he said. "The oath, though obtained by guile, cannot be broken without sinning against the Law. But the Law also makes provision for consequence. The sojourners will not be destroyed, but neither will they be permitted to share in the inheritance of Israel as equals."

A hum of assent rolled through the benches, but it was tinged with the unease of men who saw in this precedent a thousand new headaches. Joshua followed, his words measured.

"We will not break faith," he said, "but neither will we make ourselves vulnerable to betrayal. These Gibeonites shall become servants to the assembly, cutters of wood and drawers of water, as a sign to all that deception buys no comfort, only survival."

The Gibeonite leader bowed his head, and for a moment it seemed he might collapse under the relief. But Gershom saw the flicker of calculation behind the man's lowered brow, the quick glance at Joshua, the half-smile caught and stifled before it shattered the moment.

One of the senior elders, a man whose beard had gone silver long before Moses' death, raised a hand for the floor. "If we make a place for them," he said, "do we not risk a dilution of our covenant? The Lord said to drive out the nations, not to graft them onto our own."

Phinehas was ready for this. "The Law is not a fence to keep men out," he replied, "but a path by which any man might learn to walk upright. Their presence among us will not corrupt us—unless our own hearts are already divided."

This rippled through the benches: some nods, some grimaces, the old argument sprouting new leaves but not new fruit.

A younger Levite, emboldened by the absence of the full crowd, leaned over to Gershom and whispered, "At least we won't have to chop our own firewood for the altar now." The joke was tasteless, but it carried the sour truth of a people tired of abstractions. Gershom held his tongue, while heat gathered within, a friction shaped not by anger but by neglect.

For years, he had made himself small, ducking the debates, letting the sharper minds and louder mouths carry the day. Now, for reasons he could not name, maybe to reconcile his actions against Tima. Either way, he found himself rising, the muscles in his legs acting before his mind could tell them to sit.

He stood, clearing his throat in the old, involuntary way that always preceded a disaster. Joshua saw him, nodded once, and gestured for the room to attend.

Gershom's voice, when it emerged, was not loud, but it carried. "My father taught that the Law was given not to end life, but to preserve it. That to walk upright before the Lord is not merely to avoid offense, but to honor the dignity of every living soul. The Gibeonites deceived us, yes. But they also placed themselves under our judgment, trusting that our Law would be more merciful than the sword."

He paused, letting the words find their mark.

"They should bear consequence. But if we turn them away, or treat them as animals, we become less than what was promised to us in the wilderness. My father failed in many things, but in this he was clear: 'The stranger who sojourns with you shall be as the native among you, and you shall love him as yourself.' We owe the Law nothing short of our best obedience, even when it is inconvenient, or hard, or ugly to our pride."

The air grew taut, the hall stripped of sound. Joshua's expression flickered, gratitude flashing before it vanished into composure. Phinehas stayed unmoving, but the rigid mouth slackened, a faint release from long-held strain.

The silver-bearded elder nodded, once, as if to concede the point and also to acknowledge the wound it opened. The

Gibeonite leader, still kneeling, looked up at Gershom and offered a nod. It was subtle, almost sly, yet unmistakably grateful.

Joshua continued. "The matter is settled. The sojourners will live among us, but in service. Let it be written, and let it be remembered." He banged the haft of his staff against a stone slab set in the dirt for such purpose, the sound echoing in the bones of the tent.

The benches scraped as men rose, the gathering dissolving into motion. The Gibeonites were ushered out, their faces lifted with relief too sharp for what they had earned. Gershom lowered himself onto the bench, his fingers twitching against the wood, the tremor left behind when the rush drained away. Beside him, the young Levite studied him with narrowed eyes, weighing whether the burst he had witnessed belonged to courage or folly.

Phinehas approached, his raiment trailing behind him like the afterthought of a storm. He bent close, voice meant for Gershom's ears alone. "Your father would have been proud," he said, "though he would have argued every point with you, twice."

Gershom managed a smile. "That sounds about right."

At the circle's boundary, Joshua's stance shifted, carved stone giving way to flesh and breath, as though he had found, if only briefly, a way to hold judgment and mercy together.

The council had adjourned long before the nights chill bit through the thin linen of Gershom's garment, but he lingered near the entrance of the hall, unwilling to rejoin the camp's ordinary rhythms. The torches at the perimeter guttered in the breeze, each one losing ground to the larger darkness encroaching from the hills. The benches, now abandoned, looked like gravestones for arguments that would be exhumed by sunrise.

He watched as clusters of elders broke into their familiar alliances, some in urgent debate, others resigned to the silence that followed judgment. The Gibeonites had been escorted to a holding tent at the far edge of the avenue, guarded more by curiosity than necessity. Scattered along the poles, older Levites leaned back, their faces lit by the glow of private pipes, their voices pitched so faintly they carried nothing beyond the mood.

Gershom had started toward the rows of cooking fires when he noticed Eliezer. His brother stood apart, the width of the ground between them, arms folded and posture stripped of expression. He hovered between approach and retreat, a man weighing the terms of his own discomfort. Gershom thought of passing him by, but the notion felt cowardly and, after the day's events, beside the point.

Their eyes met across the clearing. Eliezer looked away, then back, then squared his shoulders and began the deliberate walk over, each step landing like a verdict.

"Your words in there," Eliezer said, when he was close enough to speak but not so near that their shadows merged, "they reminded me of Father."

Gershom blinked, surprised by the lack of accusation in the tone. "Did they?"

Eliezer shrugged, a motion so practiced it was almost un- conscious. "You always said you had no taste for oratory. But today—" He hesitated, as if weighing whether the compliment was safe. "Today, you spoke with more sense than the rest of them combined."

A faint laugh escaped Gershom. "I suppose anyone can

sound wise if they're desperate enough."

They moved unevenly, drawing close, then drifting apart as their steps threaded through the remnants scattered across the ground. At last they came to the central brazier, its coals pulsing faintly in the dark. Gershom stooped, lifted a stick, and pressed it into the embers. Sparks leapt upward, spiraling before dissolving into the night.

Eliezer watched him, jaw working, the words trapped in the architecture of his teeth.

"You hated these assemblies," Eliezer said, finally. "I remember you as a boy, always trying to run off, always asking why we had to listen to the same arguments, the same old men, over and over."

Gershom kept his eyes on the fire. "I still hate them. But sometimes you have to listen anyway."

Eliezer's mouth twisted. "I used to think that made you weak. Or lazy. Or—" He stopped, then finished with a shrug. "But you were right about the Gibeonites. About mercy. I don't know if I could have done what you did."

Gershom let the words settle. The silence was no longer hostile, just unpracticed. But the truth of the matter was that the words were not his but Tima's

"You always wanted to be Father," Gershom said, the words emerging more gently than he had intended. "You studied the Law, you memorized the lists, you did everything they asked. I think I resented you for that. Maybe I still do."

Eliezer smiled, but it was thin, the skin drawn tight at the edges. "And I resented you for not caring. For being able to walk away from it, when I never could."

A pause, long enough that the sound of the camp intruded: the clatter of a dropped pot, the distant laugh of a woman, the bark of a dog chasing something into the dark.

"I was afraid," Eliezer admitted, voice low. "Afraid that, if you kept refusing the Law, you'd dishonor Father. That I'd have to bear it for both of us."

Gershom nudged the stick deeper into the coals. "Maybe I did. Maybe I still do."

"But today," Eliezer said, "you spoke like him. Not in the words, but in the... I don't know. The weight of it. Like you finally wanted it to matter."

Gershom turned, met his brother's eyes. "Maybe I finally do."

They stood that way for a time, the orange light painting the lines of their faces with a harsh, flattering honesty. Behind them, the camp began its gradual surrender to sleep, the last disputes of the day dissolving into the muted communal hum that marked the end of business.

Eliezer shoved his hands into the sleeves of his robe. "What now?" he asked, not as a challenge, but as a brother.

Gershom looked past the fires, past the tents, to where the stars crept out in their ancient, indifferent constellations. "Now," he said, "we keep walking. One foot in front of the other. Like always."

Eliezer nodded. "And after that?"

Gershom smiled, the expression unfamiliar but not unwelcome. "We figure it out. Like father showed us."

For the first time in recollection, the two brothers stood together at the boundary of the camp, their old rivalry softened by exhaustion and something near to understanding. They watched the sky, the embers of the central fire mirrored in the pinpricks of starlight overhead, and for once the world was, if not simple, then at least survivable.

They did not speak again that night. Words had done enough. Instead, they sat and watched the flames flicker, content to let the questions wait until morning.

Alter by the Jordan

Rumor moved through the avenue faster than fire. By the third day after the Gibeonite affair, it had grown so definite—so lavishly embroidered with names, details, and motives that the only ambiguity left was whether the burning would commence at sunrise or whether the elders would wait until the morning fog cleared enough to make it spectacular.

The story, in its most vulgar telling, was simple: the tribes across the river, Reuben, Gad, and the half-tribe of Manasseh, had raised a new altar along the Jordan. An altar to the Lord, they said, but not the Lord's altar. They had built it high and visible, a taunt from the bluffs above the ford, its stones mortared and tiered to rival the one at Shiloh. Not a day passed before some shepherd or runner or peddler of news returned with a sketch, traced hastily in earth: see, the horns at the corners, the altar wide enough to butcher an ox, the strange adornment of river stones worked smooth by centuries of current.

To those who nursed suspicion as a way of life, it was proof. To the rest, it was an alarm so sudden and so plausible that by nightfall, even the children had learned the choreography of outrage, parading up and down the avenue and chanting, "New god! New altar! New curse!" until the old women began to stuff rags in their ears or else threaten to slit the tongue from whichever grandson started the next round.

Gershom heard it first at the water-drawing, the rumor bobbing from mouth to mouth like an apple at the harvest festival. The men at the front of the line were already calculating how long it would take to send a punitive column eastward. The women behind them had moved to the immediate concerns of tents, livestock, and the orphans who might be left if both men and boys were taken in the first wave. It was a subject with gravity, and Gershom, by now practiced at detachment, observed the drift and accumulation of fear as one might track the slow silting of a river: inevitable, but always surprising in its particulars.

He passed Tima on his way back to the Levite tents. She was filling a jar at the lower cistern, and he could not help noticing her beauty, even in the midst of such a simple task. He caught her eye, attempted a wave; she answered with a glance so brief and so curt it felt like a door closing. And though his heart sank a bit, he moved on, weaving through the clusters of men who had stopped working entirely and now devoted their energies to prophesying disaster. As he neared the tent row reserved for the sons of Aaron, he heard the unmistakable voice of Phinehas, loud even at a distance, carrying the cadence of command.

"It is not the building of the altar that is the crime," Phinehas said, "but that they have done so without the Lord's command. Have we not seen enough judgment for this generation? Must we invite another?"

A chorus of assent, bitter and overlapping, rose in answer. Some cursed the names of the eastern tribes; others speculated that perhaps it was the Gibeonite precedent, the Law's loophole, that had emboldened the rebels. A few, too young or too old for nuance, simply called for war.

Gershom skirted around the people, slipped into the tent where Eliezer waited, and found his brother already pacing the narrow aisle, hands clenched and unclenched as if kneading an invisible argument into shape.

"Did you hear?" Eliezer said, voice pitched low to avoid eavesdroppers but unable to hide its urgency.

"I heard," Gershom replied.

"They say the altar stands as tall as a man. That they built it in a single night. That they used no iron tools, simply the stones from the riverbed, stacked so tight not even a blade of grass could find a way in."

Gershom raised an eyebrow. "It's a miracle anyone can agree on the height of anything, these days."

Eliezer pressed on, heedless. "The council meets at sundown. They say Joshua himself will decide whether to summon the fighting men, or send a delegation, or—" He paused, uncertain. "Or wait. Can you imagine? After everything, to just wait."

Gershom could imagine it. In fact, he could imagine nothing less likely than a sudden, violent solution to a problem that had not yet had the chance to metastasize into the full theater of disaster. He saw Joshua as a man who preferred the luxury of time, a man who understood that the most effective weapon was often the one left sheathed.

He did not say this aloud. Instead, he changed the subject. "Are you going?"

Eliezer hesitated. "I have not been called."

Gershom glanced around the tent, as if to confirm the lack of summons. "Maybe that's for the best."

His brother frowned, the old resentment returning for an

instant before being swallowed up by the urgency of the moment. "You think so?"

"I think sometimes it's better to let the elders talk themselves hoarse before the rest of us get involved."

Eliezer did not answer. He resumed his pacing, the soles of his sandals raising a faint mist of dust with each turn.

Outside, the camp's soundscape had shifted. The usual chorus of children's voices was gone, replaced by the measured drone of men discussing strategy, or the sharp, metallic edge of women gossiping as they shredded herbs and roots for the evening meal. Gershom stood at the tent's threshold, watching as the light dimmed and the first torches flared to life along the avenue.

At the center of camp, near Joshua's own dwelling, a knot of men was already forming, a cluster of the most senior elders, their cloaks pulled close against the cold, their faces drawn in the half-light like masks from a drama whose script had been lost. Gershom recognized several: the high priest, the sons of the other tribes, even the Gibeonite leader, who had not been exiled after all but remained as a permanent, uncomfortable reminder of the previous compromise. At the edge of the group, Phinehas gestured with a stick, using it as both baton and pointer, tracing diagrams in the sand that only he could see.

As the company reached critical mass, Joshua emerged from his tent, the act answering the unspoken question in every mind. He did not climb onto a dais or raise his voice for effect. He stepped directly into the ring, paused until the murmurs subsided, and spoke with the measured authority of a man who had already weighed every outcome and found each one wanting.

"We have heard the reports," he said. "We have seen the

altar. We know that the tribes beyond the river have done this thing without counsel, without invitation. The Law is clear on the matter."

A hum of agreement, like the buzz of hornets.

"But the Law is also clear about the consequence of civil war. A brother's blood calls out more sharply than that of any enemy. We will not rush to judgment. We will send men to inquire, not to accuse. We will hear what the builders have to say, and if there is repentance, we will offer mercy. If there is not..." He let the sentence taper, unfinished. The effect was more terrifying than any threat.

He looked around the circle, his gaze landing briefly on each elder before settling, unexpectedly, on Gershom.

"You will go, and be sure to take your brother with you. May your relation show the other tribes, that we are brothers in the same manner," Joshua said, "Phinehas and the heads of the tribes will also go along. Speak not as spies, nor as judges, but as brothers. Let the truth be made plain."

Gershom felt the eyes of the assembly turn, the recognition as immediate as it was unwelcome. He bowed his head, not out of humility but to avoid the certainty that someone in the group—perhaps several—was already cataloging the decision as a sign of favoritism, or, worse, as an attempt to fix the outcome by sending Moses' own blood.

He stole a glance at Eliezer, who stood at the back of the crowd, he gave a simple nod of acknowledgment.

Joshua finished with a gesture, dismissing the circle as easily as he had called it to order. The elders broke off in pairs and trios, their voices now pitched lower, the arguments turned from the question of going to the harder question of how to interpret whatever evidence the journey would reveal.

Phinehas approached, his runic billowing behind him like the wake of a small, determined ship. He wasted no time in protocol. "We leave at dawn," he said. "Bring only what you need. The more we resemble ordinary travelers, the better."

Gershom nodded, then started back toward the Levite row to pack. He noticed, as he walked, that the mood in the camp had shifted again: where before there had been outrage, now there was a kind of nervous anticipation, as if everyone expected the next day to end in blood, whether from the altar's builders or from those sent to demand an accounting.

He passed Tima a second time, this time near the lamp-lit path that led to the women's working tents. She stood in profile, her arms crossed, her face fixed on the horizon where the last blue of the day was leaking out into darkness. She did not see him, or if she did, she gave no sign.

That night, the camp slept poorly. The usual lullabies were absent, replaced by the low, restless murmur of men rehearsing their roles for the coming drama. Gershom lay awake on his mat, the skin at the back of his neck prickling with the sense of unfinished business. He wondered what would happen if the altar truly was a new start, a rival to Shiloh. He wondered what kind of man he would be if he returned and found that, by some accident or miracle, nothing had changed.

Before dawn, he joined the others at the edge of camp. Phinehas was already there, surrounded by the heads of the tribes: the stooped elder of Judah, the grizzled captain from Benjamin, the twins from Naphtali who always spoke in tandem. Eliezer was present as well, his cloak pulled tight against the morning chill, his face unreadable.

Joshua gave his instructions in a voice barely above a whisper, as if to avoid waking the camp to the possibility of disaster.

"Ask questions," he said. "Do not accuse until you have heard every word. Remember, a brother's blood is the price of haste."

The delegation set off in single file, crossing the hard ground to the east with nothing but walking staffs and the odd bundle of dried meat. Gershom was near the back, content to let the others shoulder the work of leadership, content to watch and listen and decide nothing until forced.

As they walked, he glanced over his shoulder. The camp was already stirring, the fires lit, the women scraping pots for the morning meal. At the edge of the avenue, he saw Tima again, her face now turned directly toward him, the line of her gaze sharp as a blade. He held it, for a second, then looked away, unsure whether the sensation was comfort or rebuke.

There was so much he wanted to say to her, yet every time he tried to form the words, his thoughts tangled and scattered. Even if he could gather them, he was not sure he possessed the courage to walk up to her and speak them aloud. The closer he came to imagining it, the more his resolve thinned, leaving him silently watching her instead, full of unsaid things. Finally, he turned his eyes forward, toward the river, toward the altar, toward whatever waited on the far side.

He walked, and did not look back again.

The road east was not a road at all, but a series of hints, a logic of compressed earth and grass-shadows that only the old traders and the sharpest-eyed Levites could follow with any confidence. By midmorning, the river's voice was always audible, though never in sight; its presence haunted every rise and declivity, the promise of water a constant companion to the delegation's measured progress.

The heads of tribes walked in a loose formation, no two men trusting themselves enough to break the peace with casual speech. Phinehas led, his stride both predatory and priestly, the staff he carried doubling as an extension of his argument with the world. The rest followed according to status, or sometimes convenience, or sometimes nothing at all. Gershom and Eliezer found themselves at the rear of the group, the only place where their companionship did not require an immediate answer to the question of which brother belonged ahead of the other.

They walked in silence, the only words exchanged those strictly necessary to the navigation of rocks or the avoidance of a bramble patch. The land here was different than the valleys and plains west of the Jordan: fewer trees, more brush and stone, the kind of earth that suggested no one had ever wanted it badly enough to make a real claim. Occasionally, they passed a cairn or a ring of burned rock, the faintest traces of others who had crossed here before. Once, Gershom caught the glint of obsidian along the trail, a razor-sharp remnant of some old war or old economy, and he knelt to pocket it, just for the shape of its history.

Eliezer saw him do it and offered a small, dry smile. "Still collecting?" he asked.

Gershom shrugged, then risked a reply. "It's something to hold onto."

They resumed their march, the brief intimacy already exhausted. Overhead, clouds massed and then dissolved, the sun alternately brutal and absent, the wind shifting from river-cool to dust-hot in the span of a few dozen steps.

When they stopped for the noon meal, the brothers sat at opposite ends of a boulder, elbows nearly touching but eyes fixed in opposite directions. Gershom chewed his bread with intentional, thoughtful bites; Eliezer tore his with a kind of methodical violence, as if the thing had insulted him and required punishment before it could be digested.

At length, Phinehas called the delegation to order. "We are less than a day from the crossing," he said. "Tomorrow by sunrise, we will see the altar. Until then, speak to no one not of your own house. We are not spies; we are witnesses. Remember that."

He looked at Gershom as he said it, the implication thick as paste.

That night, they camped in a hollow between two small hills, the river's song now closer, a murmur behind every word spoken at the fire. The Levites assembled a crude altar from the available stones, nothing elaborate, a place to stack the offerings and place the light so that their God would not be a stranger in this borrowed country. Phinehas led the prayers with a precision that revealed both habit and hunger. The words, though familiar, bore a force that made it impossible to ignore the subtext: the Law was not a comfort but a sword, and tonight it waited in stillness for the next infraction.

Eliezer joined the prayers with easy fluency, bowing and responding at all the right moments, his voice blending with the others as if the anger and doubt of the day had never touched him. Gershom stayed back, sitting on a wedge of stone a little beyond the glow of the fire, watching as the men performed the choreography of faith. It looked, from a distance, like nothing so much as a rehearsal for something that would never arrive.

He let the others sleep first, volunteering for the night watch so he would not have to share the darkness with Eliezer or Phinehas. He was not entirely sure why he made the choice. Perhaps it was old habit, or perhaps it was simply the need to avoid speaking about everything that had unfolded.

Alone, he walked the perimeter of the camp, the staff of the tribe of Levi in his right hand, the obsidian flake in his left. The moon was a mere sliver, the stars sharp and insistent overhead. Somewhere beyond the ridge, a wolf sang to its own loneliness, a high, broken sound that made the skin along Gershom's arms rise up in response.

He found himself scanning the sky, as his mother had taught him to do when he was a child: find Orion, find the Pleiades, find the trail of fire that marks the ancient crossing. Zipporah had insisted that every night sky was the same, if only you learned to read it properly. Even in Egypt, she'd said, you can look up and know you are never truly lost.

He thought of her now, her hands always busy, always shaping dough or braiding hair or tracing the line of his brow to see if he had grown since the last time she checked. He wondered what she would make of this journey, of these men, of the altar that might or might not be a portal to disaster.

Near midnight, a shifting in the brush signaled Eliezer's approach. Gershom heard the footfalls before he saw the silhouette. He recognized the awkward cadence, half hesitation and half bravado, that had defined his brother's movements since childhood.

"You're supposed to be sleeping," Gershom said.

"I couldn't too much on my mind," Eliezer countered.

They sat together at the fireless borders of camp, the only warmth that of memory or accident.

For a while, they watched the stars and let the silence do its work. Then, in a voice so soft it seemed borrowed from a younger self, Eliezer said, "Do you remember the night before Father climbed Nebo?"

Gershom did. The air that evening had been electric, the camp so tense that even the children refused to play. Moses had eaten little, spoken less, and spent the hours before dusk simply walking among the tents, touching a shoulder here, a cheek there, as if to anchor himself to the world he was about to leave.

"I remember," Gershom said.

"He called us both in, that night," Eliezer went on. "Told us to take care of each other. Told me I would have to carry the Law now, that it would be my turn to set the example."

Gershom smiled, but it was thin, the kind that lives mostly in the eyes. "He never asked that of me. Not once."

Eliezer looked at him, the question naked on his face. "Did that make it easier, or harder?"

Gershom considered. "Both, I think. Easier, because no one ever expected me to rise to anything. Harder, because it meant I could never fail."

A breeze stirred the grasses, carrying with it the faintest tang of smoke from the Levite altar.

"He was proud of you, though," Eliezer said. "Even when you doubted. Especially then, I think."

"Did he say that?"

"No. But I could see it. In the way he watched you when you argued with him, or when you fixed something in the camp that the others said was hopeless." Eliezer paused. "He wanted to be argued with. He needed it."

They sat for a time, the only sound the small animal noises that mark the border between sleep and morning.

"I miss her more," Gershom said, and the admission shocked even himself.

"Mother?"

Gershom nodded. "She had a way of making every fight seem like it could be survived. With Father, it was always life or death. With her, it was just another day."

Eliezer's eyes shone in the starlight. "I wish she'd lived to see this. The land, the camp, the way it finally, almost, works."

"She would have laughed at us," Gershom said. "At the altar, at the fighting, at the way we still manage to lose ourselves even with all the maps and all the prayers."

They lapsed into a silence more natural than before, the old grievances smoothed by the act of remembering.

At length, Eliezer broke it with a question that rang with the sound of iron. "Why did you never try to take his place? Not even once?"

Gershom turned, drawn into his brother's eyes, and found he could not answer. Not honestly. Not yet.

He let the pause linger, the answer deferred, as the first gray line of dawn stretched across the eastern sky.

They watched it together, and said nothing more.

From Disaster to Union

The sun had barely broken over the eastern rim when the delegation first glimpsed the altar. It was exactly as rumored: a mass of uncut stones, mortared with the pale clay of the riverbanks, its corners squared by the careful alignment of boulders that must have required the combined effort of a dozen households. It stood at the highest point above the ford, visible from both banks, a monument not only to piety but also to the human compulsion for symmetry, for grandeur, for the staking of a claim in a world that often refused to acknowledge ownership.

At its base, the leaders of the eastern tribes waited, arrayed in a tight crescent. Gershom counted at least fifteen men of consequence, each flanked by a pair of younger warriors who stared down the delegation with the slack-faced suspicion of men unused to playing defense. Their clothing was travel-stained and utilitarian, but their weapons were polished to the point of absurdity. One of the elders, tall, his beard the color of river mud, stepped forward as the delegation approached, palms outstretched in the ancient gesture of greeting, perhaps even of peace.

Phinehas wasted no time. He raised his staff and called out, the words carrying across the space with the force of accusation.

"Why have you done this thing?" he said, the phrase as formulaic as a curse. "Have you built a rival altar to turn from the Lord? Is this not the very sin that brought ruin to our fathers in the wilderness?"

The river elder did not flinch. He stood for a moment, the silence dragging long enough for several in the delegation to begin exchanging uneasy glances. Then he let the words emerge, drawn out but unmarked by shame or bravado.

"We built this altar not for sacrifice, nor for the burning of flesh," he said. "We built it because we feared, in days to come, your children would say to ours: 'What part have you in the Lord? The Jordan is a boundary. You do not belong to us. Your offerings are an offense.'"

A murmur ran through the delegation; Gershom saw the ripple travel from man to man, surprise overtaking anger, the body language shifting from attack to calculation.

The elder continued: "We know the Law. We know the altar at Shiloh is the only true place for offering. But this—" he gestured to the structure behind him, massive and inert— "this is not an altar for burnt offerings or for sin. It is a witness between us and you, and between the generations to come, that we have not made ourselves strangers to the covenant."

Phinehas opened his mouth, then closed it again. For the first time, his confidence faltered, the script running out of lines.

Another of the easterners, shorter, broader, with a gravel-rough voice, spoke up. "If this is a sin, let the Lord Himself judge it. But do not say we sought to build a new faith, or a new priesthood. We only wished to remain remembered. We feared you would forget us."

A long stillness took hold. At first, no one moved. Then, one by one, the delegates relaxed their posture, lowering their staffs and letting their hands drift from the hilts of their knives. Even Phinehas was diminished, the energy once animating him giving way to a kind of blankness.

Gershom watched as the men around him recalibrated: anger replaced by relief, then relief replaced by a rueful amusement at how close they'd come to a war over what was, in essence, a monument to unity. He caught Eliezer's eye, and in that glance he saw the full circle of their last conversation— a reminder of how easily brothers could mistake each other's intentions, how much energy could be wasted on guarding against the very wound they had both been raised to fear.

Phinehas found his voice at last. "If this is the truth, let it be said before the Lord. Swear by the altar at Shiloh that you will offer no sacrifice here, nor divide yourselves from the rest of Israel."

The river elder bowed his head. "We so swear."

The ritual was completed. The men clasped hands, the phrase repeated in the cadence of legal binding, the argument resolved by the substitution of oath for offense.

For a moment, there was nothing left but the sound of water below, and the wind riffling the grass along the slope.

Gershom walked to the side of the altar, let his palm rest on the cool surface of the stone. He felt nothing, no tremor of sanctity, no echo of forbidden sacrifice, only the roughness and the solid proof of a community's terror of being left behind.

He turned to see Eliezer watching him, a tentative smile lurking behind the seriousness of his features.

"Close call," Eliezer said.

"Too close," Gershom replied.

They stood together, the rest of the delegation already preparing for the return journey, the easterners forming a loose perimeter around the altar as if to shield it from some last-minute change of heart.

"What do you think Father would have done?" Eliezer asked, the words unguarded now, free of rivalry.

Gershom considered. "He would have waited," he said, "until he was sure the fight was necessary."

Eliezer nodded. "He would have hated being here."

"Probably," Gershom said. "But he would have come anyway."

They stayed at the altar, the two of them. They watched the sun climb a little higher. They saw the delegation's anger shift into a story that would be retold in a hundred camps. Each time it would carry less violence and more humor.

It was a good ending, as such things went.

But Gershom wondered, even as they turned to leave, whether there would ever be a story so perfect that it could not, by the right misreading, become the cause of another war.

The journey back was different. Where the road east had been tense, bristling with the possibility of violence, the return felt disarmed, almost weightless by comparison. The men no longer walked in formation; the lines blurred, conversations happened in twos and threes, and the general mood had loosened enough that one of the twins from Naphtali told a joke that was nearly obscene, and the others laughed as if the sound itself were a sacrament.

Gershom and Eliezer drifted ahead of the main party, the distance both deliberate and, for the first time, comfortable. They followed the curve of the river, the air thick with insects and the scent of wild fennel, the bank on their left teeming with the white flowers that Zipporah had once called "ghosts of the drowned." For a while, they said nothing, letting their steps synchronize, the rhythm of their feet a counterpoint to the hush behind them.

It was Gershom who broke the silence. "I want you to know," he said, "that I'm relinquishing any claim to leadership. Formally, if you need it. I never wanted it, and I won't take it, even if it's offered."

Eliezer kept walking, his face a study in neutral. "You don't get to resign from something you never did," he said, but the words lacked heat.

Gershom smiled, a thin line. "I'm serious. You always thought I was biding my time, waiting for the moment to step in and take the mantle."

Eliezer stopped, forced Gershom to face him. "Why now?"

Gershom considered. "Because the altar changed everything. I watched men almost kill each other over an argument that turned out to be a misunderstanding. I saw myself in that. I saw us." He paused, searched for the right words. "You were always the one who cared. About the Law, about Father's legacy. I was just... there."

Eliezer's brow furrowed. "You think I want it? The leadership?"

"I think you deserve the chance to find out," Gershom said. "Without me in the way. Without anyone wondering if I'll step in and undo your work."

Eliezer exhaled, a long, "You're doing this for me?"

"I'm doing this so we can stop hurting each other. So we can be brothers without it being a competition." Gershom looked away, watched a dragonfly hover above a patch of weeds. "If there's anything I learned from that altar, it's that the worst wounds come from people trying too hard to protect what they love."

They resumed walking, the quiet now soft and full, the kind that suggests everything worth saying has already been said.

They reached the camp as the sun was setting, the rows of tents aglow with the scattered fires of a people who, for all their appetite for drama, still preferred the comfort of routine. Word of the delegation's return traveled faster than the men themselves, so by the time they approached Joshua's tent, a semicircle of elders, Levites, and curious bystanders had already assembled.

Joshua greeted them at the threshold. He looked older than when they'd left, the creases around his eyes deeper, his shoulders drawn with fatigue. He listened as Phinehas delivered the report, the cadence of the story edited to emphasize how close they'd come to disaster, and how simple the answer had turned out to be. The tension in the air eased with each sentence, until by the end, many were grinning, clapping backs, or whispering "Thank the Lord."

Joshua addressed the gathering, his voice measured but heavy with relief. "Let this be a lesson to us all. The enemy is not always across the river, but sometimes in our own doubt, our own fear. We are one house. Let it be remembered."

That night, the camp put aside the week's anxiety with a vigor that bordered on the reckless. Gershom found himself drifting among the rows, accepting bowls of lentils from women he barely knew, letting children tug at his garment as they reenacted the scene at the altar, each appointing themselves the hero. He watched the spectacle from the margin, smiling, but acutely aware of the absence at his side, a presence that, until recently, had been as constant as his own pulse.

He found Tima in the Levite quarter, her hair pulled back with a cord of blue, her hands busy at the table sorting wild mint from a basket. She looked up, caught his eye, then returned to her work with a deliberateness that dared him to interrupt.

He approached, the words he'd rehearsed collapsing the instant he needed them.

She finished a sprig, placed it aside, and waited.

"I wanted to say—" he began, then faltered.

Tima's lips twitched, the faintest hint of a smile. "You want to say you're sorry. For betraying me."

He nodded, the heat rising to his cheeks.

She regarded him, her eyes not soft, but not hard either. "You did what you thought was right. I don't blame you for that. But it hurt."

"I should have trusted you," Gershom said. "Or at least tried to."

She snipped another stem. "Maybe. But if you had, the Law would have broken us both. You chose it over me. I see that now. But I don't hate you for it."

He reached for her hand, stopped himself, then forced the gesture anyway, awkward and honest. "I want to do better."

Tima laid her fingers atop his, the contact light as a feather. "What does that mean, for a man like you?"

He searched for the answer, and for once found it ready. "It means not hiding anymore. Not from you, not from myself, not from what I believe."

She studied him, the old shrewdness in her expression. "And if it happens again? If the Law and I are on opposite sides?"

Gershom smiled, a real one this time. "Then I'll fight for you. Even if it means losing."

Tima laughed, a soft and unguarded sound. "Let's hope it doesn't come to that. But thank you. For saying it." She gave his hand a gentle squeeze. She began to pull away. Gershom seized the moment, drawing her close and kissing her.

They stayed like that for several seconds, long enough for a few nearby women to exchange knowing smiles. When they finally parted, Tima's face was glowing.

"What was that for?" she asked, her smile bright and unable to hide her joy.

"For forgiving me," Gershom said, returning her smile, "and for showing me how the simplest misunderstanding can grow into disaster. It is wiser to hold back judgment until one has full understanding."

"Well, I am glad to know that even the son of the great Moses can still learn a thing or two," she teased, wrapping her arms around him in a warm hug.

Gershom looked into Tima's eyes, his expression settling into a seriousness she had rarely seen from him. "I promise," he said quietly, "that by tomorrow I will ask your father if I may make you my wife."

For a heartbeat she said nothing, as if the words needed time to reach her. Then her breath caught, a soft gasp slipping out before she covered her mouth with her fingers. Her eyes filled, not with tears of sorrow, but with a bright, trembling joy. When she finally spoke, her voice was barely above a whisper.

"You mean that?" she asked, searching his face for any hint of doubt.

He nodded once, steady and sure.

Tima let out a breath that turned into a laugh, half-shy and half-overwhelmed. She touched his cheek with both hands, her thumbs brushing lightly against his skin, and for a moment she simply looked at him, as if memorizing this version of him, the one who only weeks ago was uncertain about most things.

"Then tomorrow cannot come fast enough," she said, her smile blooming like sunrise.

They stood together as the moon rose, the noise of the camp swelling around them. Laughter rolled like a tide, prayers droned steadily, and hands beat time on empty water jars.

Later, as the stars reclaimed the sky, the camp gathered for a ceremony at the Tabernacle: a song of thanks, improvised but fierce, each tribe lending its own chorus. Gershom took Tima's hand and guide them to a place among the Levites, this time not at the fringe, with Tima by his side, they sat shoulder to shoulder with the others, his voice blending with the hundred more around him.

He saw Eliezer across the aisle, saw the nod of acknowledgment, the unspoken blessing. He felt Tima at his left, her shoulder pressing into his, her harmony threading through the melody like a scar that had healed over into something new.

As the last note faded, Gershom found himself smiling—not for his father, not for the memory of anything lost or regretted, but for the simple fact of being there, alive, unfinished, and, at peace with what he was.

He sang the final line a little louder, to feel it settle inside him.

And this time, the echo came back, whole and undivided.

Division of Lands

Weeks passed like a dream half-remembered, blurred at the edges, real only in the small evidences they left behind: the sun crawling higher by increments, the ash from Jericho's pyres long since scattered, the faces in the avenue replaced with new configurations of hope and fatigue. In that gentle vacuum, the marriage feast of Gershom and Tima was not an eruption but a flowering, a canopy of color and sound unfurling above the drab geometry of tents.

The avenue had been transformed, not by the hand of artisans but by the practical magic of women: old sailcloth dyed in improbable hues, lengths of blue and scarlet traded long ago from Tyre, a roof stitched from the best fragments and patched, where needed, with flour sacks too threadbare for bread. Strings of dried fruit and willow branches looped from pole to pole, their shadows dancing in the breeze like the ghosts of the wilderness. The musicians, placed at a respectful distance, played soft and insistent, flutes and hammered reeds, the rhythm kept on a battered goatskin stretched across a hollowed plank. The sound was not grand, but it was stubborn, refusing to be drowned out even by the laughter and the crush of bodies.

The feast was, by any standard, excessive. Baskets overflowed with smoked fish and salt-brined olives, the bread stacked in precarious pyramids that leaned against clay jars sweating with barley wine. Children wove through the throng, cheeks sticky with honey, their hands darting like minnows at any unguarded morsel. The men stood in clusters at the perimeter, talking politics and weather, their speech roughened by months of dust and disappointment. The women, who had done most of the work sat together, heads close, their laughter brittle with exhaustion but also, somehow, victorious.

At the center of it all was Gershom, his hair newly trimmed, his robe brightened with a sash of undyed linen. He wore the dazed, slightly hunted look of a man who had expected to die an obscure Levite and now found himself the object of community fascination. Tima, at his side, was luminous in a tunic dyed the deep green of tamarisk needles; her hair was braided back in a crown, studded with river pebbles and the tiniest possible bells, so that every movement sent a ripple of music into the air. She looked, if not happy, then at least resolved, and there was in her eyes a calm that made even the most persistent of the old gossips hesitate before whispering.

Eliezer was there, too, seated behind his brother, his own garments unadorned but his posture gave way to a rare ease. The old lines of rivalry had softened; he watched the proceedings with a kind of detached pride, a man who had finally accepted the limits of his own shadow.

It was well into the meal, after the first round of speeches, after the children's song and the blessing from the priest that Joshua rose. He did not clear his throat or demand silence; rather, the shift in the air was so sudden even the musicians played more softly, as if an unseen hand had dampened the room. The guests, sensing the arrival of a moment, turned as one toward the head table.

Joshua's face, so often unreadable, tonight held the ghost of a smile. He raised a cup, waited for the last stragglers to notice, then addressed them in a measured cadence that had become his signature.

"It is fitting," he said, "that we gather tonight to mark the union of two souls, and, through them, the union of many hopes. For years, we wandered as strangers in the world; tonight, we are not strangers to each other."

The people exhaled, the mood relaxing by degrees. Gershom felt the stare of every eye on him, and for the first time, he did mind being the focal point of discussion.

Joshua continued. "There will be more such feasts, in time. The land has not finished giving up its mysteries. Already, some among you speak of new cities, of vineyards where today there are only rocks. It falls to us, then, to decide not only how to live in the world, but how to become the kind of people who deserve it."

He let the words hang. A baby wailed at the far end of the avenue; a woman shushed it, the sound small and comforting.

"In the weeks to come," said Joshua, "we begin the division of land among the tribes. The work will be hard, and the decisions will not please all. But tonight, I ask your patience—for one more day, for one more request."

Here he turned, not to the company but directly to Gershom and Eliezer. "The sons of Moses," he said, and the phrase rang with an unexpected kindness. "The Lord did not set you over all Israel, as your father once feared. But he did set you among us, to bear witness and to remind us what the Law looks like, in the ordinary."

A murmur ran through the guests, a current of approval surprising even those who uttered it.

"To that end," said Joshua, "I am appointing you, both of you to assist in the recording and the setting of the new boundaries. The task is not only of lines and numbers, but of memory and judgment, of fairness and, above all, of the kind of patience your father showed every day of his life."

Gershom blinked. The room tilted, just a little. Eliezer gave a measured nod, as if testing the offer before taking it. Tima, for her part, squeezed Gershom's hand so tightly he thought the bones might fuse.

Joshua raised his cup again. "It is not leadership that I ask of you, but something harder: that you serve as witnesses. That you see the work through to its end, and that you tell the story when the rest of us are gone."

He drank. The guests did likewise, the noise swelling at once to fill the vacuum his words had left behind.

Gershom, still reeling, glanced at his brother. Eliezer's expression was unreadable, but within it lay a kind of challenge, a dare not to fail. He turned to Tima, and her eyes met his with such piercing clarity that, for an instant, he felt stripped bare.

A few seats down, one of the old warriors from Judah called out, "So! Will the sons of Moses redraw the river? Or rewrite the rules?" Laughter, warm and forgiving, rippled across the avenue.

Gershom found himself laughing, too. It was not the brittle, defensive sound he remembered from his childhood, but something freer, closer to delight. He looked at Tima, who had begun to clear plates in the way of women who have no time for ceremony. She leaned in, her lips at his ear.

"Don't disappoint them," she said, but the words were a

tease.

He reached for her hand, then stood, feeling the eyes of the room as a kind of lightness. He raised his own cup, empty but unnoticed, and said, "I will do as I am told. But only if Tima agrees to keep me from wandering off."

The line landed better than he had dared. Even Joshua smiled, this time with something like relief.

The musicians, sensing the moment, picked up the tempo. Tima, quick as a cat, pulled Gershom into the avenue, her hair scattering bells into the night. They danced, not well but without apology, the people clapping along in time. Children darted between their legs, the old men grumbling about knees and backs but grinning as they were cajoled to their feet.

Eliezer watched for a moment, then let himself be pulled into the fray by a trio of Levite girls, their laughter a rebuke to the gravity of the past months. For the first time, the avenue was not an encampment but a village, and the music was not a borrowed thing but their own.

Later, when the fire had burned down and the food was picked clean, Gershom sat by the tent, Tima's head on his shoulder, his eyes fixed on the patch of stars visible through the torn canopy. He did not think of Moses, or of the battles to come, or of the burden of judgment that had so often warped the air around him. He thought only of the wine pressed to Tima's lips, and of the strange, giddy sense that, for tonight at least, nothing was expected of him except to remember, to witness, and, if possible, to be happy.

He found that it was not impossible, after all.

Days later, the tent appointed for the boundary work was a lean structure, its walls pieced from whatever could be spared. An old cloth here, a stitched-together patchwork of animal skins there, every seam evidence of a compromise between permanence and the necessity to move on short notice. Inside, the table was a slab of unpolished cedar balanced atop a pair of overturned grain bins, its surface pitted with the scars of a hundred hasty meals and now, overlaid with a palimpsest of ink stains and the delicate dust of carbonized parchment.

Gershom and Eliezer sat across from each other, the apparatus of the work arrayed in careful rows: ink pots and reed pens, the scrolls of the census, a spool of braided twine to measure distances on the scale map. The tent flap had been staked wide to admit the morning sun, which threw long bars of light across the table, transforming each motelike particle into a brief, glowing filament before it vanished into shadow.

Their work had the rhythm of old habit, even if the context was new. Gershom unrolled a sheet, anchored it with two river pebbles, then traced the outline of the Jordan with a measured sweep of the pen. Eliezer, eyes narrowed in concentration, cross-checked the names against the tally: tribe, family, clan, the geometry of people distilled to the language of boundaries.

"South of Merom," Eliezer said, not looking up. "That's the line for Zebulun."

"Merom's changed its course," Gershom replied. "It runs three lengths west now. The marker at the old crossing is useless."

Eliezer grunted, the sound halfway between agreement and frustration. "Redraw it," he said. "The men from Zebulun can argue the point themselves when the time comes."

Gershom made the correction, careful not to smear the ink. He had always possessed a steadier hand than his brother, a skill he attributed less to talent than to an ability to let go of mistakes. Eliezer, by contrast, operated from a baseline of tension, every muscle tuned to the possibility of error.

They worked for a long time in silence, the only sounds the occasional creak of the table or the soft slap of a page as Eliezer turned it.

"You remember," Eliezer said, voice breaking the quiet with unexpected gentleness, "how Father would check every letter three times before he let us copy a scroll?"

Gershom smiled, a small, private gesture. "He made me redo the whole Torah section once, because I wrote the aleph in 'Adonai' a hair too narrow."

Eliezer allowed himself a laugh, the sound rare enough to seem like a borrowed thing. "I once watched him spend a whole afternoon on two lines. He said the Lord judged the Law by the care of its scribe. That each mark had to be a prayer by itself."

The memory settled between them, recalling the old alignment, the impossible standard, the strain of being watched.

"Mother thought he was mad for it," Gershom said, his tone light. "She always said his attention to detail was both his glory and his affliction."

Eliezer dipped his chin, "She said he could have ruled Egypt if he'd spent half as much effort understanding people."

The room felt warmer for the memory. They soon returned to the work, but now, when they spoke, the tension of a contest gave way to the matter-of-fact tone of craftsmen repairing a thing that had almost come apart. The boundaries came into focus, not as lines of division, but as the bones of a future in which both would have a hand, and perhaps they would remember the details, not as burdens, but as gifts.

They worked until the sun angled sharply through the tent flap, and the first of the day's visitors arrived with new maps, new numbers, new corrections to debate. Gershom poured fresh ink into the well, laid the next page with a firm palm, and wondered how many generations it would take for any of it to matter.

But for today, it was enough to mark the world as it was, and to do it in the company of a brother, the memory of a father, and the faint, persistent possibility of grace.

The weeks gathered themselves into a pattern, and in that repetition there was something resembling peace. At twilight, when the camp's heat leached away and the main avenue emptied of all but the night-haunters and the desperate, Gershom and Eliezer would retreat to the family tent. It was the one luxury untouched by war and judgment, never unhouseable. There, Tima laid out the evening's meal on a woven mat, her hands deft with the old motions, the flick of a knife or the coiling of a bread round into something almost ceremonial.

The tent, repaired so many times it was more patch than original fabric, exuded a comfort that no new construction could hope to match. Each repair was the story of a storm weathered, a child's mistake forgiven, a moment of clumsiness that, in the retelling, became part of the mythos of the family. On these nights, they sat cross-legged, knees touching, their heads bent over a common bowl of barley or the dried fruit Tima favored. Oil lamps, fashioned from clay scavenged at Jericho, lit the inside with a subdued, golden warmth that made even the most ordinary meal look like a feast staged for the eyes of heaven.

The rhythm of their conversation matched the gentle cadence of the meal: pauses broken by bursts of memory, laughter bearing traces of old battles but not their bite. Tima joined them sometimes, settling herself between the brothers with the easy grace of someone who had learned, early, how to enter a male space without apologizing for it.

On one such evening, as dusk leaned against the tent walls and the scent of roasting lentils hung sweet and heavy, Eliezer placed his cup down and said, with a hesitation it nearly faltered, "You remember the law about the inheritance of the sojourner?"

Gershom looked up, his hand stilling on the crust of bread he'd been about to tear. "Which part?"

"The one that says a sojourner may dwell among us but has no share in the land. Only a place in the city."

Tima's eyes flicked from one to the other, but she did not interrupt.

Gershom chewed the thought, then answered. "It's a matter of borders. The land is not ours to divide without permission. We are its tenants, not its owners."

Eliezer nodded, but his brow stayed furrowed. "I read it today, three times. I still don't know if I agree. After everything, after Gibeon and all that, it feels... incomplete."

Tima, kneeling by the brazier, said softly, "Maybe it's not meant to be complete. Maybe it's meant to make you ask."

Eliezer looked at her, then at Gershom, as if seeing the same answer reflected back twice, from different angles.

"I've always wondered," Eliezer admitted, "if the Law was less about rules, and more about reminding us that nothing ever fits perfectly. That the gaps are what keep us honest."

Tima smiled, the line of her mouth softened by the lamp's glow. "I think your father would have argued both sides, just to make sure the question stayed alive."

The thought lingered, a pleasant dissonance that neither

brother rushed to resolve.

After a while, as the meal thinned and the conversation ebbed, Gershom said, "You know, I used to think you hated me. Or at least, the part of me that refused to fall in line."

Eliezer laughed, the sound more genuine than any they'd shared since childhood. "I did. Sometimes I still do. But I envy it more, now. I see how you can live with uncertainty. I still can't, not really. Not for long."

Gershom shrugged, his smile lopsided. "It's not a skill. When you doubt everything long enough, you get used to the company.."

Tima reached across the mat and laid a hand on Gershom's wrist, the gesture light but unambiguous. "You could have left," she said. "After the first round of judgments. After your father died. But you didn't."

"I thought about it," Gershom confessed. "But the world outside is often more of the same, with fewer people who remember your name."

Tima turned to Eliezer. "And you? Did you ever think of leaving?"

He shook his head, quick and certain. "I always thought I'd become the Law, if I only studied it hard enough. That I'd be the fixed point when everything else was shifting." He looked at Gershom, then Tima. "Turns out, I like the shifting. At least when I don't have to do it alone."

They sat like that for a long time, the three of them, the tent a small ark bobbing in the current of the camp's restlessness. Outside, the avenue had gone dark, save for the erratic flare of a torch or the laughter of the women who took the late water-drawing shift. Inside, there was only the rhythm of their breath, the ebb and flow of small talk, the easy quiet of people who had finally, after much trial, earned the right to occupy the same space without fear of collapse.

At the end of the meal, Eliezer rolled onto his back, hands folded across his chest, and said, "When we were boys, I used to dream that one day we'd be neighbors. That our tents would face each other, and we'd spend the evenings trading stories about how much better we'd done than the other."

Gershom smiled. "You never told me that."

"I thought it was childish," Eliezer said. "But now I think maybe it was the only thing I ever wanted."

Gershom looked at Tima, who nodded, her eyes shining with something that was not tears but could have been. He lay back as well, and together they watched the lamp's flicker ripple across the canvas roof, the patterns shifting with the breeze. In that silence lay the truth that nothing, old wounds or ancient law, was ever permanent.

They would work together again tomorrow, dividing the land, arguing the boundaries, marking the world as best they could. But tonight, they were simply Gershom, Eliezer, and Tima, bound by the gravity of shared bread and the stubborn framework of a family rebuilding from within.

The day of the formal ceremony arrived with the hush of expectation: no wind, no birdsong, only the murmur of a thousand men and women arrayed around the Tabernacle. The structure, its skins newly stretched and its cords re-tied, rose from the dust like a promise kept. In front of it, the tribes assembled by family and by seniority, each man in his appointed place, the effect more like thought in formation than chaos, a mind arranging itself for a final, clarifying argument.

Joshua stood at the center, flanked by the priestly caste, his garb perfectly plain, his hair combed flat by water and intention. The Levites gathered in their own block, a monochrome band distinguished only by the occasional child peering out from behind an uncle's leg. Gershom and Eliezer stood together, and if there was a difference from all the other assemblies of their childhood, it was that both seemed hesitant to step forward first. They were content to wait, to let the world come to them at its own measured pace.

The ceremony was more recitation than spectacle, a deliberate, measured walk through every article of allocation: which city for which clan, the boundaries of pastureland, the rotation of sacred duties. The scroll Joshua read from was nearly as long as he was tall, and he unspooled it with the care of a man who felt the gravity of each syllable. The names of the cities were intoned in the order they had been conquered, each paired with its new stewards: "Kedesh, for the sons of Gershon; Shechem, for the Kohathites; Hebron, for the descendants of Aaron..." And so on, the list a drumbeat of inheritance.

There were no protests, no interruptions. The silence of the crowd was complete, almost reverent, the only punctuation a collective shifting of feet or the dry cough of an elder who had outlived his patience. When the allocations ended, Joshua rolled up the scroll, passed it to the high priest, and signaled for the assembly to disperse. It was over in under an hour, but the recollection of it felt as though it would last the rest of their lives.

Afterward, as the people melted into smaller, more intimate knots, Joshua found Gershom standing outside the shade of the Tabernacle's awning. He approached alone, a courtesy that did not go unnoticed by those who had come to expect the relentless choreography of public leadership.

"Walk with me," Joshua said, his voice gentle enough to

make the request an invitation rather than a command.

They moved away from the avenue, through the narrow lanes of tents and empty cooking fires, past children playing at swords with sticks, their laughter bright and oblivious. For a while, neither spoke; Gershom waited, the old urge to fill silences now replaced by a willingness to let them breathe.

Finally, Joshua said, "You understand the Law differently than your father did."

Gershom looked at him, unsure if this was accusation or compliment.

Joshua smiled, reading the question. "I do not mean lesser. Just different. Your father saw it as a wall: high, unbreakable, a thing to keep the chaos at bay. You see it as... what? A path?"

Gershom considered. "Sometimes it feels like a riddle. Or a trap. But most days, I think of it as a net, something that holds together what would otherwise unravel."

Joshua nodded. "There are those who fear that difference. But I do not. The Law needs its defenders, yes. But it also needs those who can teach it to men who do not know its music. Or who, knowing it, cannot sing the tune."

He stopped, placed a hand on Gershom's back, an unexpected presence, warm and solid. "There are cities that need teachers. Men who can explain not only the rules, but the reasons. Who can make the children believe in the stories, even when the miracles run out."

Gershom swallowed, the implication settling on his tongue like a drop of cold water.

"You want me to teach."

Joshua did not hesitate. "I want you to remind them that the Law is not a cage, but a promise. That it can make men better, even if it sometimes fails to make them happy."

He released Gershom, stepped back, and let the silence hang.

"I am not my father, and I'm not a leader as is evident," Gershom said, the admission softer than he expected.

Joshua's smile deepened. "That is why I am asking."

As they turned back toward the avenue, and Joshua went his own way, Gershom caught sight of Tima. Her hair was pulled back in a single braid, and her eyes shone with quiet satisfaction, the kind a person wears when they have watched an argument resolve without spilling into ruin. She walked to him, a little ahead of the others, and when she reached his side, she slipped her arm into his as if she had been doing so for years.

"Good news I hope?" she asked.

"I have been conscripted to teach," Gershom replied, dead-pan.

Tima grinned. "You'll make a poor soldier. But perhaps a fair teacher."

They walked together, the evening drawing in around them, the sky painted with the pink and ochre stripes of a day that had managed, somehow, to deliver on its promises.

Later, as dusk settled over the camp and the lamps lit up one by one in the rows of tents, Gershom stood outside his own, a small scroll of statutes in his hand. He read by the last of the light, his posture easy, the knot between his shoulders finally slackened by the simple act of being wanted for what he was, not what he was meant to be.

Tima called to him from inside. Eliezer was there, too, already arguing the finer points of a passage he'd barely finished reading. Gershom smiled, rolled the scroll closed, took a deep breath and smiled before he ducked inside, the world behind him fading to a pleasant, manageable hum.

Joshua's Farewell

The day announced its arrival long before sunrise, a solemn quiet pressed against the thin pale sky, broken only by the hammers and the men's calls as they prepared Gilgal for a gathering greater than any since the conquest of Jericho. The city, if that is what the encampment had become, sprawled in a geometry that defied logic but not the practical needs of food, shelter, and gossip. The smell of roasting millet and mutton hung over the avenue, thickening the air, drawing even the late risers to their morning tasks.

Gershom walked in measured steps, the rolling pace of a man projecting patience, though his muscles slightly tense with what awaited him. At his left hand, Tima guided the smaller of their children, a girl of perhaps five, sharp-eyed and silent except for the occasional yawn that threatened to fold her in half. At his right, a boy, not yet eight, moved with the restless energy of one who has only recently discovered the world is not designed to prevent him from running at full tilt. They made a mismatched parade: the son of Moses, graying at the temples but upright as a poplar; the wife with the hands of a baker and the eyes of a mathematician; the children, each the sum and remainder of their improbable union.

They settled near the boundary of the great field, where the earth lifted slightly, granting a view of the unfolding scene. Already, the avenue below was clogged with men in every conceivable configuration of tribal finery: the Reubenites with their gold-stitched sashes, the Benjaminites in narrow bands of indigo, the Levites (Gershom's own people, though he had long ago ceased to think of them as kin) in a washed-out white that seemed both practical and, given the company, oddly flamboyant. The air teemed with the murmurs and elbowing of men who had not seen each other since the last war or the last harvest.

Gershom scanned the people, his eyes settling at last on the small knot of priests assembling near the makeshift dais that had been constructed at the center of the field. Eliezer stood among them, taller than most, his ceremonial raiment so new the creases had not yet learned to relax. There was in his posture a calculated restraint—a man who understood both the necessity of spectacle and the risk of overplaying it. Their eyes met briefly, a flicker of acknowledgment that held the unspoken text of decades: rivalry, resentment, the gradual accretion of respect. Gershom raised his chin in greeting; Eliezer returned it, then turned his attention to the knot of elders now moving up the steps to the platform.

The Tabernacle formed the backdrop, skins freshly stretched and poles capped in newly-burnished bronze. Through the open curtain the Ark gleamed, its gold catching the morning sun so fiercely it swallowed the light. Around it, Levite guards stood in two concentric rings: the inner rigid with proximity, the outer looser, as though certain no one would risk defiance under so many watching eyes.

Tima surveyed the assembly, then nudged Gershom with a deliberate, practiced motion. "You think he'll actually say it this time?" she murmured, her voice pitched soft enough to avoid neighboring ears.

Gershom smiled, the expression more a folding of the lips than a true display of feeling. "He'll say it, if only to make certain we're listening."

"And will you?"

He glanced at her, then at the children, who had begun to amuse themselves by tracing patterns in the dust with the soles of their sandals. "I think that's the point," he said, "to be reminded."

A ram's horn sounded from the dais, not the shrill wail used for battle but a measured, almost lyrical note that coaxed the people to stillness. The heads of each tribe, arrayed in a deliberate hierarchy, gathered at the front, their faces arranged in what they imagined to be expressions of grave responsibility. The old man Joshua emerged from behind the curtain with careful steps, a staff in his right hand and a cloak of undyed wool thrown over his shoulders. The years had carved their signatures in the planes of his face, with deep furrows at the brow and a mouth permanently bracketed by lines of endurance, yet his eyes, when he looked out over the camp, were bright and unyielding.

He did not ascend the dais at once. He stopped at the threshold, letting the calm gather, letting every man, woman, and child see the effort it cost him to stand so straight, so unbroken by all that had come before.

"My brothers," he began, his voice neither booming nor grandiose, but tuned to a frequency which resonated in the chest before it registered in the ears, "my time is nearly finished. I have served as your witness and your judge, but now the land is yours to keep or to lose, according to your faithfulness."

There was a lull, then a shuffling of feet as the people attuned themselves to the gravity of what was unfolding.

"Many of you remember the first crossing," Joshua continued, "when the Jordan stood up in a heap, and we walked through on dry ground. Some of you remember Egypt, and the plagues, and the night when the Lord passed through and spared only those who had marked their door." He let this hang, and a few heads nodded, some out of memory, some out of reverence, some perhaps to be seen. "We have seen walls fall, kings tremble, the impossible made ordinary. But it is not the miracles that keep us. It is not the victories, or the punishments. It is only this: that we serve the Lord, and not ourselves."

The line landed with a soft impact, rippling out through the assembly in concentric circles of comprehension and resistance.

Gershom watched Eliezer, who stood utterly motionless, his eyes fixed on the old man. He wondered, for the first time in years, whether his brother still believed in the simple version of the story—the one in which obedience led to blessing, disobedience to curse. Or whether, like Gershom, he had come to suspect that the truth was both more complicated and less satisfying.

"Choose this day," Joshua said, the staff rising in his hand, "whom you will serve. As for me and my house, we will serve the Lord."

The phrase was echoed at once, first by the priests, then the elders, then, in a ragged but growing chorus, by the men arrayed on the field. Even the children, sensing the moment, abandoned their dust games and joined in the refrain, their voices high and unschooled but urgent.

Tima leaned in, her shoulder pressing against Gershom's. "You could have been up there, you know," she whispered.

He shook his head. "No. I could only ever be here, watching."

She smiled, the line of her mouth softening. "I think it's better, sometimes, not to be the center."

At that, their daughter tugged at Tima's garment, her face upturned. "Can we go to the river? The other mothers are already there."

Tima nodded, shot Gershom a look that said, This is your legacy, too, and shepherded the children away from the gathering, leaving Gershom alone with the echo of Joshua's words and the resuming hum of the assembly as the speech dissolved into a series of administrative announcements: the designation of cities of refuge, the appointment of new judges, the ritual passing of torches that, while solemn, was also riddled with the absurdities and politics of every human institution ever invented.

Gershom watched from his post on the hill as the men below fell back into their old patterns: arguing, boasting, forming new alliances before the echo of the previous ones had faded. He saw Eliezer, now surrounded by the other priests, fielding questions and handshakes, his smile practiced but not entirely insincere. He saw, too, the Gibeonites, standing a little apart, their faces unreadable, a study in the art of occupying space while pretending not to need it.

He let his attention drift to the Tabernacle, the Ark's gold still catching the sunlight. It occurred to him that, for all the ceremony and all the words, nothing ever really changed. The Law endured, but it endured as much by being questioned as by being obeyed. The story was not one of conquest, or even of faith, but of persistence, of men and women who, lacking miracles, made do with memory.

He stood a long while, the morning fading into afternoon, the sounds on the field thinning as men were called away to other duties. When at last he turned to go, he found himself looking forward not to the next gathering or the endless debates that would surely follow. His thoughts turned to the river, where Tima and the children would be waiting, and where, if he hurried, he might still catch them before they walked home without him.

Gershom had made it halfway down the rise when he heard his name being called out, not the flattened, common version but the one sharpened by formality and intent.

He turned. The man who stood before him was not a functionary or scribe, but one of Joshua's own, a face he remembered from the old councils and the long, sleepless nights before Jericho. "The master requests your presence," the man said. "Both you and the priest Eliezer, at once."

Gershom came upon Eliezer as the people dispersed, already speaking intently with a group of Levites. He signaled, a sharp tilt of the chin, and Eliezer extracted himself, approached with the wary, deliberate pace of a man called too often to judgment.

"Is it urgent?" Eliezer asked, when they were within earshot.

"It is final," said the messenger, and for once there was no exaggeration in the phrase.

They followed the man through the narrow arteries of the camp, past the lamp-lit faces of women preparing the evening meal, past the old men who lingered outside their tents to listen for news. The way narrowed, then widened again, then turned abruptly into the small compound reserved for the assembly's leaders. The tent was plain, but its position, set apart with the entrance facing east, marked it as a place of reckoning.

Inside, the air was thick with the smell of beeswax and olive oil. Three lamps burned at different heights, throwing restless shadows on the walls and pooling their light around a low table heaped with scrolls and fragments of reed. At the rear, a pallet was made up with meticulous care, and beside it, a wooden chest stood open, exposing its contents: a folded tunic, a set of tablets, a clutch of river stones blackened by age and handling.

Joshua waited in the center of the room, seated not on a bench but on a low stool, his staff braced across his knees. He did not rise when the brothers entered, but he lifted his chin in greeting, the gesture spare and unadorned.

"You may leave us," he said to the attendant, who bowed and withdrew without a sound.

For a moment, no one spoke. The only noise was the soft, uneven draw of Joshua's breath, a sound like sand being sieved through a coarse screen. Eliezer looked at Gershom, his face a mask of unpreparedness, then cleared his throat.

"You summoned us," he said, the words heavier than intended.

Joshua smiled, the expression slow and deliberate. "You have always been impatient, Eliezer," he said. "Even as a boy, you wanted the answer before the question was finished."

He turned his gaze to Gershom. "And you, always the opposite—waiting so long to speak that the conversation had already ended."

The judgment, if it was meant as such, landed with the weight of a compliment.

Joshua gripped the staff, adjusted it so it stood upright between his knees. "I will not keep you long," he said. "But there are things I have carried too long, things that should not go with me into the grave."

He let his eyes linger on the lamps, as if gathering strength from their pooled light.

"I knew your father better than most," Joshua began, his voice softer now, a shade above the murmur of the lamps. "Not as a prophet, not even as a leader. As a man." He glanced at Eliezer, then back to Gershom. "Did you know that, in Midian, your father was once lost for three days trying to count sheep?"

Eliezer blinked. "Sheep?"

Joshua nodded. "He had a flock. Not a large one, but more than he had ever managed in Egypt. He was proud, and so he would not ask for help. He left the fold to chase a straggler, and when he looked back, the land had erased every sign of his passing. He wandered in circles until the third morning, when he stumbled back into camp, lips cracked and voice gone. He never spoke of it, but he could not look at a sheep again without a certain dread."

Gershom felt a smile begin, but it faded into something more complex, a mix of embarrassment and a peculiar gratitude.

Joshua continued: "When the Lord called him to Pharaoh, your father was so terrified of stammering that he spent whole nights reciting his words to the rocks. Sometimes, I would wake and hear him arguing with a stone as if it were a king. He would lose the argument, every time, and begin again."

Eliezer laughed, a brief, incredulous bark. "You're making this up."

"I am not," Joshua said, and for a moment he was the boy again, the apprentice sent to fetch water while the elders debated strategy. "He did not want to lead. He only wanted to be left alone with the Law."

The lamps flickered, and for a moment the creases in Joshua's face deepened, the shadows gathering at his eyes.

"He never told us," Gershom said, the words small and uncertain.

"Of course not," Joshua replied. "What father tells his sons the truth of his fear?"

He let the question settle, then adjusted his stance, wincing as he did so. The effort cost him, and when he spoke again, his voice was thinner, more translucent.

"When your father died, there were many who expected you, both of you, to take up his place. Some even hoped you would challenge me, make a contest of it."

Gershom watched Eliezer, who stiffened at the words, his hands tightening in his sleeves.

"I feared it, at first," Joshua admitted. "I am not your father. I am not even myself, most days. But you did not challenge. You served. Quietly, faithfully. You made yourselves small, so that the Law could be large. I do not think I ever thanked you for that."

Eliezer's mouth twisted, the conflict plain on his face. Gershom, for his part, felt nothing so much as relief, relief that there was at least one thing he had managed not to break.

Joshua leaned forward, his hands trembling as he reached for the container beside the pallet. He drew out a small wooden box, plain except for the ring of soot around the rim of the lid.

"This is the last thing your father gave me," he said. "It is not gold, or a miracle. Just a stone. He said it came from the Nile, that he picked it up on the morning of the exodus. He carried it all his life, as a reminder that nothing, not even a river, could hold a man if the Lord had other plans."

He opened the box, revealing a single black stone, polished

by time and touch.

"He would want you to have it," Joshua said, and held it out in his cupped palm.

Gershom hesitated, then took the stone, feeling the unexpected warmth of it, the smoothness worn into it by years of worry or hope. He closed his fist around it, the action both intimate and irrevocable.

Joshua sagged back onto the stool, his energy spent. For a long moment, the three men sat without speaking, the only sound the steady, persistent tick of oil in the lamps.

"It has been an honor," Joshua said, at last, "to serve with you. To serve your father. And to see that the Law is not a monument, but a living thing. I am old. I am finished. But I would not change my life, even if it meant another forty years in the wilderness."

He let the words stand, then gestured toward the entrance. "You may go. The night is for your families, not for old men."

Eliezer stood at once, his face turned away, the tears raw and unhidden. Gershom lingered, wanting to say something, to express the gratitude that hovered out of reach. In the end, he simply bowed, the movement stiff and awkward, and let himself be led into the coolness of the open air.

They walked together for a time, saying nothing. The stone rested in Gershom's palm, solid and persuasive. Above them, the stars had begun to multiply, the avenue slowly emptying as men found their way home. Eliezer stopped, wiped his eyes with the back of his hand, then looked at Gershom.

"Did you know he hated sheep?"

Gershom smiled, the laugh breaking from him before he could stop it. "No. But it makes sense, somehow."

They stood in the avenue, two men made suddenly small by

the knowledge of how little it took to tip the world from legend into history. The sounds of the day replaced the crick of sandals on hard-packed earth. Gershom and Eliezer walked together, not side by side but in that staggered alignment peculiar to men unused to sharing the same path.

At first, both were silent for a moment. Gershom turned the stone over in his hand, its heft surprising, the surface cold and oddly greasy from decades of skin and oil. Eliezer kept his arms folded, his posture hunched forward, moving with a pace that suggested reluctance rather than fatigue. The air here smelled not of spice and lamp smoke, but of wild onion, of mown grass, and of the vibrant, living river that curved out of sight to the west.

They reached the top together. Below, the plain stretched wide, darkness settling into every gully and crease, the hills of Canaan a pale, improbable blue against the last line of sky. The land promised to them, the land that had cost so much, lay perfectly still, as if holding its breath.

"Do you think he's dying?" Eliezer said, after a time.

Gershom rolled the stone in his palm, hesitated, then nodded. "If not tonight, then soon."

"He seemed at peace with it." Eliezer sat, folding his legs, the movement abrupt but somehow final. "I never thought I would envy a man for that."

Gershom joined him, and together they looked out over the plain. From here, the camp was impossibly small, a grid of hope clinging to the border of an unfinished world.

After a while, Eliezer spoke again. "When I was a boy, I thought you would be the one to lead Israel. Not Joshua. Not anyone else."

Gershom laughed, the sound escaping before he could stop

it. "You hated me for it."

"Yes," Eliezer admitted, "and I hated you more when you refused. I thought you were a coward. Or that you thought it was beneath you."

He picked up a pebble and flicked it down the slope, watched as it vanished out of sight. "But now I think maybe you were the only one who understood the cost."

A breeze stirred, carrying with it the faint, overlapping shouts of children playing near the tents, their games undimmed by any awareness of history or loss.

"It's not that I didn't want to lead," Gershom said, and the words surprised even him. "I just wanted to matter. To be… necessary."

Eliezer looked at him, his face shadowed but the old edge gone. "Do you remember Mother's hands? The way she could quiet anything, sheep, children, even Father, simply by holding them?"

Gershom nodded. "She said that to lead was to carry, not to command."

Eliezer smiled. "She was right. She always was. I wish she could see us now."

They sat in stillness for a time, each turning the new knowledge of the other like a stone between their hands.

"Joshua gave me this," Gershom said at last, holding out the black river stone. "He said Father carried it from Egypt."

Eliezer touched it, ran his thumb across the polished face. "It's a rock," he said, but the words were gentle.

"That's what I thought, too," Gershom replied. "But then I remembered the night before Father told us he had to leave. Do you remember what he said to us?"

Eliezer shook his head.

"He said, 'Everything ends. Even the wilderness. Especially the wilderness.' And then he laughed, as if it was a joke."

Eliezer's smile flickered, then steadied. "Maybe it was."

Behind them, a patter of running feet, then Tima's voice—low, conspiratorial: "There you are. I was about to send out a search party."

She approached, the two children in tow. The boy barreled ahead, launching himself into Gershom's lap, heedless of the presence of his uncle or the seriousness of the moment. The girl hung back, watching with the careful caution of someone who had already learned the cost of being too forward.

Gershom lifted his son into his arms, the act effortless and astonishingly familiar. The boy reached for the stone at once, his fingers curling around it, feeling its smoothness and heft.

"Can I keep it?" he asked, eyes wide.

"Someday," Gershom said. "When you're ready."

The boy frowned, unsatisfied, but then glimpsed the sun setting behind the distant hills and lost all interest in arguments over inheritance.

Tima settled beside them, her hair loose now, the ends catching the faintest shimmer of light. She said nothing, simply folded her legs and watched the sky deepen into a wash of remarkable colors as the sun slipped away.

The girl eased in beside Eliezer, who offered her a place without comment. For a while, the family sat that way, five small bodies at the rim of a continent, none of them speaking, all of them held together by the gravity of the thing that lingered in the dark.

Eventually, Eliezer spoke. "He's going to die soon," he said, not looking at Gershom but at the horizon, where the blue had finally given way to black.

"Yes," said Gershom. "But the story won't."

Tima smiled, her hand resting on Gershom's knee. "That's what matters, isn't it?"

Gershom nodded. "It is now."

He looked down at the boy, at the girl, at Tima's hand, at the stone that rested between his own fingers and those of his son. He felt the old envy, the old failure, dissolve into something weightless, something almost kind.

Reflective Journey

Gershom parted the heavy curtain and ducked inside, the tent's interior already a balm after the harsh flare of the sun beyond. The air hung with the twin scents of lamp oil and baked earth, a combination so familiar it was now a comfort. Within, the home was nothing remarkable, though to Gershom it was the very geometry of peace: three woven rugs layered over bare sand, the largest threadbare and patched with darker wool at the edges, the next a child's project, the third so thin it served only to catch the grit from their feet. The small wooden table by the south wall held a neat stack of scrolls, their edges straight as a scribe's ruling, a clay lamp casting its pool of trembling light exactly in the middle. On a shelf above, a handful of river stones, trophies or keepsakes he could never decide, kept silent vigil over the comings and goings of the tent's inhabitants.

A soft murmur rose from the next partition, then the regular shuffle of sandals. Then the curtain parted and both children appeared at once: the boy leading, his face smeared with the black from burnt olive seeds, the girl trailing with a look of wild exasperation.

"He's taken the charcoal for his eyes," she complained, as though this were a capital offense.

Gershom crooked a finger. "Come here," he said, and the

boy obeyed, hunched as if expecting a blow that would never come.

He lowered himself before the child, his body protesting the effort. "Why the war paint?"

The boy grinned, unfazed by his own guilt. "To scare the sons of Levi," he said, as if this were self-evident.

"It will not work," said Gershom, and reached out to rub the charcoal from the boy's cheek, leaving behind only a stubborn shadow. "But go, play until sunset, and bring your sister with you. She is to return unharmed and unpainted."

The girl gave a sly, conspiratorial smile, then seized her brother's hand and pulled him out, their laughter rising in quick staccato as they tumbled into the blue of early dusk.

Gershom straightened, the ache in his legs a steady echo, and turned back to the middle of the room. He let out a measured breath and settled himself on the low wooden stool by the table. He closed his eyes, long enough to calm the whirring in his mind, and felt the world contract to the gentle pulse of the oil lamp and the muffled sounds of the world playing out beyond the tents.

He opened his eyes again to find Tima standing at the partition, the curtain draped loosely in her hand. She had a way of appearing without sound, and yet the entire space shifted toward her in a gentle tilt as she entered. Her hair was pulled back as she always had, shot with gray now, but her eyes had not lost the clarity that, years before, had so often made him feel naked and found-out. She wore her working garment, cinched with a belt so old the threads had taken on the color of every food ever spilled on it, and her hands, strong with the long, spidery fingers of a woman born to knead, were dusted with flour.

She regarded him for a moment before moving into his lap, folding herself there with a fluid grace despite her years. Gershom adjusted to make room, his body yielding to her as it always had. She let her head rest on his shoulder, her cheek against the line of his collarbone.

He kissed the top of her hair, the action automatic and, even after all this time, still slightly daring. "You smell like bread," he said.

She smiled into his neck. "And you smell like old sheep."

"Better than new sheep," he replied, and she laughed, the sound small but genuine.

They sat like that for a while, the stillness so full that it hardly deserved the name. Tima traced the line of his jaw with her thumb, deliberate and careful. The touch made him shiver, a reaction he could never suppress.

"I have been thinking," he said, "about the old days. About the way I used to worry that nothing I did would ever measure up to the men who came before me."

She drew back, just enough to meet his eyes. Her face was still and composed, but her eyes sparkled with something both knowing and amused.

"And now?" she asked.

"Now," said Gershom, "I am too tired to care."

She snorted, the sound almost undignified. "You are not tired," she said. "You are content. There is a difference."

He let the words settle, then reached up to cradle her cheek. "I could never have done any of this without you," he said, the confession so raw that he had to look away from her eyes as he uttered it.

She held his chin, turning his face back to hers. "I know," she said, "but I also know you would have tried. And you would have failed, magnificently."

He smiled. "You have always been good at the truth."

She ran her hands over the planes of his face, stopping at the corners of his mouth as though to confirm the presence of a smile. "You remember our first winter in the camp together?" she said, her voice lowered to the register reserved for secrets.

He did. The valley had been lashed for weeks, the tents collapsing under the weight of rain and the certainty that none of them would survive until spring. Tima had managed to keep their small patch of world together, weaving and reweaving the torn fabric, scrounging for anything that would burn, stitching shut the wounds of every fool who thought they were immune to cold or steel. He remembered the nights when the whole camp curled inward, waiting for death, and how Tima's joy had, impossibly, held the dark back.

"You saved me," he said.

She brushed a lock of hair from his brow, the gesture both maternal and tenderly intimate. "I only kept you warm," she replied. "You did the rest."

They remained still for a time. The lamp's flame flickered and then steadied, a single insect circling in the halo of light before vanishing into the upper reaches of the tent.

"When the men speak of you," Tima said, her lips near his ear, "they say you are stubborn. That you are unhurried to anger and quick to forgive. They think it makes you weak."

Gershom shrugged, his hands settling at her waist. "Perhaps it does."

She shook her head. "They do not understand. Mercy is a strength only the strong can afford."

He considered this, then nodded. "You have always been my voice of judgment."

"No," she said, almost fierce. "Only your voice of sense."

They laughed together, the sound rising and falling like the sway of the trees around them.

The light from the lamp trembled again, painting the inside of the tent with shifting patterns. Tima stood, then pulled him to his feet. They stood near, their bodies almost but not quite touching, and for a moment the years, the scars, and the burden of legacy fell away, leaving only the raw, unvarnished fact of their union.

He reached for her hand, and she took it, her grip as sure as the day she had first taken it on the far side of the river.

"Promise me," she said, "that when the time comes, you will not let the world make you hard."

He hesitated, then squeezed her hand. "I promise. But only if you do the same."

She smiled, and it was the same smile that had undone him from the start.

From the camp, the children's sounds rose again, a shout followed by a burst of joy.

Within the tent, the air was warm, the oil lamp burning lower but still holding its ground against the night. Gershom let himself be drawn toward the cot, the world beyond the tent fading until only Tima and the soft rhythm of their shared breath remained.

They lay together, not as conquerors or teachers or heirs, but as two bodies with nothing left to prove.

At length, Tima brushed her lips against his and whispered, "We are as one."

He smiled and allowed the muscles of his face slackening.

Right before night seized the camp, Gershom slipped from the tent. The air beyond the tents was a study in stillness, its coolness settling over the rows of dwellings and making the ordinary world new again. He lingered at the threshold, breathing in the fresh air.

He moved through the encampment, sandals brushing the compacted earth, each pace carrying him further from the warmth of home and deeper into the stillness that settled when the last child had been called into the tent. He wandered the familiar paths, past the Levite quarters, past the water jars lined up for morning, past the refuse pit where two goats argued in muffled urgency over a cabbage leaf left too long in the sun. Every landmark was both changed and unchanged.

He did not know where he was headed until his feet brought him to the boundary of the camp, where the ground sloped gently toward the river. There, arranged in a precise and patient circle, stood the stones of remembrance, the ones the elders had retrieved from the riverbed when the nation first crossed into Canaan. They were notched and pitted by years of weather, the edges dulled by sun and by the hands of curious children who could not resist the urge to measure against the past.

Gershom approached, his pace slowing as he neared the ring of stones. He stood for a long time, caught between being fully within them and drifting beyond their bounds, his arms folded and his breath rising in a pale plume in the chill.

The stones were not grand, nor were they uniform. Some rose to the height of a man's hip, others barely reached his knee. Moss grew in the cracks where the morning dew lingered, and at the base of one was a pile of what looked like children's offerings: a broken toy, a feather, a sprig of wild rosemary tied in a knot.

He reached into his tunic and drew out the black river stone, the one Joshua had given him in the final days before his death. He turned it in his palm, tracing the familiar, greasy smoothness, its heft exactly as he remembered. He had kept it for years, letting it drift from hand to pocket to the bottom of a pack, always holding on to it but never quite deciding what to do with it.

Tonight, it felt heavier than ever.

He knelt at the largest stone, the one that bore the faintest of carvings: two parallel lines, notched at intervals, as if the man who marked it had been interrupted and never returned to finish. He gripped the stone tightly, as though releasing it would cost him something essential.

He closed his eyes and tried to pray. For a long time, nothing came. His mind chased its old circuits, always returning to the image of his father, to the stories of greatness and failure that had defined the contours of his youth. The shame of not being enough, the terror of being too much, the sick, familiar envy of men who wanted only to be left alone and yet were tasked with the fate of a people.

But the longer he stayed, the more those feelings melted, their edges rounded by the chill in the air, at last, no one expected anything from him. He found himself thinking not of Moses or even of Joshua, but of Zipporah, her hands callused from years of work, her irreverent, unbreakable joy, her way of turning every rule into a challenge and every responsibility into a dare.

He remembered how, as a child, he had once broken a neighbor's tool and lied about it, the guilt eating him alive until Zipporah found him curled behind the tent, fists clenched and eyes swollen from shame. She had not scolded him. She sat beside him in the dirt, giving him space until he was ready to speak.

When at last he confessed, she nodded, as if this were only the first, necessary act in a much larger story.

"Guilt is the stone in your shoe," she said. "It slows you, but it also keeps you honest about where you've been. The trick is not to let it make you stop walking."

He had never forgotten those words.

He let his fingers wander the cold surface of the memorial, then bowed his forehead to the stone. All was silent except for the river, a ceaseless mutter. It was not the voice of God, and it was not a summons to anything greater than the moment. It was only water, and history, and the passage that had changed everything.

He let the words rise into the air, though they were as much for his own sake as for any unseen listener. "I have spent my life trying not to be you," he said, unsure whether he meant Moses, the men who came after him, or the entire notion of inheritance.

He lingered, half-expecting an answer. But the stones said nothing, offering only their stillness and the reminder that, whatever they were meant to commemorate, they had endured.

He opened his palm and stared at the black stone. It was ordinary, unremarkable, and yet it was his now, in a way nothing had been before.

"Thank you," he whispered, to no one in particular. "For the burden. For the freedom."

He rose, brushed the dust from his garments, and tucked the stone back into his tunic.

He lingered a moment more, then turned toward the camp, toward the thin, golden line where the first lamps of night already begin to blink into being.

As he moved forward, the heaviness inside him lifted, giving way to something lighter, if not simpler. The world ahead remained uncertain, but he now knew he could step into it without apology or regret.

The air stirred, rattling the tents and carrying with it the faintest, familiar scent of both fragrances and burning oil. He made his way home, his steps unhurried, the stone in his pocket a solemn task he was, at last, prepared to carry.

Afterword

Thank you for taking the time to journey through this story, one woven against the vast and sacred backdrop of the Israelites entering the Promised Land. The events surrounding that era remain among the most powerful in biblical history, filled with struggle, hope, divine intervention, and human uncertainty. To stand with them at the river's edge, to walk in the dust of their wilderness years, and to witness the first steps into a land long promised is to step into a narrative that continues to shape faith and imagination today.

This novel sought to explore that familiar landscape through unfamiliar eyes, following Gershom, a figure scarcely mentioned in Scripture but rich with creative possibility. Through his path, I hope you experienced not only the wonder and weight of Israel's transition but also the quiet, personal battles that often unfold behind great moments in history. If even for a moment the world of the wilderness, the Jordan, and the early days of settlement felt more alive, more human, or more spiritually resonant, then this story has done what it set out to do.

Your willingness to invest your time, attention, and imagination in these pages is something I do not take lightly. In a world filled with countless responsibilities and endless distractions, choosing to sit with a story is a gift. I am grateful for every chapter you read, every thought or emotion stirred, and every moment spent walking alongside these characters.

May the themes within this tale, faith, growth, reconciliation, and the search for purpose, stay with you long after the final page. And may the ancient journey of Israel, both its triumphs and its lessons, continue to inspire your own steps toward whatever promise lies ahead.

About the Author

Dameon Gibbs holds an BA in Anthropology and World History and an MA in Classical Studies. For the past five years he has worked with inner-city youth in Baltimore, Maryland. He has been an avid writer since his days in high school during the late 1990's. He enjoys the creative process of all writing genres, whether it be religious, poetic, science fiction, historical, biographies or action adventure.

Dameon is married to fellow author Tiffany Michele.

You can connect with me on:

🌐 https://gibbspublishingconglomerate.com

f https://www.facebook.com/GibbsPublishing

Also by Dameon Gibbs

He has been an avid writer since his days in high school during the late 1990s. He enjoys the creative process of all writing genres, whether it be religious, poetic, science fiction, historical, biographies, or action-adventure.

Found in the Storm

Found in the Storm is a gripping tale of faith, redemption, and survival that will keep you turning pages until the very end. When Antonio—a flawed but determined Army vet—takes a risky job flying a mysterious package across snowy Minnesota, what starts as a quick payday spirals into a life-or-death battle against a deadly winter storm.

As the blizzard rages, Antonio is forced to confront his past, his choices, and the fragile line between survival and surrender. Through betrayal, forgiveness, and the raw testing of faith, Tiffany and Dameon Gibbs deliver a heart-pounding story rich with emotion, tension, and unforgettable characters.

Perfect for readers who crave thrilling adventure with depth, Found in the Storm is a powerful reminder of how resilience and redemption can rise—even in the fiercest storm.

Guardians of the Realm Beneath

Kylia Wilks never expected to find a portal under her bed—but when she and her brother Demetree fall through it, they land in a world full of strange, magical creatures...and big trouble. The creatures aren't scary by choice—they're being forced to frighten kids by a wicked ruler.

Now it's up to Kylia and Demetree to uncover the truth, stand up to the villain, and help their new friends fight back. But freeing the realm won't be easy—it'll take smarts, bravery, and a sacrifice they never saw coming.

A World Can Exist Anywhere

www.ingramcontent.com/pod-product-compliance
Lightning Source LLC
Chambersburg PA
CBHW020053310726

48970CB00002B/306